Yours for Eternity

HANNAH HOWELL
ALEXANDRA IVY
KAITLIN O'RILEY

http://www.kensingtonbooks.com

ZEBRA BOOKS are published by

Kensington Publishing Corp.
119 West 40th Street
New York, NY 10018

All Kensington titles, imprints, and distributed lines are available at special quantity discounts for bulk purchases for sales promotion, premiums, fund-raising, educational, or institutional use.

Special book excerpts or customized printings can also be created to fit specific needs. For details, write or phone the office of the Kensington Special Sales Manager: Attn. Special Sales Department. Kensington Publishing Corp., 119 West 40th Street, New York, NY 10018. Phone: 1-800-221-2647.

Zebra and the Z logo Reg. U.S. Pat. & TM Off.

ISBN-13: 978-1-4201-1228-3
ISBN-10: 1-4201-1228-7

First Kensington Books Trade Paperback Printing: September 2010
First Zebra Books Mass-Market Paperback Printing: September 2011

10 9 8 7 6 5 4 3 2 1

Printed in the United States of America

"Adeline," he groaned against her throat, "I think we had best cease. The tether on my desire isnae a verra strong one. I am but a heartbeat away from spreading your fine little body out beneath me."

"Nay, kiss me again," she demanded. "And again and again until I cannae breathe or think."

"If I kiss ye again, I willnae stop until ye are fully mine."

"Oh." She trembled, passion tearing through her at the mere thought of what they were about to do. "I ken it. Kiss me again."

Lachann growled softly and kissed her, making no attempt to govern his need. She did not pull away as he had feared she might but pressed even closer. When she tentatively parried the thrust of his tongue with her own, he cast aside all doubt and restraint and pushed her down onto the rough pallet. It took what little willpower he had left not to tear off the thin linen shift she wore, hurl aside his own clothing, and bury himself deep inside her . . .

Books by Hannah Howell

ONLY FOR YOU * MY VALIANT KNIGHT
UNCONQUERED * WILD ROSES
A TASTE OF FIRE * HIGHLAND DESTINY
HIGHLAND HONOR * HIGHLAND PROMISE
A STOCKINGFUL OF JOY * HIGHLAND VOW
HIGHLAND KNIGHT * HIGHLAND HEARTS
HIGHLAND BRIDE * HIGHLAND ANGEL
HIGHLAND GROOM * HIGHLAND WARRIOR
RECKLESS * HIGHLAND CONQUEROR
HIGHLAND CHAMPION * HIGHLAND LOVER
HIGHLAND VAMPIRE * CONQUEROR'S KISS
HIGHLAND BARBARIAN * BEAUTY AND THE BEAST
HIGHLAND SAVAGE * HIGHLAND THIRST
HIGHLAND WEDDING * HIGHLAND WOLF
SILVER FLAME * HIGHLAND FIRE
NATURE OF THE BEAST * HIGHLAND CAPTIVE
HIGHLAND SINNER * MY LADY CAPTOR
IF HE'S WICKED * WILD CONQUEST
IF HE'S SINFUL * KENTUCKY BRIDE
IF HE'S WILD * COMPROMISED HEARTS
HIGHLAND PROTECTOR

Books by Alexandra Ivy

WHEN DARKNESS COMES
EMBRACE THE DARKNESS
DARKNESS EVERLASTING * DARKNESS REVEALED
DARKNESS UNLEASHED * BEYOND THE DARKNESS
DEVOURED BY DARKNESS

Books by Kaitlin O'Riley

SECRETS OF A DUCHESS * ONE SINFUL NIGHT
WHEN HIS KISS IS WICKED * DESIRE IN HIS EYES

Published by Kensington Publishing Corporation

Contents

Highland Blood

HANNAH HOWELL

Prologue

Scotland
Summer, 1511, In the Reign of James IV

The sound came in on the wind. Voices and a soft mewling. Adeline sat back on her heels and put the blackberries she had just picked into her basket as she strained to listen. She hoped it was not the blacksmith's boys torturing a cat again. Unable to hear clearly and determined to discover just what was going on, she crept toward the sound, pausing only to pull the hood of her cloak over her head. Her cursed red hair could easily be visible even in the shadows of the trees.

When Adeline drew near enough to not only hear but to see what was happening, it took all of her willpower not to rush forward and confront the couple standing over a wounded child. The child was bleeding from a slash on his small arm and neither the woman nor the man was doing a thing to help. She pushed aside the anger pounding in her head and listened. It soon became clear that Anne Drummond was the child's mother but Robbie MacAdam was not the father. What also became clear was that they were arguing over the best way to dispose of the child.

"Nay right to just leave him here to get eaten by the beasts," said Robbie. "Ne'er liked that, though 'tis done from time to time. Why dinnae ye just kill the little bastard?"

"And have that sin on my soul?" Anne shook her head. "Nay, this will do."

"He will still be dead at your hand."

"Nay, he willnae. 'Twill be the beasts what kill him, nay me."

"Dinnae see much difference, woman. Ne'er have. Dead be dead whether ye kill him yourself or leave him for the beasts to gnaw on."

"If ye think this is so wrong, then ye kill him!"

"I willnae kill a bairn."

"I dinnae see ye doing anything to save him, either."

"He be a demon, the devil's own son. I dinnae want naught to do with him."

"Then can we leave now?"

"Still doesnae seem right," muttered Robbie, but he hurried to catch up with Anne, who was already striding away through the trees.

Adeline did not move until she was certain the couple was gone and would not return. It hurt to see the child sitting there, fat tears falling from the little boy's wide eyes, but she fought the urge to immediately go and comfort the child. Anne and Robbie wanted the child dead. She could not give them any reason to think the boy had survived.

Then the boy looked in her direction. Adeline knew he was aware of her but she did not know how he could be. She had not moved and had made no sound. Cautiously, she stood up and moved toward him. When he showed no sign of fear, she quickly hurried to his side to tend to the cut on his arm. She frowned when she found that it no longer looked as bad as it had first appeared. It did not even need to be bandaged. Shaking away all thoughts of that oddity, she began to plan how she could help him.

"The only curse ye have, my bonnie laddie, is your mother, aye? Now, what to do to make them think they succeeded in their crime?"

She looked at his bloody, ragged clothing. The thought that it was a lot of blood to have come from a cut that was already closed slipped through her mind, but, again, she shook it aside. Murmuring soft words to ease whatever fears the child might feel, she stripped him of his clothes. Tearing the rags, she scattered them over the ground, hoping it would appear that some animal had taken the child.

"Now, ye look a sturdy lad," she said as the little boy toddled up to her side. "I wonder what your name is."

"Demon," the boy said.

"Nay."

"Debil."

"Nay."

"Battird."

"Most certainly nay. I believe I shall name you. Ye will be called Osgar from this day forward. 'Tis a proud name. My father carried it weel. Now ye can grow up to do the same." She picked him up in her arms and gently kissed his cheek. "Will ye come home with me, laddie?"

The boy nodded, his wide golden eyes fixed un-blinkingly upon her face. "Aye."

"And your name is?"

"Othgar."

Adeline laughed and hurried back to her bas-ket. She knew it would not be easy to keep the child safe but she was determined to do so. Anne would never get another chance to kill the boy. Osgar was now hers and woe to anyone who tried to take him away or hurt him. Looking at the boy who smiled up at her, she shook her head. How could anyone think he was a demon?

She stroked his cheek and smiled when he grabbed her by the wrist. He was a strong little boy. They would make a home together, she thought. Finally she would no longer be alone. Adeline's soft, happy thoughts about the future came to an abrupt halt when Osgar sank his teeth into her wrist.

Chapter One

Enough was enough. Adeline finally accepted the fact that she could not keep Osgar safe as she bathed the dirt and blood from his shaking body. For two years she had struggled to keep him hidden but she had failed. This was the third time someone had hurt him. All she had accomplished with her cautions was to make everyone for miles around think there was a demon running free in the woods. The hunts for the demon were growing more frequent. People not even from the village had joined in, strangers who chilled her blood. It would not be long before the hunters cried her a liar when she claimed that she had never seen the little demon they all looked for. They would tear her tiny cottage apart looking for Osgar.

This time the wounds Osgar had suffered were little more than scratches and a few bruises. The next time her beautiful golden-eyed boy could die. Osgar's death was what the hunters sought. Although she could not understand this fear of a child, she had to accept that it existed. Adeline swallowed the urge to weep as she sat down on the bed next to Osgar, her dream of their becoming a family in ashes.

Osgar crawled into her lap and Adeline held him close. Burying her nose in his thick raven curls, she blinked back the tears in her eyes. Love was making her weak and she had to fight that weakness. She needed to be strong enough to think only of Osgar's safety. That meant she had to be strong enough to give him up.

"I dinnae hurt this time," Osgar said.

Adeline smiled, knowing he meant he did not need her blood. "Good. Ye escaped in time but laddie, ye came too close to dying this time. Three times I have almost lost ye. It cannae go on anymore. We must leave here."

"Where will we go?"

"To your kinsmen."

Osgar looked up at her and frowned. "I have kinsmen?"

"Aye, ye do. Ye are of MacNachton blood. The last time those hunters came here to look for you, I followed them when they left. I heard them talk of a clan called MacNachton and that Anne Drummond claims ye are one of them. The men spoke of them as a clan of demons. All they said made me verra certain that ye are kin to them. There were too many similarities for me to doubt it. So, we must seek them out."

"Where are they?"

"At a place called Cambrun. 'Tis high in the mountains."

Adeline could still hear the men speaking of how others who had gone hunting there had never returned. It was not something she could tell a little boy of five, however. He lived with enough fear and she did not want him balking at going to Cambrun. The thought of going there terrified her, but it sounded like a place where Osgar would be safe and that was all that mattered.

Osgar sat up and looked around the little cottage. "But I like our home."

"So do I, love, but 'tis nay longer a safe place for us. Cambrun will be safe."

"I could keep hiding."

"Spending hours hidden beneath the floor is no life for ye, laddie. And, thrice ye have nearly been caught. Nay, we must pack what means most to us and seek out your kinsmen for help."

It proved to be a heartbreaking chore. By dawn, Adeline had reduced her possessions to a few sacks tied to the saddle of one of her ponies. She hated leaving anything behind, for everything in the cottage held a memory of her father or her mother. The only items she could call foolish were her cats, two ratty-eared felines she had saved from the cruelty of the blacksmith's sons. The animals huddled in the sturdy cage she had made for them and stared at her. Her decision to take them had wavered nearly a dozen times but she had finally, irrevocably, given in to what her heart wanted. She just prayed that she did not lose them on the journey.

"I dinnae think Tom and Meg like their cage," said Osgar as Adeline put him up on the pony they would ride.

"They would like being left behind even less." Adeline settled herself behind Osgar and took up the reins. "Who would feed or shelter them?" She checked to make sure the lead to the pony carrying her belongings was secure. "They will settle and they have that nice piece of plaid to keep them warm, aye?"

Adeline stared for another moment at the house she had grown up in. It hurt to leave even though the people she lived amongst had never accepted her. Her father and mother were buried here and it felt as if she were losing them all over again. Then she straightened her spine and squared her shoulders, knowing that her parents would understand. Osgar's life was threatened. She had no choice. Her parents would always live in her heart and memories, and that had to be enough. Whispering a farewell, she lightly kicked her pony into an easy, steady stride and started her journey north.

The moon was high by the time Adeline made camp for the night. She did not like riding at night but Osgar had to be sheltered during the middle of the day, when the sun was at its full strength. Riding into the night was the only way to make up for that lost time.

She unpacked and unsaddled the horses and then started a small fire. Osgar helped her attend to the cats, making certain they did not escape as she gave the animals food and water. Adeline cleaned out the small box of dirt she had secured inside the cage, something she felt quite proud of.

"Will we be there soon?" asked Osgar as they sat by the fire eating cold chicken and oatcakes.

"I cannae say when we will get there, laddie," Adeline replied. "I just ken that 'tis in those hills we can see to the north. Once we get closer I will try to get some better directions."

"Those are verra far away."

"A few days' ride. Nay more than that, I am thinking. Weel, a few days if we can keep going straight toward them and the weather doesnae stop us. I think if we were closer, Anne would have left ye with them."

"I am glad ye found me."

"So am I, love."

"Will my kinsmen like me?"

"How can they nay do so? They will be verra pleased to have such a fine lad returned to the clan."

Adeline prayed that was the truth. She had never met any of the MacNachton clan. Yet, if they were all like Osgar, she could see no reason why they would turn the boy away. They would certainly understand the danger the child was in while living outside their protection. The men she had eavesdropped on had called Cambrun an impenetrable fortress and that was just what Osgar needed.

She would not mind living in such a place, either. Adeline was weary of being an outcast, a woman eyed with suspicion and fear even as she was called to heal an injury or birth a child. She was always but one misstep from being decried as a witch, just as her mother had been. A shiver went through her as the dark memories of her mother's brutal death flooded her mind. It was not a fate she wished to share. She prayed that the MacNachton clan had a place for her even though she was not their kind, and not just so she could remain with Osgar. For once she would like to feel safe.

When they were done eating, Adeline spread a blanket on the ground. She urged Osgar onto the rough bed, ignoring his muttered complaints about how hard that bed was. Settling down next to him, between him and the fire, she drew another blanket over them.

It did not surprise her when his muttering soon ceased, his breathing growing slow and even as sleep conquered him. Adeline wished she could find the sweet oblivion of sleep as easily, but her mind was crowded with worries and fears. Traveling alone with a child was dangerous. Traveling to a place that might be filled with ones like Osgar, ones full-grown with all the power and cunning of men, was terrifying. She closed her eyes and sternly told herself that she had no choice.

The gray of approaching dawn met Adeline's eyes when she next opened them. Her first clear thought was one of relief when she realized she had managed to get some sleep. The snap of a twig banished the lingering lassitude of sleep. She did not move, but looked around and tensed. Four men were creeping toward her. They were armed and grim of face.

Adeline yanked her knife from beneath the blanket she rested on and leapt to her feet. "Osgar—run."

Osgar stumbled to his feet and stared at the men. *"Maman?"*

"Run, Osgar. Now."

Even as she spoke Adeline knew it was too late. Two of the men moved quickly to get behind her and Osgar, cutting off all chance of the child escaping. There were four of them against one of her. There were four swords against her one knife. They were free to move as they pleased, while she had to protect Osgar. Adeline wanted to scream in fury. She had failed Osgar once again.

Lachann MacNachton idly rode along the rough drover's track. He would easily reach the next shelter before the sun was high, even at his leisurely pace. For two long months he had searched for ones carrying MacNachton blood but found only one. He had sent the young boy home to Cambrun with Martyn and continued the search on his own. Now he was finally headed home, eager to be back amongst his own kind. He was tired of constantly needing to find shelter when the sun was high and of hiding who he was.

The clan had been ignorant of the Lost Ones, those of MacNachton and Outsider blood, for far too long. For every Lost One they found, they heard of too many others who had met with brutal deaths. It made his heart sore. So many of their people lost and far too many of them killed before they even had a chance to truly live or defend themselves. He yet again cursed all the fools who had never taken the time to be sure that the seed they had so freely spilled everywhere they went had not taken root.

"Maman?"

It was only a whisper on the wind but it yanked Lachann out of his dark thoughts. He halted and looked around, idly stroking his mount's neck to keep the animal quiet. Lachann waited to hear more, to discover where the voice was coming from.

"Run, Osgar. Now."

Not far, Lachann thought as he dismounted and

secured his horse's reins to a branch. Unsheathing his sword, Lachann began to silently make his way toward the voices he had heard. One did not tell someone to run unless there was some danger. He was not sure why he was compelled to walk into what was none of his concern, but he did not resist the urge to do so. That first word told him that a child was involved. The second voice had been a woman's.

"Now, lass, do ye really think ye can stop us from doing what we must with that wee knife? This be God's work ye interfere with."

The man's voice was coarse and weighted with scorn. *Why would men attack a woman and child?* Lachann wondered as he slipped into the shadow of a tree and studied the scene in a small clearing only a few feet away. A small woman with a young child clinging to her skirts stood within a circle of armed men, a knife in her hand. Her rough gown revealed a slender yet fulsome figure but it was her hair that fully drew his gaze. Gloriously red, it hung in thick, wild waves to her nicely curved hips. His palm actually itched with the urge to touch it. The expression on her pale, beautiful face was one of cold determination. She had no chance at all of fending off four men armed with swords but obviously intended to try. Lachann was just as determined not to let her die. The strength of that determination, one that went far beyond the simple need of a man to protect the weaker, was something he would think about later.

He stepped into the clearing and smiled at the four men who looked at him in surprise and then horror. Lachann made no attempt to hide his fangs, the urge to kill now running strong in his blood. "Ye best leave the lass and the bairn be. If ye do, I just may allow ye to live."

"So, the demons come to collect their spawn," said the tallest of the four men.

Lachann was intrigued by that statement, but his gaze on his enemies never wavered. He would consider the meaning of the words when the battle was done. "Four men against a wee lass and a bairn? Such bravery."

"She is naught but a witch, bred of a witch, and she now protects the devil's spawn. Can ye nay recognize your own?" The tall man turned all his attention on Lachann, his men quickly doing the same.

"What I recognize is four swine who badly need gutting." Lachann tossed his sword from hand to hand. "Brave enough to face a mon?"

"Aye! Brave enough to do God's work and cut down one of Satan's dogs!"

Adeline stared at the man who challenged her enemies. He had appeared out of the shadows without making a sound until he spoke, his deep voice cutting like a well-honed knife through the tension that had held them all in place. She was spellbound, his height and broad shoulders heralding a champion in her eyes. Then she saw his fangs and nearly gasped. Was he like Osgar or was he, too, a threat? His black hair hung past his shoulders, rippling slightly in the dawn breeze. He had a face to make a woman's heart beat faster, despite those inhuman teeth. Even in the dim light she could see the glint of gold in his eyes.

Shaking free of her bemusement with her rescuer, Adeline realized no one was watching her or Osgar. She began to edge away from the men, nudging Osgar along behind her. Guilt pinched at her heart. She was leaving the man to face four armed men alone, but she quickly smothered the feeling. Osgar was not able to defend himself. His safety had to be first and foremost in her mind.

She was almost to the trees when the men attacked her rescuer. He moved so fast that she could barely see each deadly motion, only heard the cries of the men who had meant to kill her and Osgar. Two of those men fell to the sweep of her rescuer's sword before they had even fully engaged him in battle. When another man leapt on her rescuer's back as he faced the leader of her foes sword to sword, Adeline prepared to throw her knife in an attempt to help him, but he saved himself. He swiftly trotted backward and slammed the man clinging to his back into a tree. The sound of breaking bones made her gasp.

Adeline scooped up Osgar, her mind ordering her to run, but she could not completely break free of her fascination with the battle. Then her savior attacked the last man with a speed and furious skill that quickly disarmed him. Adeline was just thinking that she could stay where she was now that she had a protector, when her savior sank his teeth into the last man's throat. She ran, praying she had the speed to escape the seductively beautiful dark angel who had just slain all her enemies.

Chapter Two

Lachann rose from the man he had just fed from and cursed. He had not meant to do that but the bloodlust of battle had claimed him. Though his wounds were small, they had bled freely and his body had demanded he feed. It did not surprise him to see that the woman and child had fled. He had loosed the beast every MacNachton had within him, and few Outsiders could face it. It struck him as odd that this time that fear should cause him such a sharp pang.

He cleaned his sword on the dead man's clothes and sheathed it. The woman had left behind all her belongings, he realized as he looked around. Lachann suspected she would not go far but he was in no mood to chase after her. He was, however, strangely reluctant to leave her. It was because she and the child were unprotected, he told himself, and a little voice in his head scoffed at his claim. Ignoring that voice, he glanced up at the sky and decided he had the time to wait for her to creep back before he would be forced to seek shelter from the sun.

After dragging the bodies away from the area and settling his horse, Lachann stood with his eyes closed and just listened, certain he would hear her approach, for Outsiders could not move silently enough to evade the keen hearing of a MacNachton. A moment later he frowned. Why was he hearing cats? Lachann opened his eyes and walked toward the sound. Hidden from view by the pair of sturdy Highland ponies was a cage with two cats in it.

Lachann smiled even as the cats hissed at him. The cage was large, and dishes for food and water and even a small box of dirt were all tied securely to the bars. An odd scrap of blanket was also set inside for the comfort of the two battle-scarred cats. The woman would definitely return. No one who took such care of two such ragged animals would then desert them.

"Lass, I ken that ye havenae gone far," he called out. "There is no need to fear me."

Adeline almost answered, reminding the man of how he had just killed four men and supped on one of them. That was enough to make any sane person fear him. She had not run far, knowing it would be both dangerous and foolish to leave behind the ponies and supplies. As silently as she could, she had crept close enough to be able to hear it when the man rode away. She had just prayed that the man would not take all her things when he did leave. Now, after what felt like hours, it was becoming clear to her that he had no intention of leaving. She was immediately wary of his reasons for lingering. Telling herself that she was now facing one foe instead of four did nothing to ease that wariness.

"If ye make me wait too long, lass, I could become hungry, aye? They say cat tastes much like rabbit and I have always been verra fond of rabbit."

"*Maman*, he is going to hurt Tom and Meg!" cried Osgar.

She grabbed the boy before he could run back to the clearing. "Hush, Osgar. He will hear you."

"Too late," called the man, the mocking tone in his voice causing her to grit her teeth in annoyance.

Silently repeating every curse she knew, Adeline tried to think of what to do next. She suspected the man was one of the MacNachtons she had intended to find, but she was no longer certain she wanted Osgar to join that clan. Adeline shivered as she recalled how the man had sunk his teeth into the hunter's throat. That was not the life she wished for Osgar, a life of killing and feeding upon men as if they were cattle. She now had to consider the possibility that some of the horrific tales she had heard about the MacNachtons were true. If they were, the MacNachtons were the very last people she wished to entrust with the care of Osgar.

The four men who had crept into her camp had intended to kill her and Osgar. She did not regret their deaths. She did, however, find many reasons to fear her rescuer. The speed and deadly skill he had shown while killing four armed men had been terrifying things to see. But the way he had drunk of that man's blood had been worse. Adeline cursed, knowing her thoughts were circling but unsure of what to do.

"*Maman?*"

"Hush, Osgar," Adeline said in as soft a voice as she could manage. "I am thinking. We need a plan."

"But, *Maman*—"

"Can it not wait?"

"Nay. The mon is here."

Adeline lifted her gaze enough to see the pair of deer-hide boots planted so firmly in front of her face she knew they were caught. How did the man move like that, like mist rising from the marsh? The brief hesitation brought on by her surprise cost her dearly. She reached for her knife but his long-fingered hand was firmly wrapped around her wrist before she even touched the hilt. A squeak of surprise escaped her as he yanked her to her feet and, in one swift move, disarmed her, wrapped one strong arm around her, and pinned her arms to her sides. Adeline struggled, drumming her heels against his legs, but he took no notice, fixing his gaze on Osgar.

"Be still, woman, ere ye hurt yourself."

The man's deep voice made her heart skip and Adeline told herself it was only fear and anger making it do so. "Put me down now," she ordered, not surprised when he ignored her.

"Put my *maman* down or I will bite ye," said Osgar.

Lachann stared at the boy facing him with his little fists raised and a dark scowl on his face. He suddenly heard the voice of one of the men he had just killed. *So, the demons come to collect their spawn.* Lachann tensed, anticipation and hope surging through him.

"What is your name, lad?" he asked.

"Osgar, and I can bite verra hard."

"Can ye now?" Lachann carefully studied the big golden eyes staring up at him. He could see the beast glinting in them despite the fact that the child was too young to be revealing it. "Who was your father?"

"Dinnae ken. Anne didnae tell me. I think I called him Papa but he went away and didnae come back."

Lachann wondered why the child paled a little but before he could ask, the boy was looking belligerent again. "And just who is this Anne that she should know what mon bred ye? This lady?" Lachann was not surprised at how tense and still his captive had become, not after all she had already done to protect the child.

"Nay. Ye are holding my mither. Anne is the lady whose body I came out of. She cut me and left me in the woods for the beasties to gnaw on. *Maman* saved me. So, ye had best put her down or I will get verra mean."

Lachann looked at the woman he held. She was staring at him, her lovely green eyes filled with fear and mistrust, her temptingly full lips made thin by the way she pressed them together as if afraid to speak. He doubted she had any MacNachton blood in her, yet she cared for a child who was plainly one of the Lost Ones, had even been ready to die to protect the boy. What Lachann needed to do now was to ease her fear and gain her trust. Considering all she had just seen him do, gaining her trust was not going to be easy. He needed it, however, if only to get some answers about why a small boy already had so many of the traits most Mac-Nachtons did not gain until they were older.

"Ye took the lad in?" After a brief hesitation, she nodded. "He is a MacNachton. He is of my clan, my blood."

"How can ye be so certain of that?" Adeline asked.

Deciding she was both weaponless and easy to hang onto, Lachann loosened his hold on her body but, the moment her feet touched the ground, wrapped his hand around her slim wrists to hold her in place. "Are ye a witch?" he asked, suddenly recalling something else the men had said.

"Nay, and neither was my mother," she snapped. "Healers. That is all she was and all I am. Healers. For that they killed her and would, undoubtedly, soon come for me. What Osgar tells ye is true. His birth mother and a man cut him and left him in the woods. I took him in. I am Adeline Dunbar. Two years ago that happened and since then the fools searching the wood for some demon have nearly killed him. Thrice. I decided we needed to leave that place."

"We are going to Cambrun," said Osgar, "where there are people like me."

Adeline was not sure why Osgar was now so calm and friendly just because the man no longer held her up like a sack of grain. "I dinnae believe that is any of this mon's business, Osgar."

"Oh, but it is," said the man. "I am Lachann Mac-

Nachton. I have been on a long search for ones we call the Lost Ones and am now headed home to Cambrun. Ye will ride with me."

"Nay, we willnae." She gave a brief attempt to free her wrists from his hold before deciding that all she was accomplishing was to use up her strength in a futile attempt to escape. "I have changed my mind about going to Cambrun."

"Because ye saw me kill those men."

"Nay, because of what I saw ye do to the last mon ye fought. That isnae what I want for Osgar."

"It was the bloodlust of the battle, lass. That and the fact that I had lost some blood. And, whether ye take the lad to his clan or nay, he will become like me." He frowned at Osgar. "'Tis unusual for the beast to be stirring in one so young."

"There is nay a beast in the child!"

He grinned at her forceful defense of the boy but quickly grew serious again. "MacNachton bairns, especially those born of both MacNachtons and Outsiders, dinnae show the"—he glanced at her scowling face—"spirit the adult MacNachtons do at such a young age. 'Tis often something else that gives away their heritage. That need for blood if weakened or wounded is usually it, or the weakness caused by the sun. How strong is his weakness? How long can he stay in the sun?"

"He cannae abide the noon sun."

Lachann nodded. "Come along, lad. We can talk o'er all this back at the campsite."

Adeline stumbled slightly when Lachann started striding back to the clearing, dragging her along at his side. The only thing that aided her in remaining calm was that the man showed no hesitation in his acceptance of Osgar as one of his own. He showed no hesitation in expecting that Osgar would take his place at Cambrun, either. The latter was not something she was feeling all that sure of at the moment, but her need to flee the man's side had eased. She was willing to listen.

"When did ye ken that the lad was different?" Lachann asked as he sat near the fire with Adeline and Osgar, passing his skin of cider around.

"Immediately," replied Adeline. "Within moments after I picked him up to take him home with me, he fed from my wrist. His wound had healed but I eventually realized that 'twas the loss of blood that made him do that."

"He fed from ye? Ye didnae have to coax him to it?"

"Nay. He just did it. Now he tells me when he hurts. He doesnae just bite."

Lachann simply could not understand how the boy could be as he was. Full-blooded MacNachton children had not been born for many, many years but there were tales of them, memories kept alive so that they could all learn from the past. No child born of Outsiders and MacNachtons revealed such a need for blood so soon, or the innate skill on how to take it.

"Why do ye look at him like that?" asked Adeline.

"I am just trying to understand something that doesnae make any sense," replied Lachann. "Laddie," he asked Osgar, "have ye always had the need to feed?"

"Nay," replied Osgar. "I did it first just after my fither went away."

"Ye were a verra wee lad when Adeline took ye in. Are ye certain ye recall anything about your father?"

"He was verra big and he said I had to be brave because he had to mark me. I was brave. I 'member that clear because then he left and he ne'er came back. Then Anne decided to put me out for the beasties."

"He *marked* ye?"

"'Tis what he said. Right here." Osgar pulled up his shirt and pointed to a crescent-shaped mark very near his heart. "See? This proves I had a fither because he said this is what fithers do when they love their sons and want to be sure they are safe e'en when he cannae be there to help them. He said if someone tried to hurt me, he would ken and come help me but he didnae come. *Maman* did."

Lachann reached out and lightly touched the scar. "Sweet Jesu, he is a Blooded Son."

"What do ye mean?" asked Adeline, gently tugging Osgar's shirt back down.

"'Tis an old ritual. Verra old. It was rarely done, for it made the child as much a MacNachton as any adult was. The father bites the child, takes a wee bit of blood, and then feeds his own to the child. Within the week the child is still a child but with an old soul, if ye will. It was a way to protect the child, to help the parent ken exactly when he was in danger. They became bonded in many ways. It can also give the child some added strength and speed so that he can better protect himself despite his small size."

Adeline lightly stroked Osgar's thick black curls.

"His father kenned that Anne had become a threat to him and Osgar."

"I would guess that is just what happened but the mon couldnae stay just then, so he did what he could to try and protect his son."

"Then where is he?"

"I fear he is dead. A parent who has blooded his child cannae stay away from him for verra long; the bond is that strong. 'Tis but a guess, but I am thinking he felt the danger was too great to try and take Osgar away with him, that he feared the peril was close enough to make any journey dangerous, and so he went alone to try and get help."

"And they killed him."

"Aye, and I suspect this Anne was the one to lead him to his death." Lachann muttered a few curses, stopping only when he noticed how closely Osgar was paying attention to every word he said. "Again and again I have heard such tales; one of our own led to his death by a woman. None of our men seem to ken that they take their verra lives in their hands when they take up with an Outsider lass."

"I beg your pardon." Adeline scowled at him, insulted even though she could understand his anger. "I believe I am one of these people ye call an Outsider and I havenae led anyone to their death, nor would I."

Lachann looked at her and sighed. Revealing his own mistrust of all who were not of his clan was not a good way to win over her trust. He realized he did not fully extend that mistrust to her but doubted she would believe that, especially as he could not explain why he did not feel it as strongly with her as he should. He hoped it was not just because he felt drawn to her, attracted to her with a strength that left him a little uneasy. Lachann did not want to think he could be such a fool. Just because she saved a child of his clan did not mean she would be as accepting of all of them.

"We need to go and talk to this Anne," he said.

"Ye want us to turn around and go all the way back?" Adeline shook her head. "Nay, that is foolish."

"I need to ken who his father is and what has happened to him."

"He is dead. Ye have just confirmed that with all ye just told us about this marking the mon did. If he wasnae dead he would have come to help Osgar. Ye want us to go to the place where he was probably murdered? Where they hunt for Osgar and think me a witch? That is madness."

"Ye willnae be without protection this time." The way she tilted her jaw up and crossed her arms told Lachann she was not going to be easy to convince. She had a right to her fears but he could not let them hold him back from what needed to be done. "I need to ken the truth. For many reasons," he said when she opened her mouth to argue with him. "It can tell me what Osgar's bloodline is, which is verra important. He could be of one of the more important families within the clan and that will make a difference in his future."

The way she frowned told him that making the return trip to the village important for Osgar's future was the way to get her to agree. Lachann began to explain just how important the boy's bloodlines were and all about how his clan was trying to put together a history that could help them to solve all the problems their clan faced now. By the time he knew they had to head to shelter, she was a reluctant partner in his plans. He did not fool himself into thinking she would cease trying to make him change his mind, however.

Chapter Three

"I still dinnae like this," Adeline muttered as she stood beside Lachann looking down the small hillside at the village. She had been grieved to leave her home but not the people who lived here.

"In truth, neither do I, lass," Lachann confessed, knowing she could not turn back now. "These are the people who tried to kill Osgar and I am certain they killed the lad's father. I suspicion they would have soon come for ye, too. Nay, I dinnae wish to be here but I cannae ignore the need to speak to this Anne. I need to ken who fathered the lad. If naught else, the mon may have close kin at Cambrun and they will wish to ken what happened to him. That and all the reasons ye have made me repeat again and again since we started the journey here."

"And ye wish to ken who may be pleased that he left a wee bit of himself behind. I ken it. Doesnae mean I like being here, but I ken the reasons for this are good ones."

"And ye couldnae have agreed from the start?"

"Nay," she replied, and made no apology for her stubbornness. "And Osgar should ken if he has family."

"Aye. Because Osgar is a Blooded Son his family may be able to ken who he is, but I cannae be certain of that. The blood bond may be clear enough for all the mon's kin to see but a name will help us save some time in kenning who he belongs to if the mark isnae strong enough."

He belongs to me, Adeline thought as she looked back toward the cluster of trees where Osgar waited with the ponies and Lachann's horse, but she bit back the words. She hated to leave the boy all alone but had to trust that he knew to flee on the pony if anyone approached him. Osgar had learned how to sense and elude danger before he could even speak clearly. Sad as that was, it served him well. She idly wondered if that was one of the things his father had given him when he had marked him.

"He will be fine," Lachann said quietly. "He is a clever lad and we willnae be long."

"As ye wish. She lives in that wee cottage next to the blacksmith's place. She is a widow now. Her husband was nay rich but he owned that wee home and Anne has a keen eye for lovers with full purses."

"Any other children?"

"Two. One by her husband and one by a lover. 'Tis whispered that she had others but that she is fond of taking the poor bairns to the wood, returning without them. I ne'er found any, though, nor any sign that she had done so. Another rumor claims that she kens how to rid herself of a bairn ere it is born." Adeline scowled at Anne's cottage.

"Unfortunately, some in the village believe the latter and think I am the one who gives Anne such potions. I ne'er have. My mother would spin in her grave if I e'en thought of it. But the priest decries my dark sin with near every mass he gives and Anne does naught to absolve me of such unfair blame."

"And yet ye stayed here, stayed near enough to these fools to be at risk."

"The cottage was my home," she explained softly. "They destroyed that when they murdered my mother but I had thought I could regain it with Osgar. I thought he and I could make it a home again."

Lachann had the strongest, and strangest, urge to pull her into his arms and soothe her pain, to tell her that she could make a home at Cambrun, with him. That was utter foolishness. He did not even know the woman, he told himself firmly and then immediately called himself a liar. She had already revealed her bravery by facing those men and protecting Osgar, her kind heart in the way she had taken in a child most of the world would run from or kill, and her stubbornness in the way she had argued with him so strenuously about returning to this village. She had done it all for Osgar's sake. Lachann also sensed an old pain, one inflicted by the superstitious people in the village, people who had killed her mother and kept Adeline an outcast.

"Let us be done with this," he said, shaking away his rambling thoughts as he started down the hill.

Adeline hurried to his side and directed him along a less obvious path to Anne's cottage. The sun was almost set and most of the villagers were indoors but she saw no reason to risk meeting or being seen by anyone. Someone might already have discovered that she had fled her home. It would not take long for people to wonder why, especially since the suspicion that she was hiding Osgar had already set down roots in the hunters' minds.

As they approached the back door of Anne's cottage, Adeline noticed the signs of prosperity. A neat, full kitchen garden, glass in the windows, a newly thatched roof, and a stout door. If Anne was ridding herself of children she was not doing so because she had no means to feed and care for them.

The smile that curved Anne's full mouth when she opened the door and first saw the strong, handsome man standing there quickly fled. Adeline was just wondering if the woman suddenly recognized something in Lachann that reminded her of the man who had fathered Osgar when Anne tried to shut the door in their faces. Lachann moved with that speed that still astonished her, shoving the door open and grabbing hold of Anne, his hand over her mouth to halt any attempt the woman made to cry out for help. He walked into Anne's warm kitchen and Adeline followed, shutting the door behind them. A quick glance around told her the children were either gone or in bed.

"Now, mistress, ye will nay scream or cry for aid, aye?" Lachann said.

The hard chill of his voice made Adeline shiver. Anne's eyes were so wide they had to sting as she stared at the man who held her captive. Fear and guilt were so strong in the woman that Adeline could almost smell them. Finally, Anne nodded.

"Be warned, woman. I can stop ye from screaming ere ye finish taking the breath needed to do so," Lachann warned as he slowly released Anne.

"Who are ye?" Anne asked as she stumbled back a few steps and fell into a chair.

"I think ye have a good idea. I look like your lover, aye? Like the mon who sired the wee lad ye tried to kill."

"I have ne'er tried to kill a wee lad!"

"Ye are a poor liar. Ye set your son, a wee bairn, out in the wood kenning weel that he couldnae survive on his own. And, just to make certain the wild beasts made a meal of the boy, ye cut him, filling the air with the tempting scent of blood. Ye may nay have killed the boy with your own hand but leaving him like that 'tis the same, as I see it. What I need to ken now is who sired the boy. Give me a name and I will leave ye be."

Anne trembled as she looked from Lachann to Adeline and back again. Then, slowly, a sly look entered her eyes and Adeline nearly cursed. It did not surprise her to see that the woman thought she could gain from this confrontation, could sell the truth Lachann sought. One look at Lachann's face told Adeline that he, too, now saw the crafty thoughts crowding Anne's mind. She had to wonder just how witless Anne was. Could the woman not see that her life was hanging by a very thin thread?

Lachann leaned toward the woman, letting Anne see the glint of the beast in his eyes. "Best ye think verra carefully about trying to play some game with me, woman. Dinnae think I will be gentle or merciful just because ye are a woman. Ye tried to kill a child of my clan and we dinnae take kindly to that. Nay, nor do we act mercifully to one who sent one of our own to his death."

Anne went so white Adeline feared she was about to swoon. A quick glance at Lachann's face told Adeline why the woman was so terrified. Lachann's beautiful golden eyes had turned hard and feral and he was showing his teeth. Adeline suspected that if she were presented with that face attached to such a big, strong man, one who could snap her neck in the wink of an eye, she might wish to swoon as well. It puzzled her a little that she was not the least bit afraid even now.

"Arailt," Anne whispered.

For a moment Adeline thought that Lachann was going to draw his sword and strike the woman's head from her shoulders. Anne must have thought so too, for she tried to press herself into a very small figure in her chair and whimpered. Deciding that although Anne certainly deserved harsh punishment for her crimes and the blood on her hands, it was not wise for Lachann to deliver it, Adeline placed her hand on his arm. It took long enough that she began to grow nervous, but then she felt the hard tension in his arm ease a little.

"How did he die?" Lachann asked, his voice rough with the fury he was struggling to hold back.

"The men hunted him down the last time he left," Anne replied, a little of her foolish bravado returning as she realized she was not about to be killed.

"Aye, as I thought. And ye told them he was here

and where he was headed, didnae ye? Ye made certain your mon wouldnae return to trouble ye again."

Anger twisted Anne's face into something far from pretty. "He wasnae a mon! He was a demon and 'tis clear that the land is swarming with them. Ye are of his ilk and ye deserve the same fate. God demands it."

"Jesu, dinnae try to cover your sins with the shield of righteousness, bitch. Ye were willing to take the mon to your bed, to do so for near to two years. Ye tired of him or found a richer purse to dip your fingers in."

"Nay, I—"

"Dinnae twist your tongue with more lies. After being his lover for so long ye must have kenned his secrets and ye used them against him. Ye sent him to his death, willingly. Aye, and then ye tried to send his son after him." He spat at her feet. "Tell me how he died."

"I dinnae ken. The men hunted him down somewhere in the wood."

"So how do ye ken he was killed?" Lachann's stomach turned when he saw how pale she went. "They brought proof of their murder back so that ye could be sure. What? His head?" He could tell by the look on her face that he had guessed right and ached to put his hands around her white throat and choke her until she ceased to breathe.

Adeline shook her head. "Ye could share a mon's bed, bear his child, and then see him brutally murdered? Why didnae ye just send him and the child away? Ye have ne'er hesitated to simply cast off one mon for another before."

"Dinnae look down your nose at me, witch,"

snapped Anne. "I shouldnae be surprised that ye have taken up with one of the demons. Like clings to like, aye? Weel, best ye run, run faster than your mother could."

Adeline felt her nails dig into her palms as she clenched her fists, fighting the urge to leap onto Anne and beat her senseless. All the anger and frustration she had suffered over her mother's death and her inability to make anyone pay for it rose up and choked her. If she had had anyplace else to go she would have walked away from them all. Instead, she had had to ignore their guilt, try not to think of what they had done, and nurse all their petty ills just to survive. They were fortunate she was not the vengeful sort, for she could easily have poisoned the lot of them before anyone became wise to her tricks.

Well, she now had a place to go, she realized, and the tide of her fury receded a little. Lachann had not just taken Osgar and left, something he could have done with ease. He was taking her to Cambrun, too, even though he really had no need of her any longer. She suddenly wanted to talk to him about that, to hear him say outright that she could stay at Cambrun. The thoughts crowding her mind actually helped her regain control of her anger and need for revenge against people like Anne, people who condemned and killed anyone they did not understand.

"Oh, aye, I am leaving," Adeline said. "Best ye pray none of ye fall ill or have a problem birthing a bairn, for none of ye thought to learn any healing skills, thinking them the devil's work."

The look on Anne's face told Adeline that need for a healer was the only reason she was still alive, her skills quite possibly the only reason they had so easily turned on and killed her mother without thought to all the good the woman had done for them. After all, they still had one healer left. Suddenly all Adeline wanted to do was leave, to get as far away from Anne and her ilk as quickly as possible.

"Fetch anything Arailt gave or left ye," ordered Lachann. "'Tis all Osgar's by right now."

"I ken no Osgar," said Anne.

"He is the bairn ye left to die. The son of the mon ye had killed. Now, I ken he would have given ye gifts or something of his, so I will take it now." He grabbed Anne by the arm and yanked her out of the chair, and he watched as she tried to hide her hand in her skirts. "I believe we will start with what ye are trying to hide."

He pulled her hand free of her skirts and stared at the ring on her hand. It was a wide silver band engraved with the badge of the MacNachtons and set with a fat, blood-red garnet. Poor Arailt had cared for this woman. Such rings were prized and not given away lightly. Lachann wondered when the man had realized he had erred in his choice of lover and suspected it had been the night he had marked his own child.

She struggled a little when he took the ring from her. Keeping a firm grip on her, he pushed and threatened her until she gave them several items. One was a medallion that Lachann was sure Arailt's kin would recognize. He was surprised the woman had not sold it yet. Vanity or the need to keep something set aside for the lean times, he supposed. He looked at Adeline as he shoved Anne back into her seat.

"Go," he ordered. "Start on the path I showed ye and I will catch up with ye."

"Nay, ye still need someone to watch your back," Adeline said.

"I willnae kill the bitch."

"I ken it. That danger has passed, but she is still a threat. The moment ye step out of this cottage, she will be screaming for men to come and help her, men to kill you."

"All of whom will have to ready themselves and run here, then listen to what she says. In that time, short as it may be, I can be gone. I think ye may need a wee bit more time than that and I have a faster mount."

She hated to leave him but knew he was right. The time had come to leave this place and, since they could not kill Anne, the woman would soon rouse men to hunt for them. Her ponies were not fast enough to outrun a man mounted on a large horse, and some of the hunters would get horses. It was best to get a good start in her retreat.

"Silence her then. A wee tap on the chin should do, although I wouldnae complain if ye broke her nose and stole away some of that beauty she uses so cruelly. I will be on the path ye showed me."

Adeline did not wait to see what he would do. Anne's gasp of shock and fear caressed her ears as she strode out of the cottage. The minute she reached Osgar and the ponies, she mounted behind the boy and kicked her sturdy little pony into a trot.

"Where is Lachann?" asked Osgar, twisting around to look behind him. "We cannae leave him."

"We are nay leaving him," Adeline said. "'Tis just that we may have to leave verra quickly and his horse can move faster than ours, so 'tis best we start out first."

"They will take his head!"

It was a struggle to hold onto Osgar as he thrashed and twisted in an attempt to get off the pony. He started crying when she got a firm hold on him and they continued to put distance between them and the village. Now she understood the child's occasional nightmares, why Osgar would grow so pale when he talked of how his father had not returned. He had seen the men return with his father's head. Adeline fought the urge to go back and beat Anne until she was little more than a mess on her fine wooden floors.

She was several miles from the village and was thinking she might need to go back and rescue Lachann when she heard the rapid approach of a horse. Before she could fully conceal herself and her little group in the trees, Lachann rode up, slowing his mount to match the trotting pace of her ponies. He looked as if he had endured a hard race and she sighed.

"Ye didnae give her a little tap on the chin, did ye?" she said.

"I dinnae strike women, nay even murdering slatterns like her," he said and then grimaced when he saw that Osgar was watching him. "It wasnae her that cried the alarum, however. Her wee son came in, saw me, and went screaming out of the house." Lachann smiled a little. "I look enough like Arailt that the poor lad thought he was seeing a ghostie. I did give the woman a light slap that knocked her a little foolish, but she had recovered by the time I had mounted and was out there screaming for my blood."

"How close are the ones who answered her call?"

"Nay close at all. There was a lot of confusion still even as I started my race to join ye here. I suspicion they have only just gotten themselves settled enough to start hunting us down and they dinnae have the skill of a MacNachton to see in this dark. Best we keep moving, though."

They rode for a few hours before Lachann decided it was safe enough to stop for a little while and rest the horses. She watched as he studied the things he had taken from Anne. It was impossible for her to understand a woman like Anne, a woman who abandoned her own child to die and who ordered her lover killed. There had to be some punishment for that, yet she and Lachann did not have the power to deliver it. She hated to think that the woman would never pay for her crimes.

The respite was a short one. Lachann took Osgar up with him and they set out at an easier pace, needing to get to the shelter he had spoken of before the sun rose too high in the sky. Unlike Osgar, Lachann could abide only dawn and dusk but she did not complain. A long stretch of traveling followed by a long stretch of rest suited her better than the several short interludes she had employed. It was a more normal mode of travel even if the times of riding and resting were reversed.

She frowned as the sun rose and they rode up a slope that had little trail to ride on. When

Lachann stopped and moved to the face of the rocky hillside to tug aside a large collection of brush, she frowned as an opening appeared in the rocky hillside. The man signaled her to dismount and she did so cautiously.

"A cave?" she asked. "Ye wish us to go into a cave? Arenae there animals in such places? Wolves and the like?"

"There are no animals in there." He grinned at her. "Afraid of caves, Adeline?"

"Nay, I am just nay sure I want to spend the day in a cave. They are dark and damp."

"They are also shelter from the sun, something both Osgar and I need. And any enemy that tries to attack us must first come through here." He pointed at the opening, which did not look big enough to let his horse through without pushing the animal's head down. "Nature's own fortress."

"Are ye certain there are no animals in there?"

"Verra certain. I can smell the beasties, ye ken, and I smell none. Nay, not even a faint scent of a bat."

"Bats?"

"Get in the cave, Adeline. Trust me, it is safe and clear of all vermin and predators." *Except for me,* he thought as he watched her reluctantly urge her nervous ponies through the opening.

Chapter Four

Tossing more peat on the fire, Lachann stared at the flames, his thoughts consumed by the death of yet another MacNachton. Outsider women were a curse. They were behind the deaths of far too many of his people, yet there were so few available women at Cambrun that there was no way to stop all the younger men from slipping away to seek them out. They sought mates and children as any man would. Even some of the older men, revealing that age and experience did not always bring wisdom. Arailt had been a good man. He had not deserved the fate dealt him by the greedy, heartless Anne. He had been robbed not only of his life but of the chance to see his child, a blessed gift too few MacNachtons were given, grow to be a man.

He was pulled from his dark thoughts by Adeline appearing at his side, a bowl of rabbit stew in her hand. Lachann had been so lost in his sorrow he had not even seen her dish it out from the pot hanging over the fire. With a nod, he took the bowl from her, as well as the crude wooden spoon she offered, and began to eat. Out of the corner of his eye he watched as she sat down next to him.

"I am sorry ye have lost a friend," she said. "Were ye close?"

"Nay. He was older than I." Lachann resisted the urge to tell her that Arailt had been a good thirty years older than his own tender age of nine and twenty. "'Tis just that too many are dying and all because they trust in some Outsider wench." He was not surprised to see her scowl and wondered why he goaded her. Perhaps, he mused, he needed to hear her defend herself, to remind him that she was not like the others.

"Are ye waiting for me to betray ye then? To turn ye over to the verra men who hunt me and Osgar?" Adeline could hear her anger over his mistrust in her voice but saw no need to hide the fact that he insulted her with it.

"Nay, and I cannae think why. Ye are an Outsider."

"I think I have guessed what ye mean by that but, mayhap, ye can tell me just what is an Outsider?"

"One who isnae of the MacNachton clan, of MacNachton blood."

"How verra nice. Nay a friendly lot, are ye?"

"And why should we be friendly? 'Tis the *friendly* ones who are being slaughtered, the ones who try to live outside of Cambrun, to mix with the Outsiders and be accepted by you. And now we have the Hunters."

Adeline sighed. "Ye dinnae need to remind me. There were men hunting Osgar, too."

"Aye, and their numbers keep growing. 'Tis why we are all searching for the Lost Ones."

"And the Lost Ones are like Osgar?" He nodded. "And the men who chase us and want to kill him are called the Hunters? A name and nay just a word for what they are doing?"

"Aye. We call them that. I dinnae ken what they call themselves. Some grand pretentious name, nay doubt, as they all claim they are doing God's work. And, aye, Osgar is a Lost One, one born of an Outsider and a MacNachton but who was nay brought into the clan. Many dinnae e'en ken that there are others like them. That is, if they survive long enough to think on the matter. I suspicion Osgar isnae the first of his kind to be set out in the wood to die."

Adeline shivered, her mind suddenly choked with the image of innocent children like Osgar tossed aside because they were different. She knew babes were discarded, especially if a family was too poor to feed another child or the babe was born with some deformity, but it was one of those tragedies of life she had given little thought to, would not allow herself to think about. Having seen what had been done to Osgar made it hard to continue to ignore such harsh realities. It took her several moments to remind herself that she could not save them all, could not possibly find where and when such innocents were set aside to die. She had saved Osgar and would certainly save any other child she might find. That had to be enough.

"Are there any of Arailt's kinsmen, or women,

left at Cambrun?" she asked, wanting Osgar to find family at his new home yet terrified of losing him.

"One. An aunt, but she is old," replied Lachann after he swallowed the last of his meal. "I dinnae think she will be able to care for such a young lad, although she will be glad to ken that one of her blood still survives. She will grieve for Arailt but she was fair certain he was dead when a year passed with no word or sight of him."

Lachann could read the fear on her face even though he knew she thought she was hiding it. She was worried about losing the boy yet she did not slow in her journey to take him to his clan, to people who could protect him better than she could. He opened his mouth to reassure her and quickly closed it again.

Now was not the time to offer assurances he might not be able to fulfill. Cambrun was not a place many Outsiders would wish to stay at. Nor was he certain he wanted her to stay there. His hunger for her grew stronger with each hour he spent in her company, but he had seen too much tragedy result from the pairing of Outsiders and MacNachtons to risk putting himself in such a position without a great deal of thought.

"Have ye saved many Lost Ones?" she asked.

"Nay enough. I dinnae care to think on how many were lost to us forever." He shook his head. "I ken of far too many who left Cambrun and ne'er returned, too. The saddest thing is that we need new blood; we need Outsiders. Yet too many who try to join with one end up like Arailt."

"Why do ye need us? 'Tis odd that ye would claim a need for people ye dinnae trust."

"Our people, the full-blooded MacNachtons,

the Purebloods, cannae conceive. We have wed amongst our own for too long. The only ones born to the clan now are ones born of a mating between a MacNachton and an Outsider." A harsh laugh escaped him. "So there is a fine choice for us, aye? We die when we stay outside of Cambrun to find a mate and we die if we dinnae. We just do it a wee bit more slowly."

Adeline could think of nothing to say to dispute that or comfort him, so she asked, "Are ye a Pureblood?"

"Nay. There is some Outsider blood in me that came through my mother. My great-grandsire brought it into the family, I believe. Unlike too many of the old ones, he actually kept an eye out for any child he might have bred on a woman and fetched it home. The reason we have Lost Ones is that too many of our men didnae do that. Why should they have? They didnae think they could breed children. It wasnae until one of our clan began to record everything he could about the clan and we found a Lost One that we realized we could breed a child, just nay with anyone of strong MacNachton blood. The man making the records bred one himself."

Such a sad tale, she thought as she inched a little closer to the warmth of the fire. The cave they sheltered in was surprisingly well supplied but it was still a dank, cold hole in the rocks and that cold damp had sunk into her bones. So had the sadness, that hint of hopelessness, behind Lachann's words. Adeline did not understand why the MacNachtons were as they were, but they were God's creatures. It did not seem right that they faced such a bleak future, that their search for a mate, for children to carry on their name, too often brought them only death. It was such a simple wish, one shared by most people.

Then again, she mused, their differences made them a threat. She did not know the full extent of those differences but life with Osgar and her brief time with Lachann gave her a good idea of many of them. The need to drink blood was, of a certainty, the most alarming. She could easily understand how that could breed fear in people. That feral look both Osgar and Lachann got, those sharp fangs, only added to that fear. It revealed the predator under the skin. So too did Lachann appear to be a lot stronger and faster than other men. Those traits alone were enough to make people antagonistic to them but she suspected there were others. The only weakness she knew of was how they needed to avoid the sun. It was one that could be used as a weapon against them.

"But ye are safe at Cambrun, aye? And Osgar will be safe?"

"As safe as anyone can be and he will be cherished as all of our children are."

Adeline nodded. It broke her heart to even think of leaving Osgar, but she would force herself to do it. Lachann had still not said that she had to leave once they reached Cambrun but he had not invited her to stay, either. She ached to ask him if she could, but bit back the words. If Lachann's attitude toward those who were not of his clan was any indication, she might well find herself a very unwanted guest. She had already had a bellyful of being an outcast.

Deciding she could not think of that or she might grab Osgar and try to run far away, she turned her thoughts to the need to wash before she sought her bed next to a sleeping Osgar. A glance around the cave told her there was no privacy to be had yet she desperately wanted to wash away the smell of pony. She was going to have to trust Lachann to be a gentleman. It was either that or go to her rough bed smelling like her pony and she could not abide the thought of that.

"I need to wash," she said and looked at him. "Can I trust ye to keep your eyes on the fire?" She blushed when he quirked one dark brow at her. "There is nary a spot in this cave where I can wash in privacy but I need to rid myself of the smell of pony."

Lachann nodded. "I will keep my gaze upon the fire." He smiled faintly. "Mayhap ye can save some of that water ye have heated for me."

"Aye, I will."

She quickly grabbed the heavy pot she had set by the fire to warm the water and gathered up what she needed to wash and to don fresh linen. The guilt she felt over using so much of the little water she had brought was easily banished. Adeline was sure she would be able to refill her small water keg soon.

The back of the cave was shrouded in shadows where the light from the fire did not reach. Adeline chose that spot for her wash, sighing a little over how meager a wash it would be. After a glance over her shoulder showed her that Lachann was staring at the fire as he had promised, she began to shed her clothes.

Lachann managed to hold to his word even as he heard her clothing drop. It was when he heard the silvery rustle of the water and the soft sighs she made as she washed that his control broke. Cautiously he turned his head just enough to see her out of the corner of his eye and caught his breath so quickly and sharply he nearly coughed and gave himself away.

Adeline might be small and slender, but she was womanly enough to tempt a saint, and he was no saint. Her hips were nicely curved, her buttocks taut and round, perfect for a man to grasp hold of as he loved her. Each time she bent to dampen the cloth she washed with, he could see the curve of her breasts, plump, round breasts with the nipples taut from the faintly chill air in the cave. His mouth watered with the need to taste them. Her skin was pale, glistening faintly where it was wet, and unmarked. She was beautiful, a temptation on two long, slender legs.

He turned his gaze fully back to the fire. His whole body ached with the need to go over there and touch her, touch that skin, and trace every womanly curve. It was going to take a while for him to rid his body of all the obvious signs of that need. It had been a mistake to sneak a peek like some untried lad just starting to be fascinated with women, he decided. The sight of her naked, of her slim, womanly beauty, was going to haunt him for a very long time.

By the time she rejoined him by the fire, Lachann was once again in control of his body. He frowned a little as he saw that her hair was wet. "Ye washed your hair?"

Adeline blushed. "I but rinsed it off in the pot. It wasnae easy, but I didnae wish to use all the water, so it seemed the only way to keep my word that there would be warm water for you and my hair would be cleaned. I left the rag to wash with and the drying cloth over there. The water was still warm but I could reheat it a little if ye wish."

"Nay. 'Tis enough that it isnae as cold as the water in a loch or stream." He stood up and grinned down at her. "I willnae make ye promise to keep your eyes on the fire. Look your fill if ye want." He laughed when she glared at him and then turned her head to firmly stare into the fire.

A moment later, Adeline decided that the man was making a lot of noise on purpose. He was even singing softly to himself. She was trying to forget his words but hearing him shedding his clothes, knowing he was standing there naked, made it impossible. Look your fill if ye want, he had said. Adeline was ashamed to admit that she did want to look her fill but the very last thing she wanted was for him to see her do so.

As carefully as she could, she moved her head only enough to see him out of the corner of her eye, using the brushing of her damp hair as a shield for any movement he might perceive. She drew her breath in hard, but as softly as she could when she saw him. He looked a big, strong man in his clothes; without them he looked like some ancient god the pagans worshipped.

His back was broad and unscarred, the taut, smooth muscles moving gracefully as he washed himself. If asked before this moment, Adeline would have heartily denied seeing any fascination in the sight of a man's backside. But one look at Lachann's well-shaped rump had her swallowing hard. His legs were long and strong yet not thick with muscle. When he turned slightly to rub the washing rag over his belly, she saw his manhood. It was not nestled in the thick hair at his groin as the few she had glimpsed in the past when tending to sick men, but long, rigid, and standing slightly out from his body.

Quickly returning her gaze to the fire, even though she did not really see it, Adeline prayed she had not gasped. She had certainly felt like doing so. And why, she wondered, did the sight of Lachann MacNachton naked make her so warm, so unsteady in heart and limb? She was trembling as if she had walked about naked in the snow yet not because she was cold. In fact, if she did not shake the image of him from her mind, she would not be surprised if she started sweating.

A few deep, slow breaths later, Adeline was calmer. She knew she would not be able to forget what Lachann looked like beneath his clothes but she was confident that she could hide the knowledge she had just gained. Then he strolled over to sit down beside her and her heart leapt up into her throat. He was sitting too close. The heat of his body was infecting her, seeping into her blood. She set her brush down and clenched her hands in her lap, fighting against the urge to touch the smooth skin she had just seen. She wondered if she could move away without looking like a fool.

Lachann grinned at the pale flush on Adeline's cheeks. He had known she was looking at him. It troubled him a little that knowing she was had excited him, sent desire burning through his veins. That had never happened before. Lachann was not sure he liked it. It was a weakness and could be used against him. A small voice in his head whispered that Adeline would never play such games but he silenced it.

He leaned closer to her, inhaling the clean scent of her. "Ye peeked," he said softly, idly wondering what she would do if he licked her delicate ear.

"Nay, I didnae," she hastily denied and was not surprised when he laughed, the heat of his breath against her ear making her shiver.

"Aye, ye did. I could tell."

She turned her head to try and deny his accusation again, only to find their faces so close their noses touched. "Ye are a vain mon to think that a lass couldnae stare at a fire rather than at ye. I was brushing my hair."

"And glorious hair it is." He reached out and ran his fingers through the thick tendrils of her hair, fascinated by how the light of the fire made the red of her hair glow. "A delight to the eye."

"'Tis a witch's hair."

"Nay. That is naught but foolish superstition. Just because it carries all the brightness and color of fire doesnae mean 'tis hellborn."

The gentle stroke of his hands in her hair made Adeline's heart beat so fast she feared it could burst. He was so close to her, his golden eyes warm and intense. If she leaned just a little bit closer she could touch her mouth to his, could taste him. Just as she began to push that wild thought out of her mind, he leaned closer to her. The moment he touched his lips to hers, she was lost in a maelstrom of sensations and emotions she had never felt before, nor fully understood. Her only clear thought was *dinnae stop*.

The voice of caution told Lachann to pull away. He ignored it. He threaded his fingers through her thick, soft hair and held her face close to his as he kissed her. Her lips were soft and warm, and he quickly grew unsatisfied with the gentle kiss they shared. He nudged at her mouth with his tongue and after a brief hesitation she parted her lips. The soft murmur of delight that escaped her as he explored the inner heat of her mouth was sweet music to his ears.

He could hear the rapid beat of her heart, the breathlessness that made her pant softly. Lachann released her mouth and touched his lips to her throat. Adeline tilted her head back in a gesture of surrender that had him desperate to push her down, to spread her lithe body beneath him. It was not until he felt the sharp ache in his teeth, realized he was but one heartbeat away from marking her, from tasting her hot blood, that he came to his senses.

Adeline found herself released and sitting by herself so quickly she suffered a moment of dizziness. She looked up at Lachann, who stood with his arms crossed over his chest glaring at the waning fire. There were no soft words, no hint that he had even kissed her with such heat and skill that she would have given him anything he asked for. A chill went through Adeline, pushing away the last of the heat he had stirred within.

"Lachann?" Adeline was not sure what to say or how to ask what had just happened without sounding like she was begging for more. Her pride would not allow that.

"That was a mistake," said Lachann without looking at her.

Those four coldly spoken words hurt so much she nearly gasped from the pain. Adeline stood up and brushed off her skirts. She stiffened her legs when she swayed slightly, not wanting him to see any sign of her pain or weakness. What she had believed a wondrous thing, he saw as no more than taking a kiss from an easily available woman. Obviously he had suddenly recalled his role as her protector, or Osgar, and doused the fire she had felt in him. It could not have been a very hot fire, she thought bitterly, or it would not have died so quickly.

"I see," she murmured. "As you wish. I will get some sleep now."

"Do so. I will wake you and Osgar when it is safe for us to journey farther."

Adeline smothered the urge to kick him hard in his handsome backside and walked over to where Osgar slept, innocent of the turmoil around him. She settled herself beside the boy with her back toward Lachann and pulled the blanket over them both. The way Osgar immediately snuggled up against her did little to ease the pain in her heart and the shame she was determined to banish. She curled her arm around his little body, rested her cheek against his soft hair, and closed her eyes.

Lachann stared blindly at the fire until he heard Adeline's breathing become slow and even. Only then did he chance a look at her. He smiled crookedly when he saw that she kept her back to him.

He had insulted her, even hurt her. He had heard it in her voice. Lachann decided that was for the best, as it would ensure that she stayed away from him. Only then could he be sure that he would not give in to the insane urge to mark her. MacNachtons marked only their mates and he was not going to bind himself to an Outsider.

Chapter Five

Adeline wanted to pace. The effort it took to stand still made her muscles ache. She knew they needed supplies but she did not trust even this tidy village by a loch. Villagers quickly recognized a stranger in their midst and they all distrusted strangers, watched them closely. That was wise but it could also be a threat to any strangers passing through. Lachann had a lot to hide. It was dangerous for him to go anywhere that he would be watched closely. He had shrugged off her concerns, however, with an arrogance that had made her ache to hit him over the head with something heavy.

Guilt nearly choked her. It was her fault they needed supplies. She had not planned well for her journey, the food she had brought quickly disappearing along with what Lachann had carried with him. The excuse that she had never made a journey before was not enough to pardon her for bad planning. Adeline did not know why they could not just eat rabbit or fish until they reached Cambrun, either.

She sighed, staring at the village even though the increasing darkness made it difficult for her to see much more than faint lights in a few windows. Lachann had so easily ignored her concerns that she suspected he had done this kind of thing many times before. Raiding a village in the night, however, felt too much like thievery to her, and thieves were swiftly hanged.

Just the thought of Lachann in danger caused her heart to pound so hard it was painful and her belly to cramp with fear. Adeline did not understand her feelings for the man. She had known him for only four days and he had not been particularly friendly. Lachann made his mistrust of Outsiders all too clear and clung to it tenaciously, keeping a polite distance from them.

Except for that kiss, she thought and touched her mouth. She could still feel the warmth of his lips, the searing heat of his kiss, even two days later. Lachann had coldly declared that the kiss was a mistake and made it very clear that he had no intention of giving her another. Adeline badly wanted another, however, weak fool that she was. It puzzled her, for she had never been attracted to a man in all her two and twenty years. She did not trust men and yet she trusted Lachann with Osgar's life, and her own. But all Lachann had to do was smile at her, something he had done little of since that kiss, and all the strength went out of her legs. Her wits went begging as well.

"Ye had best come back safe and hale, Lachann MacNachton," she muttered.

"He will," said Osgar from where he sat by her feet piling up little rocks. "He is a big, strong mon."

Adeline looked at Osgar. "Big, strong men can

still be hurt, my bonnie lad. But, aye, mayhap I worry too much."

"Aye, ye do." Osgar scowled. "I dinnae like villages. Bad people live there and always want to do bad things."

"I am certain there are some good people there, too, Osgar." Adeline sighed when Osgar looked at her as if she were completely lacking in wits. "I ken we havenae met any, sad to say, but I am certain there are some." *I just pray Lachann meets only good people if he has to meet any at all.*

The sound of rustling leaves drew Adeline's attention away from her concern for Lachann. She frowned, for there was no wind. It was also too much noise to be made by some small forest creature. She turned to look behind her and tensed. The Hunters had found them.

Three men rushed forward as she grabbed Osgar up off the ground. Adeline tried to run to the ponies but the men moved faster than she could. Cursing them, she struggled to hold fast to Osgar when one of the men tried to pull the child from her arms. She kicked the man, aiming for his groin but only catching him high on his thigh. The blow staggered him enough that for one brief heady moment, he loosened his hold on Osgar. Just as she tried again to move toward the ponies something very hard slammed into the side of her head.

Adeline stumbled and fell to her knees, the pain in her head blinding her for a moment. She cried out when Osgar was torn from her arms. The three men ran even as she tried to get to her feet, determined to go after them. Lachann would come, she told herself as she swayed on her feet, her vision clearing but the pain making her dizzy and nauseous. All she had to do was try to slow the escape of the men who had stolen Osgar so that Lachann could reach the men in time to save the child. She staggered forward a step and prayed she could regain her wits and strength in time to accomplish that.

Lachann hefted his sack of supplies more firmly onto his shoulder and almost grinned. He knew Adeline thought he had crept into the village to steal what they needed and he had let her think it. When they next halted their journey he would tell her the truth, that he had paid for everything. Old Beaton was a man the MacNachtons often dealt with on their travels. The man never asked why they came buying goods at such odd hours, nor did he talk about them. It appeared that his son was more than ready to continue that tradition, which would please the laird of Cambrun.

His good humor faded as he made his stealthy way out of the village. Adeline was tying him up in knots. He had never wanted a woman as fiercely and constantly as he wanted her. MacNachton men were taught to control the passions that could ride them as hard as the need for blood, but every time he looked into Adeline's wide green eyes he grew hard with need. The warmth in her gaze told him that she returned his need and that made it almost impossible to fight the urge to take her, to make her his woman. The urge to mark her as his own was so strong it made his teeth ache, and that was what worried him the most.

"Fool," he muttered. "Ye ask her to trust ye but 'tis clear that ye dinnae want to trust her in return. And just what has the poor lass done to make ye so wary, hmm? Taken to her heart one of the Lost Ones, a Blooded Son who takes a wee sip of her now and then? Saved the wee laddie's life and put her own in constant danger? Left her own home to take the lad to a place many Outsiders say is naught more than a room in hell filled with demons? Ah, aye, such a treacherous lass she is."

He needed to stop blaming Adeline for the sins of others like Anne. Lachann knew he also had to accept the fact that she was fated to be his mate. He knew all the signs, had heard all the tales. Every MacNachton was told the ways to recognize his mate. His fierce need to mark her after only a kiss was hard proof that Adeline Dunbar was his. It was not going to be easy to explain it all to her when he finally gave in to the need gnawing at his innards. And it was definitely *when,* not *if.*

The sound of Adeline cursing yanked him from his thoughts. Lachann fought the urge to forgo all stealth and caution and rush to her side. She was in trouble, and charging blindly into the midst of it would not help her. He moved with more speed but held fast to the silence needed to surprise an enemy. The sound of Osgar crying nearly broke his control.

By the time Lachann reached the place where he had left Adeline and Osgar he was eager for a fight, bloodlust pounding in his veins. Seeing Adeline swaying on her feet as she staggered in an attempt to go deeper into the wood only increased that eagerness. He put down the sack of supplies and grabbed her when she started to crumple to her knees. Osgar's crying faded in his ears as fear for Adeline consumed him. He cursed viciously when she faced him and he saw the blood running from a wound on the side of her head.

"Ye are injured," he said, the need to hunt down the ones who hurt her and his fear making his voice a harsh growl as the beast reared up within him.

"'Tis but a scratch," she said as she steadied herself. "Head wounds always bleed freely."

"Where is Osgar?"

"They took him. Three men. That way." Adeline weakly pushed him toward the thicker section of the wood.

His fear for her receding when she sensibly answered his questions, Lachann could once again hear the men running through the trees and Osgar crying. He abruptly kissed Adeline and then started to hunt down the men who had stolen his child and hurt his woman. For the space of a heartbeat Lachann was startled by that thought. *His child. His woman.*

Then he realized that it was the truth, the truth he had been foolishly fighting since the moment he had seen them, seen her. Osgar was his child and Adeline was his woman. It was as if a weight had been lifted off his shoulders to finally accept that. Now he would see that the men who had hurt Adeline and stolen Osgar never left the forest alive.

The moment the men caught sight of him they separated, each running in a different direction, and Lachann cursed, knowing he would not be able to fulfill his vow. The frustration that surged through him nearly made him howl. He fought down the demands of his beast and set out after the man who held Osgar. Just as he came within reach of his prey the man turned and threw Osgar at him. Lachann easily caught the boy and watched the man run as if all the demons in hell were barking at his heels. The fool would be right if Lachann dared to put down the child clinging to him and go after the man, but he knew he could not do that.

"Did they hurt ye, Osgar?" he asked the shaking, sniffling child as he rubbed the boy's small back.

"Nay, but one of them hit *Maman* and she fell down," replied Osgar, rubbing his hands over his tear-stained face. "We got to go help her."

"I ken it." He sighed and muttered, "But I truly wished to kill those fools."

Osgar patted his cheek with his small, damp hand. "Ye can do that after we help my mither."

Lachann bit back a laugh. "I think we had best get her somewhere safe first."

"Aye. Men shouldnae hit lassies."

"Nay," agreed Lachann as he hurried back to where he had left Adeline. "Men shouldnae try to hurt wee lads, either, but I fear nay all men learn those rules."

The sight of Adeline sprawled on the ground made Lachann's heart leap up into his throat. He put Osgar down and hurried to her side. The sound of her steady heartbeat made him nearly weak-kneed with relief. When he knelt by her side and looked at the gash on the side of her head some of that relief faded, however. Even small head wounds might bleed freely but, upon a closer examination, this one looked like a great deal more than a scratch.

"Did ye see what the mon hit her with, Osgar?" he asked the child.

"A big rock," replied Osgar as he sat down on Adeline's other side and patted her hand.

Lachann cursed softly.

"Is it bad?"

"I ken little about wounds, but it doesnae look good to me," admitted Lachann.

"We can give her some blood. That always makes my hurts go away."

"She isnae one of us, Osgar."

"So it willnae help her?"

"It will, I think, but she may nay like it."

"I dinnae like some of the things she gives me when I hurt or cough, but she stills make me take them. I can give her some of my blood."

"Nay, if I think she needs it, I will give her some of mine. Now, let us bathe the wound and put a bandage on it. Do ye think ye can get me a clean rag and a wee bit of water?"

Osgar nodded as he scrambled to his feet. "I ken where she has her mending-people bag." He ran toward the ponies with a speed and grace that firmly held Lachann's attention for a moment. "I think I begin to ken why his father made him a Blooded Son," he murmured, recognizing that the ritual marking had given the boy a lot of survival skills most young children did not have.

The moment Osgar returned with the bag and some water, Lachann tended to Adeline's wound. When she did not rouse or even moan as he bathed and bandaged her injury, he grew worried.

One thing he did know about head wounds was that they could do a lot of damage that one could not see. The whole side of her face was already bruising, the colors livid, and that also troubled him.

"Can ye ride the pony without help, Osgar?" he asked the boy.

"Aye, but I needs to go slow," Osgar replied.

"We dinnae have far to go, lad, and if ye ride close to me I can lend a hand if ye have trouble." Lachann picked Adeline up in his arms and then gently set her back down again so that he could settle Osgar on the pony and secure the bag of new supplies. "Nay, I think I will lash your reins to my horse so that all ye have to do is hold on."

"*Maman* did that once. Have ye mended her?"

"We will see." Lachann wanted to see Adeline awake and talking sensibly before he offered the child any assurances.

By the time they reached the cave where they would shelter for the day, Lachann had no assurances to give the boy anyway. He did not like the way Adeline's breathing had grown unsteady, or the slower pace of her heart. With every yard they traveled she had grown weaker. Something was wrong. The blow to her head had done more than simply knock her senseless and open a gash in her scalp.

Lachann had Osgar spread some blankets on the floor and gently set Adeline down on them. He quickly built a fire and settled the animals. By the time he returned to her side, he knew he was going to have to do something more than bathe her wound and hope for the best.

"She is verra sick," said Osgar in a quiet voice as

Lachann handed him some cold chicken, cheese, and bread.

"Aye, laddie, she is," Lachann replied. "Sometimes when a person gets hit in the head it can do things inside them that just keep on making them sicker and sicker." He helped himself to some food and a hearty drink of cider. "As soon as I have filled my belly, I will do as must be done if she hasnae gotten any better."

"She willnae get angry."

"Ye cannae be sure of that, can ye? Ye havenae given her any of your blood to heal her, have ye?"

"Nay. She has ne'er had anything save a wee scratch or bruise."

Seeing how the child's bottom lip trembled, Lachann patted Osgar on the shoulder. "Dinnae look so afraid, lad. We ken how to help her and we will do it, will she, nill she. I think we are strong enough to endure her being angry, dinnae ye?"

"Och, aye. She just yells a wee bit, nay more."

Lachann doubted Adeline yelled at the little boy very much at all, although he held little hope that she would restrain herself from yelling at him. He was going to make her take some of his blood even if she did sound and look a little improved by the time he had finished eating. The fact that she had gotten worse at all was enough to convince him to do it, and chance her anger, even her disgust.

When he returned to her side, Lachann was almost glad to see that she had not improved. It gave him a good reason for what he was about to do, one she could not argue with. He suddenly smiled, knowing that Adeline could argue about anything.

Gently biting his wrist, he held it against her

mouth. If he could not get her to take any of his blood this way, he would mix some in cider and force it down her throat. Lachann would rather not do that but, as he waited for her to react to the moisture on her mouth, he knew he would. Adeline would survive. She would recover from this wound hale and as sharp-tongued as ever, he vowed to himself.

After a moment so long it felt like an hour, her mouth moved against his wrist. Lachann firmly grasped her chin with his free hand and tugged on it, forcing her mouth open enough for the blood to drip in. She made a face much like a child forced to swallow bitter medicine and he relaxed a little. Adeline had to be aware in some part of her mind if she could react like that.

The feel of her mouth against his wrist, the stroke of her tongue as she lapped at what her mind thought was much-needed moisture, made his innards tighten with need. He knew sharing his blood could be a sensual experience, as he had had a few lovers amongst the MacNachtons, but he would never have thought that giving his blood to an insensible woman could be so. It was. Too much so. He was almost sweating from the heat rushing through his body. Lachann suspected that if Adeline suddenly woke up and smiled at him, he would be on her like a starving wolf.

Lachann gave her only a little blood before he forced himself to pull away from her and lick at his wound until it began to close. He looked at Osgar, who sat down beside him, leaning on him lightly. The boy was so tired he could barely keep his eyes open.

"Ye need to rest, lad," he said as he stood up and began to make a pallet for the child.

"*Maman* will get better, aye?"

"Aye. I have nay doubt about it." He smiled at the boy. "She is too stubborn to do anything else." He did not hesitate to give the boy hope this time, for he had seen far worse wounds on an Outsider mended by a few sips of MacNachton blood.

"Then may I sleep in the wee room o'er there with Meg and Tom?"

A quick glance into the far corner of the cave revealed a deep, narrow niche in the wall. "Ye will be far away from the fire."

"I ken it but it doesnae matter. I can see weel in the dark."

Lachann nodded and went to make the boy a bed inside the niche while Osgar relieved himself and cleaned his teeth. After carefully looking over the opening to the cave and the tunnel at the back to assure himself that both were well sealed with rocks, he released the cats. He and Osgar laughed as the animals raced around the cave with such exuberance he was surprised they did not bounce off the walls. After he got the giggling Osgar settled in the poor bed, the cats quickly curled up around the child and Lachann made his way back to Adeline's side.

"Ah, lass, ye have raised a fine lad," he murmured. "He will have no trouble finding his place within the clan. Neither will ye but I have the strongest feeling that ye will need some convincing ere ye will believe that."

Chapter Six

Another cursed cave, Adeline thought as she woke to find a stone ceiling over her head. She sucked a breath in through clenched teeth as she became aware of far too many bruises and pains. Her body felt as if someone had tossed her around a room and made certain that she hit every wall.

"Adeline?"

She looked to her right to find Lachann seated by her bed of blankets. "Osgar?" she asked, her fear for the child rapidly building as she recalled what had happened in the wood.

"He is fine," Lachann assured her. "He is sleeping in his own wee room but feet away."

"Room? But are we nay in another cave?"

"Aye, but there is a small room cut into the rock. Osgar claimed it as his room. The cats are in there with him." He patted her hand when she looked at him in alarm. "They cannae get out of here."

"If we can get in, they can get out, Lachann."

"Nay. The way we came in is now fully covered

with large rocks, the sort I can move but many another mon cannae. The only openings are small cracks to allow air in and the smoke of the fire out. There is a wee bolt-hole in the back of the cave but it is also completely covered with rocks. I am nay sure where it leads." He grimaced. "Should have studied the maps more closely."

"Maps?" Adeline asked, although she was distracted by how much better she was feeling except for a very odd taste in her mouth.

"Aye. We carefully map each route, the shelters that lie along it, and the places where we can get new supplies." He carefully touched the bandage on her head. "How does your head feel?"

Adeline thought about that for a moment and then frowned. "Nay bad. And all the aches and pains I woke with are already fading away. The blow I took on the head must nay have been as bad as I thought it was."

Lachann briefly contemplated not telling her about what he had done and then quickly cast the thought aside. Osgar would soon tell her if he did not. He took a deep breath as he prepared himself to make his confession. How she reacted to what he had done would settle whatever last doubts he had.

"I gave ye a wee bit of my blood," he said. When he saw only confusion on her face, he continued, "One of the MacNachton differences is that we heal quickly."

"Aye, I have seen that in Osgar. 'Tis wondrous," she said.

"Weel, we have discovered that our blood can help to heal Outsiders as weel." He sighed, his hope that she would fully accept him shattering as her curious expression turned to one of utter horror and fear.

"Sweet heavens, Lachann, ye best be verra careful who learns of that." She shook her head slowly. "It chills me to the bone to think of the danger that would put ye, and all of the MacNachtons, in."

He had been an idiot, he thought as he smiled at her and carefully removed her bandage, not surprised to find the injury healed. Adeline's horror and fear were all for what could happen to him and his clan. Lachann decided that he needed to think more on the matings between Outsiders and MacNachtons that were good, solid, and happy, instead of only on the bad ones. He had committed the sin of prejudging her, just as so many people prejudged the MacNachtons, fearing and hating them without even trying to come to know who they were.

"'Tis naught to smile about, Lachann," she said as she cautiously sat up, noticing that she was feeling better by the moment. "Ye would have trouble with far more than the Hunters if word of how your blood can heal e'er spread. Everyone would be after a MacNachton just to make use of your blood, to cure themselves or their loved ones, or to sell to make themselves wealthy and powerful. I shudder to think of the tortures that would be visited upon ye and your people. They would tap ye like a barrel of ale."

Lachann leaned forward and kissed her forehead, then smiled into her wide eyes. "We ken it. We are all verra careful. We have e'en killed to keep our secret, although the ones who died deserved their fate for far more reasons than that. Several of my clan are now carefully studying the matter. My laird's wife wonders if it works only when given freely, willingly, when there is a bond between the giver and the taker."

"A bond?" Adeline sternly told herself not to let her own needs and desires make her foolish, make her see more behind his words than there was. "Ye think we have some sort of bond between us?"

"Aye, I do." Lachann struggled to think of some way to explain without touching upon the fact that he was certain she was his mate, all his doubts about that having faded away with each passing hour. "Do we nay flee the same people? Do we nay face the same dangers? Are we nay both feared and distrusted by Outsiders? Do we nay both love that wee lad, would willingly die to protect him? I think all of that makes for a verra strong bond between us." She could not completely hide her disappointment over his answer and that delighted him. "Do we nay feel the same need, the same desire, for each other?"

His low, husky voice warmed her. He did not speak of love or marriage, but, at that precise moment, she did not care. Lachann had just confessed that he desired her. The way he had ended the only kiss they had shared had made her begin to think that he did not feel the same fierce wanting that plagued her. Adeline's heart pounded out the message that need and desire could easily grow into love. She ignored the more sensible part of her that warned her to tread slowly, that her heart could be blind and foolish.

"I think we do," she answered quietly, ignoring the heat of the blush stinging her cheeks.

Lachann stroked her long, bright hair. "I ken we do. That kiss we shared told me so."

"But ye thought it was a mistake and ye havenae tried for another."

"Cowardice and unkind thoughts. Unfair judgments just because ye are an Outsider. I wanted ye to trust me but I wasnae willing to trust ye. Despite what ye have done for Osgar, a bairn who showed ye the beast within him from the verra first time ye held him in your arms, I allowed the sins of others to taint ye. That was wrong of me but it took a while for me to see that."

Adeline nodded and smiled faintly. "Aye, it was, but I can understand the why of it. That doesnae explain why ye should call yourself a coward, however. That just isnae true. No mon who faces four armed men for a child and a woman he doesnae ken is a coward."

"Facing four armed men is naught but a nuisance compared to facing what I felt when I kissed you. I was fiercely stirred by an Outsider female and that set me back on my heels." That and the fact that he had ached to mark her as his own, but he knew it was too soon to tell her that.

"So, ye didnae kiss me again because ye didnae trust me, because I am nay a MacNachton."

He winced to hear how his prejudice sounded when spoken so bluntly. "Aye, but I finally shook off that foolishness."

Anticipation raced through Adeline's veins when Lachann slipped his arms around her shoulders and tugged her closer to him. His beautiful eyes held a warmth that quickly seeped into her blood. Her mouth watered, eager for the taste of him again.

"I should leave ye be," he whispered as he followed the delicate lines of her face with soft, teasing kisses. "Ye were badly injured today."

"I feel as if naught happened to me, though I ken that my injury was far more serious than I had thought it to be." She shivered with delight as he kissed her ear and then gently nipped the lobe, astonished that such a simple thing could make her so breathless.

"It was." He moved back just enough to study her face. "E'en the bruising has faded to little more than a faint color."

"'Tis wondrous." She slowly wrapped her arms around his neck, a little afraid that he was thinking of leaving her again. "'Tis a shame that ye must keep it a secret, that people would prey upon ye for it instead of allowing ye to help them of your own free will."

"Right now, lass, I dinnae think I want to discuss the wondrous healing power of my blood."

"Nay? What do ye want to do?"

"First I wish to kiss you."

"Oh, aye. Please."

Lachann covered her mouth with his. He planned to seduce her slowly, gently, but the moment his lips touched hers all the hunger he felt for her broke free of the chains he had put on it. The way she softened in his arms, her lithe body fitting against his in eager welcome, only added to the sharp, demanding need he suffered. He had almost lost her and he ached to assure himself of how alive she was in the most primal of ways. Lachann wanted to revel in the sweet heat of her desire, to learn all the secrets of her body, and to mark her as his own.

"Adeline," he groaned against her throat, "I think we had best cease. The tether on my desire isnae a verra strong one. I am but a heartbeat away from spreading your fine little body out beneath me."

His rough words had Adeline nearly panting from the strength of her need. She wanted to strip him of his clothes so that she could touch his skin. She wanted to look at his strong body without having to hide her delight in it. Although she had never even kissed a man before now, she knew all that could be shared between a man and a woman. A healer saw and heard a lot. Despite a tiny pinch of virginal fear, Adeline wanted to share that with Lachann.

"Nay, kiss me again," she demanded. "And again and again until I cannae breathe or think."

"If I kiss ye again, I willnae stop until ye are fully mine."

"Oh." She trembled, passion tearing through her at the mere thought of what they were about to do. "I ken it. Kiss me again."

Lachann growled softly and kissed her, making no attempt to govern his need. She did not pull away as he had feared she might but pressed even closer. When she tentatively parried the thrust of his tongue with her own, he cast aside all doubt and restraint and pushed her down onto the rough pallet. It took what little willpower he had left not to tear off the thin linen shift she wore, hurl aside his own clothing, and bury himself deep inside her.

It was not until she heard herself moan as Lachann kissed the skin between her breasts that

Adeline realized she wore only her shift and he was rapidly removing that. Uncertainty pushed aside a little of the haze his kisses and caresses had clouded her mind with. She knew a man as handsome as Lachann must have had many women, beautiful women. Suddenly, Adeline was not sure she wanted to be naked, not even if he was also naked.

The sudden tension in Adeline's body was enough to remind Lachann that he was dealing with a virgin. Her body had been untouched, and unseen, by any other man. He quickly finished removing her shift, allowing her no time to act upon her sudden attack of maidenly modesty.

Straddling her with his legs, he sat up and removed his shirt. He ached to remove his breeches as well but did not dare let her loose. The way her gaze settled on his chest, her green eyes darkening with renewed desire, made him inclined to preen, but he resisted the urge. He needed to be skin to skin to her, to feel her full, soft breasts against his chest. Even as he returned to her arms, he stealthily unlaced his breeches so that they would be easily, and quickly, removed when the time came to be free of them.

"Ye are so verra beautiful, Adeline," he said and then he kissed her.

When his warm, smooth skin pressed against hers, Adeline lost all concern about her nudity; she began to revel in it. She wrapped her arms around him again and stroked his broad back with her hands. Adeline savored the feel of his taut skin and strong muscles. She tipped her head back as he kissed his way down her throat. He slid his hands up her rib cage and over her breasts, using his fingers to tease and stroke her nipples until she thought the aching he stirred there was too fierce to endure.

"Lachann!" she cried out in shock and delight when he took the hard top of her breast into his mouth, licking and suckling until she was half mad with need.

"Hush, love," he said even as he continued to torment her. "Ye are a virgin."

"And that is why ye must drive me to madness with this play?" she asked, a little confused by his statement.

He chuckled hoarsely. "Nay. I but prepare ye for your breeching," he said and stroked his hand over her soft stomach and then between her legs.

The hot, damp welcome he found there nearly undid him. Lachann gritted his teeth, determined to hold on to enough control to stir her passion to such heights that she would feel no pain when he finally joined their bodies. He wanted to kiss her there, to taste her sweetness, but promised himself that delight later when she became more accustomed to having him as her lover. Such an intimacy done too soon could chill the desire she now felt. He plunged his finger into her heat and worked to prepare her for his entry. To his relief, she was ready for him, so caught up in passion's snare that he knew it would not take long before he could seek his pleasure.

Adeline feared she was about to break apart. She had not realized passion could be so fierce, forcing everything within her to its will. Certain she was on the brink of madness, she called Lachann's name and, suddenly, he was there, kissing her. She lost herself in his kiss, only faintly aware of how he spread her legs.

It was not until she felt him start to join their bodies that she was able to grasp some control of herself. A sharp pain made her gasp but then a heady surge of desire washed it away. They were now one. Adeline wrapped her legs around his trim hips and heard him growl his approval. He began to move and she quickly caught his rhythm. Her body grew taut and something curled tighter and tighter low in her belly until it was both a pleasure and a pain. She had the fleeting thought that something must have gone wrong with the joining and she shattered. As she tumbled down into a deep pool of blinding pleasure that had her calling out to Lachann, she felt another sharp pain—in her neck. The bliss that was sweeping over her increased tenfold.

Lachann groaned as Adeline's body clenched around his as her release tore through her. Even as his own release shook him, he sank his teeth into her neck. The sweet, hot taste of her blood in his mouth combined with the hot clasp of her flesh around his had him emptying himself deep into her womb. She was still gasping and trembling in his arms when he licked the small wound on her neck, closing it. He knew, however, that this mark would never fade.

Adeline began to come to her senses as Lachann gently bathed her, wiping away the signs of her lost innocence. She blushed and closed her eyes, embarrassed by such an intimacy. A moment later he was beside her, pulling a blanket over them and then taking her into his arms. She looked up at him and suddenly recalled that second sharp pain she had felt before she had lost all ability to think. Touching the side of her neck, she felt a slight mark beneath her fingertip.

"Ye bit me," she muttered. "Why did ye bite me? Do ye hurt?"

"Nay." He kissed her and then turned her so that her back was pressed against his front. "The passion between us raged so hot, I couldnae help myself." He inwardly sighed with relief when she relaxed against him. "Did I hurt ye?" he asked as he kissed her shoulder.

"Och, nay." Adeline was glad they were not face-to-face as she admitted, "I was a wee bit crazed at the time and didnae e'en notice much more than a pinch."

"Good." He kissed her ear. "Rest now, love. We still have a lot of miles to go before we reach Cambrun."

Love, she mused as she closed her eyes, more than ready to sleep. She wished he meant it.

Lachann smiled at how quickly Adeline fell asleep. He could not help but feel a touch of pride over how completely he had exhausted her with his lovemaking. Making love to her had been all he could have hoped for and more. He kissed the mark he had left on her neck. She was his mate. All he had to do now was figure out the right way to tell her.

Chapter Seven

Passion was a wonderful thing to wake up to, Adeline thought as she heartily returned Lachann's kiss. Her body already sang with hunger for him, her blood pumping hot with demand. The dream she had been enjoying had obviously not been a dream. The kisses and caresses that had stirred her blood as she roused from sleep had been very real. When Lachann settled himself between her thighs, she wrapped her legs around him, eagerly welcoming him into her body. He smothered her cries with his mouth as they reached the blissful heights of desire as one.

Lachann grinned as he nuzzled her neck while his body recovered from their lovemaking. Adeline was a very passionate woman. Her desire ran as hot and fierce as his did. The satisfaction she gave him was unmatched by anything he had ever known before. Fate had chosen well when sending him his mate.

"I would love nothing more than to stay right here and make ye cry out in pleasure again and again, until we are both too weary to lift a finger, lass, but"—he kissed her—"'tis time to rouse Osgar, gather our things together, and be on our way."

She stretched lazily and watched him as he dressed, fascinated by such a mundane thing and regretting the fact that he was covering that fine, strong body. It was difficult to believe that such a handsome man could desire her, but she could not doubt it any longer. Last night, their second night as lovers, had been as hot and fierce as the first. And now he had shown her that he was well pleased to wake with her in his arms.

Adeline shook aside such thoughts and hastily pulled on her shift. Now was not the time to indulge in them, to puzzle over all she had and did not have with Lachann MacNachton. There was work to do and Osgar would soon be awake. She did not really want to try and explain to the child why she and Lachann were sleeping together, naked. Just the thought of it made her hurry to get dressed and put away their rough bedding.

When they finally stepped outside into the gloom of a cloudy late afternoon, Adeline had to blink a few times. The sun was low in the sky, the clouds hiding it, but there was still more sunlight than she had seen since Lachann had joined her and Osgar. She prayed her future would not be one of continued darkness and caves. At least this time they had found shelter in a small stone house instead of a cave.

Somewhat relieved when Lachann took Osgar up before him on his horse, she mounted her pony and fell into line behind Lachann as he started down the hill. It was going to be nice to ride without having to worry about a child on the saddle in front of her. A part of her could not help but be fascinated by all she was seeing. She had never traveled far from her little cottage, so each sight was new to her. However, she was going to be very glad when they reached Cambrun and her journey was at an end. Hours in the saddle became tiresome very quickly.

They had been riding for several hours when Lachann abruptly signaled a halt. Adeline could tell by the way he sat so tensely in the saddle, his eyes closed, that he was listening to something she could not hear. She did envy him and Osgar their superior sight and hearing. She could think of many ways she could make use of such gifts in her life.

She tensed when Lachann dismounted, set Osgar on his feet, and then walked over to help her dismount, for she was certain they were not stopping for a respite. "What is wrong?" she asked.

"Mayhap nothing but I dinnae wish to ride on until I have had a look about," he replied.

"Could we nay just take another path?"

"Nay, that will solve little. Ye just wait here, lass." Lachann kissed her, ruffled Osgar's curls, and strode away.

Adeline watched him until he was out of sight, admiring his long, strong legs and manly stride. She was annoyed with him despite her admiration of his form, however. Yet again he had left and given her no explanation as to why. He was always leaving her behind, telling her to wait. It made her feel useless, too much like a burden to him.

Yet, it was difficult to get very angry with him despite her annoyance over his actions. Adeline had to admit that she liked having someone to look out for her, to protect her and Osgar. She had been alone for too long, facing every trial and danger by herself, fear a constant companion especially after she had found Osgar. Her lover had taken most of that fear away and she certainly did not feel all alone now.

Her lover, she thought, and sighed. While the knowledge that Lachann MacNachton desired her was heady, she tried not to let his passion for her overwhelm her common sense. Passion did not equal love. A man could show desire to the most ragged, plain-faced wench and yet forget her before he finished tugging up his breeches. It had long been the way of men. Being Lachann's lover for only two days did not give her any claim to his heart.

"*Maman?* Are ye going to marry Lachann?" asked Osgar. "Is that why ye sleep with him?"

Adeline inwardly cursed. Osgar had obviously woken up at least once and seen her and Lachann sleeping together. She heartily thanked God that the boy had not seen them when they were busy indulging their passions, and then turned her mind to the boy's question. She could not lie to the child because he would undoubtedly share her lie with Lachann, if he did not call her on it first. Osgar had a sharp nose for a lie.

The problem came in how to tell the little boy the truth without hurting his growing accord with Lachann. Or, worse, making him disappointed in her. Osgar knew most of the rules society and the church espoused, but to him everything was black and white; there were no *buts,* no *wee sins,* and no *mayhaps.*

"I dinnae ken," she finally answered, deciding

honesty might not be comfortable for her but it was best, if only because Osgar would not let it go if she lied. "We havenae discussed it."

Osgar scowled at her. "But ye were in the same bed. I saw ye and I dinnae think ye had any clothes on."

"That doesnae mean we are married or soon will be."

"Ye mean 'tis like Anne when she has men share her bed and doesnae marry them? Ye want to do that?"

"Nay!"

"If ye are cold, I could share your bed and then ye wouldnae have to let Lachann sleep with ye and then no mon can say any bad things about ye."

"Oh, dear."

Adeline shook her head and stared at her feet. She needed to think of a simple way to explain the situation, something a child of five could understand. Osgar was a very bright five, quick-witted and well spoken, but he was not old enough to understand the intricacies of passion and love. She frowned as she rethought that opinion. Osgar could understand love, and, if she swore him to secrecy, it might be the easiest way to answer his questions. Adeline knew that if she did not answer the boy's questions to his satisfaction, he would only keep asking them.

"I dinnae share my bed with Lachann because I am cold, Osgar." She took a deep breath and confessed. "I do it because I love the mon but I want ye to swear to me that ye will ne'er tell him so. If I think he needs to ken that, I will tell him myself. Understood?"

"He hasnae told ye so ye dinnae want to tell

him." Osgar nodded and then frowned in the direction Lachann had gone. "He should tell ye."

"That would be verra nice and make me a verra happy woman, but he must do it of his own free will. 'Tis best that way, Osgar."

"Well, when I am grown and sleep with a lass, I will tell her I love her right away."

"Only if ye truly mean it."

"Why would I lie?"

That question nudged too close to the topic of sex and passion, Adeline decided. "I dinnae think ye would. 'Twas but a rule I thought ye should be told of." When Osgar solemnly nodded and turned his attention to all the sticks and leaves on the ground, she inwardly sighed with relief.

Adeline tried to be patient as she waited for Lachann but soon began to pace. She truly hated waiting when she knew how dangerous it was for a MacNachton outside of Cambrun. The last attack had made her certain that someone had started a hunt specifically to get Osgar, as well. She desperately wanted to get the child safely behind the walls of Cambrun.

Her legs ached from all her pacing by the time Adeline became truly worried about Lachann. He should have been back, either to report that everything was well or to get them hurrying away from this place. Something was wrong. She was sure of it, but she did not know what to do about it. She did not even know where he had gone, what he had heard, or what he had been looking for.

"I think something bad has happened," Osgar said as he stepped up next to Adeline and clutched at her hand.

"I begin to fear the same," murmured Adeline. "I just wish I kenned where he is."

"I can find him."

She frowned down at the child. "Ye dinnae ken where he went, either."

"He went to where the men are talking."

"What men? I dinnae hear any men."

"I can. I closed my eyes and listened real hard like Lachann taught me and I can hear men talking."

"What are they saying?"

"I cannae hear that. I can just hear the sound of men talking. Got to get closer to hear all the words, ye ken. I think that is what Lachann was doing. He wanted to see if it was bad men talking."

Adeline argued with herself over the best thing to do now, the wisest thing to do. The wisest thing would be to go on to the next shelter, as Lachann had told her to do if he was ever late returning to them, and then wait for him there. She could not bring herself to do that, not even for Osgar's safety. She knew she would never forgive herself if she fled while Lachann was in trouble. On the other hand, she would not forgive herself if Osgar were hurt, or worse, while she tried to help Lachann. Osgar's tug on her hand drew her out of her confused turmoil of uncertainty.

"We must go find him," Osgar said. "He needs our help."

"We are nay warriors, Osgar. We are but a small woman and a wee lad." She sighed. "And Lachann would be angry if we put ourselves in danger for his sake."

"Why? He puts himself in danger for us all the

time." His bottom lip trembled. "And I love him. Ye said ye loved him, too. We cannae let him get killed."

"Hush." Adeline put her arm around the child's shoulders and held him close to her side. "We will go the way he did but verra quietly and cautiously. We shall try to get close enough to the men talking so that ye can hear exactly what they are saying, but nary a step closer. If they have done something to Lachann, we will soon ken it and we can decide what to do at that time."

It took only a few yards for Adeline to realize that little Osgar could move through the wood with a great deal more stealth than she could. She had never truly paid attention to how silently the child could move. Every time a leaf rustled as she walked, she felt as if she had just sent out a clarion call announcing her arrival. Osgar moved so silently she wondered if his feet were even touching the ground.

She was finally able to hear the murmur of men's voices when Osgar stopped, held himself very still, and closed his eyes. The dark scowl on his small face told her that what he was hearing was not good. When a soft growl escaped the boy, Adeline realized that, although Osgar had been born of an Outsider like her, he was also a Mac-Nachton to the bone. He was far more like Lachann's people than hers and that truth hurt a little. When they reached Cambrun, Osgar might well be accepted so completely, so wholeheartedly, that he would have no more use for her.

"The men have Lachann," Osgar whispered.

His words cut through her sudden fear of losing

him to the MacNachtons. One for Lachann rapidly replaced that fear. The fact that the men had not immediately killed Lachann when they had a chance was not the cause for relief it should have been. Adeline recalled all too well Lachann's tale about his cousin who had been captured and viciously tortured. He had made it very clear that no MacNachton wanted to be captured, that they would rather die, even by their own hand. It was not cowardice that prompted that dire feeling either, but the dread of being used to expose the tightly held secrets of the MacNachtons.

"I had best get closer," she murmured.

"They want me," Osgar said. "They are trying to make Lachann tell them where I am."

Adeline sat down and put her head in her hands. She did not want to hear what the men were doing to Lachann to try to get him to give up Osgar. The child's pale face and clenched fists told her all she needed to know. Lachann was a captive and he was being tortured. He must be loudly railing at the fates right now as he faced his greatest fear.

And who was there to help him? A healer and a small child. She was no warrior. About all she could do if she confronted several armed men was to give them a potion to incapacitate them. Adeline doubted the men would give her the opportunity to mix up such a potion or drink anything she might offer them. She might be able to gain Lachann a few extra minutes of life or a brief respite from the pain he suffered while the men who held him decided when they would kill her and how. She had brought Lachann nothing but trouble since he had first met her.

"I will go see what is happening," said Osgar.

"Nay, I should do that," she protested and hastily stood up.

"Nay, *Maman*. Ye are good at sneaking about but I am muches better. I will be back."

Adeline reached out to grab him and stop him, but he was already gone. She bit back the urge to call him back and began to pace again. It felt as if hours crawled by but she knew it was her fear that caused that. Then, suddenly, Osgar was back, standing in front of her. She could tell by the feral look upon his usually sweet face that what he had seen had roused the predator Lachann claimed lived within every MacNachton.

"They have hurt him," Osgar said, a growl of fury in his childish voice. "There are three men, the ones who tried to steal me and hit you. They have Lachann tied to a tree near the wood and they have been whipping him. He is bleeding."

She knew all too well what that meant. Lachann had already lost so much blood he could no longer heal himself. He was truly weak and helpless now, or would be so very soon. She could not leave him. A glance at Osgar's furious little face told her that the boy would never cooperate with her if she tried to flee, might never forgive her for it if she did. Then she looked back to where the ponies were, the ponies and a very large gelding she suspected had been well trained for battle.

"I think I may have an idea about how to help Lachann, Osgar," she said. "Ye have to hide yourself verra weel while I fetch Lachann's horse. 'Tis my thought that the horse can help us save Lachann."

Once assured that Osgar was thoroughly hidden

beneath the leaves, Adeline ran back to the horses. The gelding eyed her warily as she moved to his side. Adeline had never ridden such a large mount before but she could not see why she could not handle the mount, if only for the short time she needed him. Nudging the animal into a slow, quiet pace, Adeline returned to where she had left Osgar.

Osgar leapt from his hiding place and the horse shifted nervously beneath her. "'Ware, Osgar," Adeline said as she dismounted but kept a firm hold on the horse's reins. "Ye must nay startle a horse."

"Pardon, Ulf." Osgar stroked the animal's neck.

"Ulf?" asked Adeline.

"Aye. Didnae ye e'er hear Lachann call the beastie by name?"

"I thought he but grunted at the beast. Now, heed me most carefully, Osgar. Tell me true, do ye think ye can creep up behind Lachann without being seen and safely use a knife to cut his bonds?" When Osgar eagerly nodded, she pressed, "Do ye tell me true, lad? 'Tis nay a time to say *aye* when the truth is *mayhap* or *nay*."

"I can do it. I can. 'Tis like one of the games I played in the garden at home, aye? Sneaking up on an enemy, pretending I am a mighty warrior, saving poor Meg or Tom from bad men, and—"

"With a knife?"

"Aye." Osgar blushed with guilt. "I did sneak a wee blade sometimes."

"Your naughtiness will serve us weel this time, but later we will discuss it. Now"—she removed the sheathed knife belted at her waist and secured the blade to Osgar's belt—"ye are to creep up on Lachann like the mist and cut his bonds. Stay hidden behind him as ye do so. Once ye have freed him, and he may tell ye when ye have done enough so that he can free himself, ye are to run back to the ponies."

"But—"

"Dinnae question me on this. 'Tis verra dangerous work we are about and there can be no arguments or disobedience. Ye get back to the ponies and be ready to ride when Lachann and I join ye."

He nodded. "But what will ye and Ulf do to help?"

"I will give ye a wee bit of time to get to Lachann and start cutting away his bonds." She mounted Ulf and tested the ease with which she could draw the sword attached to the saddle from its sheath.

"And?"

"Ah, aye, and then I intend to ride to Lachann's rescue, of course."

Chapter Eight

"He isnae going to give us the lad. Best we just kill the bastard and start looking for the lad again."

Lachann looked at the too thin, dirty man who spoke and was pleased when the fool paled slightly and stepped farther away. He also cursed his own folly, that arrogance that had him stumbling into a trap like some beardless boy on his first hunt. One solid hit to his head had quickly brought him to his knees, too dazed to fend off his attackers. A second blow had sent him tumbling into blackness. It was humiliating. Worse, he had bled enough that he no longer had the strength to break free of the ropes tying him to the tree.

"Give us the lad and we will let ye live," said the burly man the other two men called Ian.

"What sort of coward would buy his life with that of a child?" Lachann asked, making no attempt to hide his scorn over even being offered such a deal.

He prayed that Adeline had the sense to take Osgar to the next shelter and wait for him there. It did not look as if he would be able to join them, but at least she and the boy would be safe. After a while, she would have to know that he was not coming to her and continue on to Cambrun. Lachann tried to find comfort in the sure knowledge that his clan would shelter them but it was hard to do so. Adeline and Osgar were his family now and he wanted to be with them. He wanted to see Osgar grow into a man and Adeline grow round with his child.

"We dinnae plan to kill the wee lad," Ian said.

The man was obviously trying to be conciliatory, reassuring even, and Lachann almost told him that he was failing badly. These men might not have any plans to harm Osgar themselves, but Lachann was certain they intended to take the child to someone who did. It chilled him to the bone to think of Osgar in the hands of such men. After the torture his cousin Heming had suffered while held captive, no MacNachton wanted to become the prisoner of the Hunters. The whole clan could see how easily the secrets they held fast to could become known under such duress, if only through the close observation of their enemies. Lachann would rather cut his own throat or stand naked beneath the noonday sun than be taken captive.

A moment later, he inwardly sighed. He realized he would do anything he could to stay alive and get back to Adeline and Osgar. Lachann admitted to himself that he would fight for life until the last breath left his body, the hope that he could see them just one more time keeping him struggling to get home.

"Ye may nay kill him with your own hands, but the bastard ye take him to will, and weel ye ken it,"

Lachann said and bit back the urge to scream when the man lashed him with the whip again.

"I told ye. He willnae give up the lad. This is useless," said the thin, dirty man.

"Shut your mouth, Keith," snapped Ian. "Mayhap he willnae give up the lad but dinnae forget the witch who rides with him and the boy. That lad isnae her child, so she may be willing to deal with us. She may nay wish to lose her lover, aye? Fine braw laddie like this. He be the type the lasses all sigh o'er, too witless to ken that he is naught but a beast from hell. We will wait awhile to see if the witch comes after him."

A surge of fear cut through Lachann's pain and he nearly cried out from the strength of it. He knew Adeline would never offer these men Osgar in trade for him, even if she could be so foolish as to think they would actually let the both of them leave that exchange alive. What he could not be sure of was that she would leave him to his fate and get the child to safety. He told himself she would think of the child's safety first but, in his heart, he knew there was a good chance she would try to save him. All he could do was pray that she did not. *Stay away,* he silently told her. *Run. Grab Osgar and run as far and fast as ye can, love.*

"And what if she doesnae come after him?" asked Keith.

"Then we will truss this bastard up and take him to the laird instead," replied Ian. "We willnae get as heavy a purse as was promised for the boy but I suspicion he willnae toss this one back. He is always looking for one of his ilk. Any MacNachton is a prize he will pay for."

Lachann was about to ridicule that plan when

he felt a slight tug on the ropes that bound him to the tree. His heart leapt into his throat, fear and anticipation warring in his heart for dominance. He slowly took a deep breath and then silently repeated every curse he knew. He recognized that scent. It was not Adeline slowly cutting his bonds; it was Osgar. The prize these men wanted so badly was now within their reach and it terrified Lachann.

In a voice so low he knew only Osgar would be able to hear him, he asked, "What are ye doing here?"

"Saving ye from the bad men," Osgar replied in the same low tone.

"Get away from here and make certain that fool lass goes with ye."

"Nay. We have a plan."

Lachann was about to deride that plan, whatever it might be, in terms that would vastly improve the child's knowledge of unacceptable words when the ropes around his ankles loosened. The three men continued to bicker amongst themselves over the best way to gain their prize or, in failing that, use him to gain some reward. They had no interest in his bleeding carcass for the moment. Hope swelled in him, but Lachann fought to keep his wits sharp, to carefully consider what his next step would be once he was free.

A faltering one, he thought with fury and despair. He had lost too much blood, his strength waning with each drop that soaked into the ground. And he feared the ground was where he would soon be once his bonds were cut, for they were undoubtedly all that kept him standing. Lachann also feared he would be of no help if

Adeline and Osgar's plan failed and they were in danger. His mind all too readily presented the many fates that could befall a beautiful woman in the hands of these men and the fate that Osgar was facing if caught, but he forced them away. Letting himself fall prey to such imaginings would be of no help at all.

"Where is Adeline?" he asked, trying to move his lips as little as possible as he kept his eyes on the men. If they thought he was talking they might draw closer to find out why, or to whom.

"She will be riding to the rescue soon."

Riding to the rescue? In his mind's eye, Lachann saw Adeline charging into camp on one of her small ponies and cursed under his breath. She would not be so foolish, would she? The ponies were sturdy but little threat to anyone. One of the men could simply snatch her out of the saddle as she trotted by.

The last of his bonds fell away but Lachann held himself in place. He hoped that he would soon overcome the urge to fall to his knees. Then Osgar pressed something into his hand. Dazed, Lachann realized it was the hilt of the sword he had been wearing when he had been captured. Although he was proud of the boy's stealth in retrieving it for him, dismay swept over him. He should have heard or seen the boy slipping amongst the enemy's horses and belongings to steal the sword. The excuse that his attention had been fixed upon his captors was judged by his mind and declared a thin one. Taking a deep, slow breath, Lachann fought to steady himself. To prepare himself to be at least some help to Adeline when she appeared.

And just where is the foolish woman? he wondered.

An ululation suddenly filled the air. His keen ears told him that it came from the south of the camp but he could not wholly blame his captors for looking in every direction. The clear, strange battle cry echoed and swirled around them. A heartbeat later the sound of pounding horse hooves came out of the dark. *Curse her beautiful eyes,* Lachann thought as he braced himself for whatever pitiful defense he might be able to offer, *she is on my horse!* No pony could make that much noise no matter how hard and fast it was ridden.

He was just moving, raising his sword in preparation for battle and heartily cursing the weakness that made his arm shake, when she burst into the camp. Adeline was leaning over Ulf's strong neck, holding the reins in one hand and his spare sword in the other. Her thick hair was untethered, flying around her like a blaze fanned by the wind. Lachann suspected he was staring at her in as gape-mouthed a way as the other men were. She looked glorious, like some ancient warrior queen.

Ulf reared when she pulled on his reins, his lethal hooves coming down on one of the men now running for his life. Lachann watched as Adeline struggled to control Ulf, her determined expression turning to one of horror as the man screamed. The other men ran for their horses, leaving their friend behind.

Lachann took a step forward, fell to his knees, and cursed. He was armed, eager to fight, but utterly useless. To his astonishment, the man he thought had died beneath Ulf's flailing hooves rolled free of the threat, and then ran for his horse. His stumbling gait revealed that he had not escaped unharmed, however. By the time Lachann looked toward Adeline again, she had calmed Ulf, sheathed the sword she had been waving around, and was dismounting with a distinct lack of grace. That awkward dismount completely shattered the image of Adeline the warrior queen. He did not know whether to laugh at the absurd but success- ful rescue she had accomplished or yell at her for the risks she had taken with her own and Osgar's lives.

"Oh, Lachann," Adeline cried as she stumbled to a halt in front of him. "They have whipped you!"

Her outrage touched him but he shook aside the feeling and clumsily sheathed his sword. "Help me to my feet, lass. We need to get away from here."

Even as she did as he asked, she said, "But they have all run away."

"Aye, but they may pause to grow a new back- bone and come back. Get me on Ulf and later we will have a talk about ye riding my horse."

He was not surprised when she ignored his threat. He needed help just to stagger over to his horse. One look at his saddle and he knew he would need her help to mount the horse as well. Lachann sighed in resignation as she pushed and steadied him while he crawled up into the saddle. She stood and stared at him, biting her lip in inde- cision for a moment, and then held out her hand to him.

"Best ye get in front of me, lass," he said. "I am nay sure I have the strength left to take the reins." It tasted bitter just to make that admission but Lachann could not allow pride to put them all in danger.

Adeline could see how that confession had stung his pride. She was glad she had not spoken her thoughts about his weakness. It was best if he saw it for himself. She was just very glad that he had.

She pulled herself up into the saddle in a graceless way that would have undoubtedly made him laugh if he were not in so much pain. Taking the reins, she rode toward where Osgar waited with the ponies, Lachann leaning heavily against her back. It was terrifying to see how weak this large, strong man had become. Adeline buried her fear for him and fixed her mind on getting them all to shelter as quickly and safely as she could.

"He needs blood, *Maman.*"

Fixing closed the last shutter on the windows of the small cottage, Adeline hurried to the bed where Lachann sprawled. He had stayed conscious enough so that she and Osgar had been able to get him onto the bed and only then had he given in to the unconsciousness that must have been lurking for a long time. It had not been easy to strip him of his clothes and bathe and tend his wounds. She had hoped that that would be enough to help him heal, but Osgar was right. Lachann was going to need blood. Adeline touched the mark on her neck and prayed she could do it with the calm detachment of a skilled healer.

When she reached Lachann's side, he was awake, staring at her, and she knew he would not ask it of her. That meant that the decision would have to be hers alone. She would have to freely offer what he needed. It puzzled her that she hesitated, for she never had with Osgar.

"I can give him some of mine," said Osgar.

"Nay, I willnae drink from a child," said Lachann.

"Of course not," said Adeline as she sat down on the edge of the bed and held out her arm. "Such a wee lad wouldnae have enough for ye anyway."

"Are ye certain, lass?" Lachann asked.

The weak, husky tone of his voice banished the last of her reluctance. "Aye. Just like Osgar, ye need it to heal."

He drew her wrist to his mouth and kissed it. It was just a simple kiss but she felt as if it was a benediction of some kind. Adeline winced as he sunk his teeth into her flesh, but then the heat began, curling through her body and stirring to life all her passion for him so rapidly it made her a little unsteady. His dark gaze remained fixed upon her as he fed and she was unable to look away. By the time he was done, she was almost panting and the way he licked the wound to close it made her shiver from the strength of her need for him. Embarrassed by her own weakness, she gently pulled away and hurried to prepare something to eat.

Lachann watched her as he felt his body immediately begin to heal itself. He had seen her arousal in her eyes, in the light flush upon Adeline's fair skin, and heard it in the way her heartbeat had increased. It had tasted sweet, flavoring her blood with Adeline's need for him. It was a need he shared and intended to feed as soon as he was strong again. By the time she brought him some bread and stew, he was able to sit up and feed himself. The way she blushed every time he looked her way told him that his desire was no secret to her.

Adeline was coming down from the small loft

where Osgar now slept when she was caught by the waist and carried toward Lachann's bed. "I can walk, Lachann," she protested with a laugh.

"Nay fast enough," he said as he dropped her on the bed and then sprawled on top of her.

"Ye are all healed now, are ye?"

"Aye, and now I wish to celebrate my health and freedom."

She opened her mouth to tease him and he kissed her. All thought of play fled her mind as passion swept over her. Lachann had them naked so quickly she fleetingly wondered if her clothes were still whole. Then she lost herself to the wonder of his touch, to the sensation of flesh against flesh, and bodies uniting. A tiny still sane part of her mind reveled in the way their cries blended as they found their release as one. When they soared to the heights together it only made it all the more intense.

Adeline faintly murmured a protest when she felt Lachann move away from her, not sure how much time had passed and not really interested in knowing. She squeezed her eyes shut in embarrassment when he washed them both clean and then wrapped her arms around him when he climbed back into bed. At first, she idly enjoyed the soft caresses and kisses he treated her body to. It took several moments for her to realize those touches were not idle ones and her body was rapidly warming to them. By then Lachann was kissing her stomach, his clever fingers slipping between her legs to torment her.

The heated touch of his mouth replacing his fingers had Adeline opening her eyes wide in shock. The protest she began died quickly. With every stroke of his tongue, fire flared through her veins, burning away all resistance. All modesty fled as well as she writhed, his intimate kisses driving her wild with need. She called to him to join her when she felt her body tightening, to share the bliss that was swelling inside of her, and cried out with relief when he joined their bodies with one fierce thrust.

Lachann gently stroked Adeline's back as she lay limp and sated in his arms. He kissed the mark on her neck and began to lecture her concerning her actions, for although her rescue of him had been successful, she had put herself and Osgar in danger. Ignoring her muttered complaints, he scolded her for not doing as he had ordered, for not taking herself and Osgar to safety, for riding his horse like a madwoman, and for waving around a sword she did not know how to use. By the time he finished she was so stiff in his arms, he was surprised he did not hear a few bones snapping. Lachann decided the only sure way to mend that and soothe her was to make love to her again and he proceeded to do so.

The last clear thought Adeline had before sinking into a sated, exhausted sleep was that Lachann was a sneaky devil. She promised herself she would tell him so when she woke up.

Staring down at a sleeping Adeline, Lachann thought his heart would burst with the strength of the joy that filled it. He was alive. His body was healed and now happily sated. He kissed her cheek and settled her comfortably in his arms.

The only problem facing him now was telling her that she was his mate. Perhaps he should have slipped that information into his lecture, he mused, and smiled. There was still time, he told himself as he closed his eyes. Even if he failed to tell her until they were at Cambrun, there would still be time. If nothing else, Adeline would not just set Osgar down at Cambrun and then walk away.

Chapter Nine

"Cambrun."

Adeline blinked in surprise. One moment they were riding through a mist so thick she wondered how Lachann could know where to go. The next, a massive stone castle that seemed to grow out of the mountain itself loomed in front of them. Its dark, high walls threatened all comers even as they promised safety to any who were allowed to shelter behind them.

"It is huge," she whispered, wondering just how many MacNachtons lurked behind its sturdy, well-manned walls.

"Aye," said Lachann. "And safe. It was built to shelter us from our enemies, including the sun."

"Can none of ye bear the sun?"

"Some can. We all test ourselves and those of us with a wee touch of Outsider blood can bear a bit more than a Pureblood. For nearly forty years now we have been trying to breed out some of the more, weel, constricting traits of our clan. We decided to seek Outsiders as mates. Unfortunately, there is some danger in that, especially since the Hunters came. But there are women and one mon within those walls who are Outsiders wed to Mac-Nachtons and the children they have bred can abide some sun, a few more than others. Many of the Lost Ones can also abide some sun." He shrugged. "It was the laird's idea. A way to solve our childless state and give us people who can mix weel with the world surrounding us. That world inches closer every day and we need to be able to slip in and out of it without too much risk."

"Is his plan working?" she asked as they rode through the huge iron-studded gates of Cambrun.

"Slowly. Verra slowly. And, we begin to think we will ne'er be able to breed every trait out of our bloodline."

Before she could ask how he felt about that, if he actually wished to breed out every trait, they were surrounded by people. Adeline was a little unsettled by how beautiful the women were and how handsome all the men were. Were there no plain-faced MacNachtons? she wondered a little crossly as Lachann caught Osgar up in his arms, dismounted, and set him down on the ground. He then came and helped her dismount.

When Osgar was presented to his kinsmen, the cheers that sang out through the bailey warmed her heart even as her fear of losing him to this clan choked her. Lachann caught her hand in his and kept her at his side as everyone struggled to welcome Osgar. It was as if some long-lost princeling had returned home to save the kingdom.

Lachann called for quiet and then told Osgar's story. There was no surprise when he told of Arailt's death, but Adeline could see the signs of grief and anger over the loss in many of the faces. The crowd parted when Lachann finished and a tall, handsome woman with streaks of white in her hair stepped forward.

"So my nephew is dead," said the woman as Lachann bowed to her.

"Aye, Nan. Nearly two years past he died at the hands of some fools sent after him by his lover," replied Lachann. "I had no time to make her pay for her crime. I am sorry."

"Nay, I have done my grieving. I kenned he was gone and I want no more of ours lost in avenging him. I felt it in my heart and soul when he died." She looked at Osgar. "But he is not completely gone, is he? He left a part of himself behind. A fine lad with much the look of Arailt about him."

"He is a Blooded Son, Nan." Lachann nodded at the shock Nan and others could not hide. "Arailt kenned that he was in danger, that his woman had betrayed him, and that the journey here to get help would be a treacherous one. He thought to protect the boy and give him skills to protect himself."

Nan knelt down and touched Osgar's cheek. "And it worked." She looked at Adeline. "Those skills and this young woman have kept the last of my bloodline alive to return to Cambrun." She stood up and kissed Adeline on the forehead. "I thank ye, Adeline Dunbar. I but ask that ye let me help in the raising of him."

Adeline was speechless and could do no more than nod. Lachann had said nothing about keeping her with him at Cambrun, but this woman clearly believed that she would remain with Osgar. It was what Adeline wanted but she feared that if Lachann tired of her and set her aside, even

Osgar's presence in her life could not make Cambrun a home to her.

"If it pleases ye, Nan, I would claim the boy as mine and raise him to make ye proud," said Lachann.

"That would please me weel, Lachann, but what does young Osgar say?" Nan smiled at the boy.

"I would like that," Osgar said and grinned up at Lachann. "A lot."

Adeline was still reeling from Lachann's announcement as she was taken away to a room where a hot bath awaited her. She sank into the water with a sigh of pleasure, but her thoughts would not be still so that she could fully enjoy such luxury. Resting her head against the edge of the large bathing tub, she stared into the fire it was set in front of. Lachann had claimed Osgar as his own before all the MacNachtons gathered in the bailey. But he had not claimed her.

"Why didnae ye claim my mither, too?"

Lachann shook aside his concerns over how pale Adeline had been when she was led away and looked at Osgar. The boy, as freshly washed and clothed as he himself, sat beside him at a table in the great hall enjoying a hearty meal. Perhaps Adeline just needed to hurry and join them, he thought, and then wondered why she was taking so long at her bath.

"What do ye mean, Osgar?" he asked.

"Ye claimed me but ye didnae claim my mither."

"Of course he did, child," said Nan as she placed some fat blackberries on Osgar's plate and covered them in thick, sweet cream. "Every Mac-

Nachton who saw her saw that. The mark was clear to see."

"What mark?" asked Osgar.

Lachann felt the heat of an unaccustomed blush upon his cheeks as everyone stared at him. The men looked amused and sympathetic, the women cross and obviously disgusted with him. Poor little Osgar just looked confused.

"Oh, Lachann." Bridget, the laird's wife, shook her head. "Ye will have some groveling to do now."

"I ken I should have told her ere now but it isnae an easy thing to tell an Outsider. 'Tis nay something they can understand and I wished her to become more accustomed to what I am." It was a weak defense and he really did not need Bridget's or Nan's looks of feminine disgust to tell him so. He had been a coward but he would rather be tied to stakes under a noonday sun than admit to that.

"She has raised and protected a Blooded Son for two years, took him into her home and heart. And, Osgar, did ye not say that ye fed from her at your verra first meeting?"

Osgar nodded. "Anne had cut me, so I bled a lot. It was so the beasties could find me quick. It was healing but I hurt. I ken now that I should ask first. She fed Lachann, too, when he was hurt."

Lachann rolled his eyes when the women scowled at him. "I didnae ask. She gave willingly. I had lost too much blood due to the gentle persuasion of my captors and was dangerously weak. I couldnae e'en help in my own rescue." He reluctantly told the whole tale and had to join in the laughter it caused, for, looking back, humiliating or not, it was funny. He did not think he would ever forget the sight of Adeline charging into that camp.

"Lachann, tell her now," said Bridget. "She needs to ken it and the more I hear of how she cared for Osgar and you, the less I think she will be shocked by how ye marked her. Or by any of the other things she will need to ken as your mate. S'truth, I think she will be most pleased. After she recovers from her anger over your silence, of course."

"Did ye nay see her face when ye claimed Osgar before us all?" asked Nan, shaking her head when Lachann just looked at her in confusion. "Ye claimed her boy and that shocked her, but I am thinking it was far more than that which had her looking but one breath from collapsing at your feet. Ye claimed Osgar but ye didnae claim her. That is how she sees it since ye havenae told her what the mark means. Ye have left her wondering what her place is now that ye have openly taken the boy she loves as her own son."

Lachann looked at his laird, hoping the man would scoff at such thoughts and ease the increasingly tight knot in his gut. Cathal looked much as he had when he had first wed Bridget about thirty-five years ago. Miraculously, so did Bridget, even though she had no MacNachton blood at all. Mating with a MacNachton appeared to give the mate the same incredible longevity MacNachtons enjoyed. It was something they were still researching and yet another thing he had to tell Adeline about. When Cathal just smiled and nodded his agreement with all the women had just said, Lachann cursed.

"Dinnae ye want my mither?" asked Osgar and

then started to look alarmed. "Ye willnae send her away, will ye?"

"Nay, never," vowed Lachann and he leapt to his feet. "I will speak to her now." He stopped at the doorway and turned to look back at the members of his clan gathered in the great hall. "One last thing, something that has begun to disturb me greatly and preys on my mind. We have all heard this *laird* spoken of by the Hunters before and most of us think he may be the leader of the fools, aye?" A rumble of agreement went through the hall. "Mayhap ye can all put your minds to the puzzle of why the mon was trying so hard to get his hands on Osgar, offering a big bounty for the boy." He nodded at the silent, grim-faced clan members staring at him. "Was it just Osgar or is it a MacNachton child he seeks?"

"We will definitely discuss it," said Cathal, his voice hard, almost a full-throated growl. "Now, go and soothe your woman. She might try to flee. Outsider women can have some verra strange turns to them." He grunted and then grinned when his wife hit him in the belly.

"She willnae be going anywhere," said Lachann. "I will tie her down if I have to."

"I have some verra fine, verra soft, silken bonds I can lend ye," called out Jankyn. "They work verra weel on a mate, e'en if she isnae mad at ye."

Jankyn's wife Efrica's outraged response to that could be heard clearly over the laughter as Lachann left the hall. He knew his kinsmen would soon return to the problem he had just presented to them. There could be a growing threat to the one thing all MacNachtons prized above anything else, the precious gift that had been denied them for too long—their children. He wondered if the Hunters would soon become the Hunted.

He stepped into his bedchamber and looked at the tub set before the fire. Adeline was still in it, her head resting against the rim and her glorious hair hanging over the edge. Lachann quietly shut the door behind him and walked over to the bath. His heart clenched with guilt and regret when he saw the tears on her face, for he knew it was his fault that she was so unhappy, perhaps even hurt.

"Adeline," he said quietly as he crouched by the tub and lightly stroked her hair.

Adeline nearly cursed and hurriedly wiped away her tears. It was just her bad luck to be caught while still deep in her misery. She drew her legs up and wrapped her arms around her breasts, suddenly embarrassed by her nudity.

"Ye shouldnae be here," she said. "I am in my bath."

"Which has grown cool." He grabbed one of the large drying cloths, stood up, and held it open. "Come out of there. We need to talk."

Not wanting to have a serious discussion while naked, Adeline quickly stepped out of the tub. Instead of wrapping her in the drying cloth, however, Lachann slowly and meticulously dried her off. By the time he was done and grasped another large drying cloth to wrap her in, Adeline was not sure she had the wits left to have any discussion at all. Even the self-disgust she felt over how easily she melted beneath his touch did not cool her ardor by much.

Lachann walked over to his bed and sat down, settling Adeline on his lap. He badly wanted to make love to her but knew he had to talk first. If she was going to be angry with him, she would be even more so if he took his pleasure of her first, for she would rightly see that as a trick of some kind to lull her into accepting what might not be acceptable to her.

"Adeline, why were ye crying?" he asked.

"I got some soap in my eye, is all," she muttered, refusing to look at him.

He grasped her by the chin and forced her to face him. "Such a poor liar ye are. Ye think I have taken the lad but nay ye, dinnae ye?"

"Osgar belongs here. These are his people. Nan was kind to suggest that I could stay and raise Osgar but—"

"Nay, no buts. That is what ye will do. Why do ye think I so openly claimed Osgar? It was so that there would be no question of ye having a place in his life. Nan is too old, has been too much alone, to suddenly take on the care of a small boy. He would have been fostered within the clan and I made my claim, got her approval, before anyone else could step in and do so. Since ye are nay his blood kin, ye would have no power to change that. Now ye do."

"Because ye say it is so?"

"Aye, and nay. It is so because ye are mine." He kissed the mark on her neck when she frowned. "Have ye nay wondered why this mark hasnae faded away?"

Adeline looked at the wrist he had fed from and saw no hint that he had ever sunk his teeth in there. Then she touched the mark on her neck. It should have faded. There should be no mark at all, if all her experience with Osgar and now Lachann told her right.

"Why hasnae it faded away?"

"Because it is the mark a mon gives to his mate. Everyone who saw ye today saw that mark and kenned that ye were my mate. I had already claimed ye in their eyes." He nodded when she stared at him in open-mouthed shock. "Best close that bonnie mouth, lass, or I will be kissing ye and we will ne'er finish this talk. 'Tis past time we had it and I need to get it all said."

"A mating mark? Ye gave me a mark that says we are mated?"

She did not sound angry, just confused, and Lachann breathed an inner sigh of relief. "That first time I kissed ye I ached to give ye that mark. 'Tis why I backed away so quickly. I still distrusted Outsiders and I didnae want to mark one. But I couldnae stay away long, could I? And, yet, I kenned that 'tis difficult for someone outside the clan to ken what the mark means and I hadnae warned ye, either. That was wrong of me."

Adeline touched the mark, knowing she should be angry at him for claiming her without even letting her know she had been claimed, but too happy to care. She was his. She, Lachann, and Osgar could be a family and live in this huge, safe castle together. It was far more than she had hoped for. Then she frowned. He had not said he loved her. Mate did not equal love.

"Does this mean ye care for me, Lachann?" she asked with a timidity that made her cross.

"Ah, lass, I more than care although I will admit that I didnae see it at the time." He kissed her. "I saw it while I was trussed to that tree thinking I might ne'er see ye again. Aye, I love ye." He laughed softly when she flung her arms around his

neck and held him tightly. "It would be nice if ye
loved me too but I am prepared to work to make
ye give me your heart."

"Oh, Lachann, ye have had it almost from the
start," she whispered against his neck as she began
to unlace his shirt.

"Love, I would like nothing more than to make
love to ye right now but there is more ye must ken,
things about being one of us that ye need to
learn."

She leaned back to look at him. "We are married in the eyes of your clan?" He nodded. "Osgar
is our son?" He smiled and nodded again. "We can
have bairns of our own?"

"I pray so and it has certainly been shown that
a MacNachton and an Outsider can breed weel,"
he said as he pushed her down onto the bed and
then began to throw off his clothes.

"Then I dinnae really need to ken any more."

"Weel, ye do, but I think we will wait a wee bit
before we finish this talk."

Lachann made love to her so tenderly and thoroughly, Adeline thought she would happily drown
in his love if that were possible. They exchanged
caresses and kisses until they were both mad with
need for each other. When he joined their bodies,
the knowledge that he was hers only added to her
pleasure. The release they shared was so strong
and sweet that she was not surprised when it made
her cry.

"Ah, love, dinnae cry," Lachann said after he
had cleaned them both off and rejoined her in
their bed, holding her close.

"Just happy tears, Lachann. I am just verra,
verra happy." She sighed. "I now have a home and

a mon I love who loves me, and Osgar has a family. It is just that my happiness is so great it overflows my heart." She kissed his cheek and teased, "And I will love ye even when ye are old and gray."

"Ah, that is something we need to talk about. It may weel be a verra long time before either of us is old and gray." He proceeded to explain all about the longevity of the MacNachtons and how that longevity appeared to pass to their mates. The way her eyes rounded as he spoke began to make him nervous. "Does that frighten ye?"

"That I may have a lot more than fifty years with ye?" She laughed and hugged him. "Oh, Lachann, 'tis wondrous. I shall have years and years and years to love ye. Could anything be more wonderful!"

He smiled down at her. "Nay, love, nothing could be more wonderful than years of loving ye and being loved by ye. I look forward to every one of them."

Taken by Darkness

ALEXANDRA IVY

Chapter One

The townhouse situated in the heart of Mayfair was predictably beautiful.

Located close to Hyde Park, it boasted a columned portico, as well as a large terrace that overlooked a tidy garden with a gazebo. The windows were high and arched, spilling light onto the cobbled street that was clogged with expensive carriages. Along the roof a row of marble statues peered down at the arriving guests, impervious to the chill in the late April breeze.

The interior was equally elegant.

There were acres of marble with gilt molding and crimson wall panels. And the furnishings offered a hint of the Egyptian influence (an unfortunate fashion introduced by the Prince Regent). There was also a profusion of artwork chosen more to impress society than with any genuine appreciation.

Upstairs the ballroom was a blaze of color as the

guests twirled beneath the glowing chandeliers, the room so crowded that it seemed as if all of England was in attendance.

In truth, Lord Treadwell's spring ball was the unofficial beginning to the London Season, and one of the most sought-after invitations of the entire year. Mothers threatened to toss themselves into the Thames if their daughters were not among the fortunate debutantes on the guest list, and politically ambitious gentlemen had been known to offer discreet bribes just to step over the threshold.

It was a collection of the most stylish and powerful bluebloods in all England, but as one they came to a breathless halt as the latest guest swept through the double doors and regarded the crowd with a bored gaze.

Victor, Marquis DeRosa, was worthy of their attention.

Although not a large gentleman, he possessed the sort of sleek, chiseled muscles that were shown to perfection in his tailored black coat and white satin knee breeches.

His countenance was carved along noble lines with a wide brow, an aquiline nose, and a full mouth that could harden with cruelty or soften with a sensuous promise. His hair was as dark and glossy as a raven's wing, and allowed to fall to his shoulders rather than being cut *à la Titus* as many of the young bucks, contrasting sharply with his pale skin.

But it was his eyes that caught and held the attention of most.

Pure silver in color, they were rimmed with a circle of black and so piercing that few would dare to meet his gaze. They were the eyes of a predator. A ruthless hunter that considered humans prey. And a mere glance was enough to make poor mortals tremble.

Some in fear.

Some in desire.

All in respect.

They might not have comprehended why they reacted so strongly to the sophisticated Marquis DeRosa, but they instinctively bowed to his will.

A small, mocking smile curved Victor's lips as he prowled toward his host and hostess, who were fluttering with a panicked delight at his unexpected arrival.

After all, Victor had been in Venice for the past six months, returning to London only the evening before. No one was aware of his presence in the city. Besides, he rarely condescended to attend such tedious human parties even before leaving London.

Why would he?

As the clan chief of the London vampires, he was the most powerful demon in England. He had only to lift his finger to have an entire harem of beautiful females, human or demon, to sate his hungers. For blood or sex.

And as for entertainment . . .

After ten centuries of indulging in the most exotic and rare pleasure to be discovered throughout the world (from being the only male on an island filled with female wood sprites, to pitting his strength against the lethal Yegni demon), a mundane society ball was laughably dull.

Or at least it should be.

He disguised his rueful grimace as his gaze covertly skimmed the crowd until he discovered the one female in London, perhaps in all the world, who could have lured him to the stuffy, overcrowded townhouse.

She was here. He'd already caught the scent of ripe peaches. Yes. There she was. Miss Juliet Lawrence.

His unbeating heart jerked with an excitement that he didn't entirely appreciate.

The female was beautiful enough. From her imp father she had inherited delicate features and a long mane of curls the vibrant color of autumn leaves. She had also been blessed with faintly slanted eyes that were the palest shade of green. But, unlike most imps, she was slender rather than lush, with an innate grace that had first captured his attention when she had arrived in London two years before.

Beauty, however, was not enough to explain his ruthless fascination for the woman. Especially considering her mother was a witch.

He hated witches.

Not only because his one weakness as a vampire was magic, but because his brother, Dante, had been abducted by a coven of witches and chained with their spells for all eternity.

Worthless whores.

And worse, Juliet was currently under the protection of a powerful mage, Justin, Lord Hawthorne.

He hated mages as thoroughly as he hated witches. Especially arrogant, pompous mages who didn't possess the sense to defer to their betters.

So why was he growing consumed with the savage need to claim Miss Lawrence as his own?

Victor had tried to accept that it was nothing more than the fact that Juliet stubbornly refused to succumb to his seduction. It had been centuries since a woman had pretended indifference to his charms. What was more enticing than a prey that was clever enough to put up a struggle?

He had even traveled to Venice to prove that his enthrallment with the female was nothing more than a passing bit of insanity that was easily dismissed.

Unfortunately, all he had managed to prove was that Miss Juliet Lawrence was destined to plague him regardless of the distance between them.

He had filled his nights with the most alluring females and lavish amusements, but he could not rid himself of the aching need to return to London.

And Juliet.

His lips twisted as he watched her stiffen and slowly turn in his direction, belatedly sensing his presence. A predictable expression of dismay rippled over her beautiful features before she was covertly edging through the crowd, clearly preparing to bolt.

He moved forward, a flare of anticipation jolting through him. The chase was on and she was not going to escape.

Beginning tonight, Juliet was going to pay for reducing him to little more than a eunuch.

"My lord . . ." Unaware how close he came to a swift, bloody death, Lord Treadwell stepped directly in Victor's path and grasped his arm. "We never expected . . . such a delight . . ."

Victor leashed his violent urge to rip out the throat of his host. Even if Juliet managed to slip away, there was nowhere she could hide.

Instead, he peered down at the pudgy fingers

that were crushing the fall of Brussels lace that peeked from the hem of his jacket sleeve.

"So I perceive," he drawled, his voice cold. "My dear Charles, have a care for my lace if not for my poor, abused arm."

Treadwell jerked back his hand, reaching beneath his puce jacket for a handkerchief to mop the sweat from his flushed face.

"A thousand apologies." The nobleman nervously cleared his throat, his customary air of smug superiority notably absent. "Please, allow me to introduce my wife." He waved an absent hand toward the plump blonde less than half his age who stood behind him. "Letty, this is Marquis DeRosa. DeRosa, my wife, Lady Treadwell."

Victor offered a graceful bow. "Enchanted."

"Oh." The woman rapidly waved her fan, her eyes wide and her lips parted in feminine awe. "Oh."

Treadwell gave a bluff laugh, clapping Victor on the shoulder as if he had every right to touch the most powerful demon in England.

"I say, you quite overwhelmed the poor gal." He winked at Victor, indifferent to his wife's sudden embarrassment. "Let me escort you round the back way to the card room. That way, you won't be bothered with the giggling petticoats. Give a man an ache in the head. Always best to avoid 'em when you can, eh?"

"Which only proves just how little you know me, Treadwell." Victor's tone was edged with a warning that made the fat idiot pale in fear. "Remain with your wife. I am capable of determining my own destination."

"Oh . . . , I say. Of course. Certainly."

Dismissing the idiot from his mind, Victor turned toward the dance floor, parting the thick crowd with a wave of his slender hand. Distantly, he was aware of the avid gazes following his slow, elegant stride and the whispers of excitement that rippled through the room, but his attention was focused on the scent of sweet peaches.

At last leaving behind the gawking crowd, Victor made his way along the dimly lit corridor, bypassing the various salons and antechambers until he reached the narrow door leading onto the back terrace.

Stepping into the chilled night air, Victor paused, his senses instinctively searching the garden and shadowed mews for any hint of danger. At the same moment his gaze was busily savoring the sight of Juliet leaning against the stone railing.

As a vampire, Victor had no need for the moonlight to reveal the pure, delicate lines of her profile or the fire in her curls that were currently pulled into a knot at the back of her head. He did, however, fully appreciate the wash of silver light that shimmered over alabaster skin and added a hint of mystery to the pale emerald eyes.

His gaze lowered to her gown, which was a delicate white lace over a gold sheath and cut in Grecian lines to emphasize the tempting mounds of her breasts. Then slowly his gaze lifted, lingering on the long, bare curve of her throat.

Victor's fangs ached with a swift, brutal hunger.

Bloody hell. He had been too long without a woman.

With an effort, Victor resisted the urge to charge across the terrace and crush the female into his arms. Although she was not a practicing witch, and her imp blood was diluted, she did possess her own share of powers. Including the ability to resist his attempts to glamour her.

If he was going to lure her to his bed, it was going to take skill and patience.

For some ridiculous reason the knowledge sent a tingle of anticipation down his spine.

Madness.

Strolling forward, Victor allowed his gaze to boldly travel over her tense body, a faint smile curving his lips.

"Did you think you could hide from me, sweet Juliet?" he murmured.

The emerald eyes flashed with annoyance, but she couldn't disguise the fluttering beat of her heart or the potent scent of her awareness.

Miss Juliet Lawrence might wish him in hell, but she desired him.

"Actually, I was attempting to avoid the sudden influx of vermin, my lord," she drawled in overly sweet tones.

"Victor," he corrected, not halting until he had her firmly trapped against the stone railing, his fierce gaze sweeping over her flushed face.

"I thought you were in Venice." She tilted her chin, her expression defiant. "What are you doing here?"

"At the moment I am enjoying the very fine view," he husked, his gaze never wavering from her wide eyes.

"I mean, what are you doing in London?"

"I should think it obvious. 'Tis hunting season."

Her brows pulled together. "You are mistaken, my lord, hunting season ended weeks ago."

His fingers lifted to trace the tender curve of her neck, his mouth watering.

"That all depends on the prey."

She shivered, pressing against the railing in a futile attempt to escape his lingering touch.

"So you are here for the Marriage Mart?"

"I am."

"You have developed a taste for tender young debutantes?" she mocked. "I thought you preferred a more well-seasoned meal."

His lips twitched at the bite in her tone. "There is no need for you to be jealous of my . . ."

"Harem?"

"Companions." His fingers lingered at the pulse fluttering at the base of her throat, his senses drowning in the scent of peaches. "You need only say the word and there would be no others."

"How many times must I tell you that I will never be a vampire's blood-whore?" she rasped, her eyes flashing with fury.

Victor laughed. "Such crude language from such beautiful lips. Does it help you to deny your body's hunger for my touch to pretend I am a monster?"

"There is no pretense. You are a monster."

His lips twisted. He could hardly deny her claim.

He was a ruthless predator who killed without mercy and was willing to use whatever violence necessary to maintain control of his clan.

That did not mean, however, that he was incapable of appreciating a woman who stirred his most primitive needs. His gaze lowered to the soft thrust of her breasts, a shudder shaking through his body as the heat of her wrapped around him.

No. It was more than mere appreciation.

Having her in his bed, tasting the potent power of her blood . . . it was rapidly becoming a necessity.

He groaned, his fingers following the enticing line of her bodice, his body hard with need.

"And yet your heart thunders and your knees tremble when I am near," he husked. "You cannot hide your reaction to me."

She trembled. "Disgust."

"Desire." He lowered his head, his lips brushing over her bare shoulder. "It perfumes the very air."

"My lord, stop this at once," she demanded, even as her hands lifted to clutch at his shoulders.

It had been like this from the beginning.

Two years ago Juliet had walked into a London ballroom on the arm of Lord Hawthorne and every other woman had faded to meaningless shadows. Victor had known in that moment he had to have her. And it had not taken his heightened senses to know she was equally aroused.

Not that she was willing to admit as much.

No, for her own inexplicable reason, she was determined to keep him at a distance.

He growled as his arms wrapped around her tiny waist, hauling her hard against his body.

"Come into the gardens with me."

"If it is time for your dinner then I suggest you find one of your concubines to slake your hunger."

"I do not hunger for my dinner." His lips traced a path down her collarbone before skimming up the curve of her throat. "Such exquisite skin."

He felt her tremble in need, her hands pressed against his shoulders. "And I do not share my body any more readily than my blood."

Pulling back, Victor regarded her with a brooding gaze. "I traveled to Venice to put you from my mind, but it was an impossible task. You haunt me, little one, and that is unacceptable."

"What is unacceptable? The fact that I am the one woman capable of resisting your seduction, or the knowledge that you could make a fortune if only I would cooperate?"

It was a familiar accusation.

Juliet's ability to sense the magical properties of objects, as well as people, was a rare talent that would be priceless to any vampire, and Victor had never hidden his desire for such a power. Why should he? Never again would he have to fear an enemy attempting to plot his early demise with a hidden spell. Or even accidentally stumbling into a trap. Juliet would always be able to warn him of the looming danger.

And, of course, there was the indisputable knowledge that her talent was worth a fortune.

The black-market trade for magical artifacts was a profitable, cutthroat business that kept any number of demons and humans living in luxury. Including the mage, Lord Hawthorne.

Bastard.

He caught and held her accusing gaze. "My wealth is more than sufficient, although I have never made it a secret that I covet your talent. A vampire's one weakness has always been magic. With you at my side I would be all but invincible."

Her chin tilted. "Which is only one of many reasons that I will never allow myself to be bound to you."

He narrowed his gaze in sudden annoyance.

"And yet you willingly offer yourself to Hawthorne. An arrogant ass—"

"You should recognize an arrogant ass easily enough. You need only look in a mirror," she rudely interrupted, her chin stuck at a stubborn angle. "Ah, but wait. You have no reflection, do you, vampire?"

"And a mage," Victor hissed, ignoring her insult.

"My mother was a witch."

"An unfortunate circumstance I am willing to overlook."

The emerald eyes flashed with fury as Juliet thrust her way past him, headed across the terrace.

"How vastly considerate of you, my lord."

With blinding speed he was behind her, wrapping his arms around her waist and jerking her back against his chest. Growling deep in his throat, Victor buried his face in the curve of her neck.

"I can be much more than merely considerate, sweet Juliet. I will give you whatever you desire . . ." His body stiffened in shock. "Bloody hell, why do you smell of gargoyle?"

Juliet resisted the urge to struggle against Victor's restraining arms.

Despite the fact that she appeared to be a mere debutante among humans, she was in fact over a century old, and she had learned long ago that battling against a predator only inflamed his instincts.

And the Marquis DeRosa was very much a predator.

A beautiful, exotic, sensually lethal predator.

Holding herself rigid, she pretended indifference to the thrilling pleasure of his unyielding arms wrapped around her and the brush of his lips against her skin. Not that she was foolish enough to believe Victor was unaware of her thundering heart and the searing excitement that coiled through the pit of her stomach. The aggravating demon was always swift to pounce on her uncontrollable reaction to his potent masculinity.

"For God's sake, stop sniffing me," she gritted. "It is rude."

He nipped at her neck, his fangs scraping her sensitive skin.

"Tell me where you came into contact with a gargoyle."

She closed her eyes, fiercely attempting to ignore the jolt of need searing through her.

She had desired Victor from the moment she had caught sight of him across a crowded ballroom. Utterly and desperately. But she was not a fool.

Women who were stupid enough to fall victim to a vampire's seduction were doomed to become mere ruins of their former selves.

"I am not your property, Marquis DeRosa, and I do not have to tell you anything," she hissed.

"Property? No. But you are mine and if you refuse to tell me, then I will simply ask the Guild—"

With a sudden gasp, Juliet was turning in his arms, her expression one of horror.

"No."

His brows lowered, the silver eyes studying her with an unnerving intensity.

"You have not allowed that foolishly soft heart of yours to put you in danger, have you?"

"Of course not."

He cupped her chin in a slender hand, his handsome features tightening with a dangerous impatience.

"Juliet."

She blew out a resigned sigh. The clan chief rarely exposed his formidable power in her presence, but when he did, she was wise enough to avoid trouble.

"A few months ago I discovered a gargoyle in Justin's attics."

"Did you?" The silver eyes narrowed. "Hawthorne must have an object of great worth to go to the expense and bother of negotiating with the Guild to provide protection for his mansion."

"This particular gargoyle does not happen to belong to the Guild."

"Impossible. He would not be allowed to hire out his services unless he was a member."

Juliet grimaced. When she had first stumbled across the gargoyle, she hadn't known what to think of the odd little creature.

Like most other gargoyles, Levet possessed grotesque features and a thick gray hide that turned to stone during the day. He also had a long tail he kept faithfully polished and a thick French accent.

Unlike most of his terrifying brethren, however, Levet was barely knee high, with delicate fairy wings that shimmered with brilliant blues and crimsons and were veined with gold. Even worse, his magic was unpredictable at best and inclined to cause more trouble than it was worth.

As a result the poor thing had been banished

from his Guild and treated as little more than a leper among the demon world.

Juliet better than most understood the pain of never truly belonging.

Which no doubt explained why Levet had so swiftly earned a place in her wary heart. She would do whatever was necessary to protect him.

"Levet did not hire out his services. If you must know, he was refused entry into the Guild because he is . . ."

A raven brow arched as she hesitated. "Yes?"

"He is unusually tiny and considered deformed by his brethren," she snapped. "Are you satisfied?"

"A deformed gargoyle?"

"Do not mock him."

The silver eyes shimmered with a wicked amusement. "I am not so clumsy as to insult your friend. My enjoyment is at the thought of Hawthorne's reaction to a miniature gargoyle cowering in his attics."

"My household is none of your concern, DeRosa." A deep male voice echoed through the darkness as Lord Hawthorne climbed the steps from the garden. "Neither is my apprentice."

Juliet rolled her eyes as Victor's arm tightened around her waist and an icy smile curved his lips.

The two men had been adversaries since Justin, Lord Hawthorne, and Juliet had arrived in London. Thus far the hostilities had not broken into open bloodshed, but Juliet sensed that it was only a matter of time.

Until then they took ridiculous delight in goading each other.

"Do you think to frighten me, mage?" Victor mocked.

Justin slowly crossed the terrace, his hand smoothing down the charcoal-gray jacket that he had matched with a black waistcoat and white knee breeches.

He was a large gentleman with a thick mane of hair that had turned silver centuries before. His face was square with strong features and black eyes that hinted at his ruthless will. Most women considered him handsome, although he would never claim the breathtaking splendor of Victor.

Halting near the stone railing, Justin folded his arms over his chest, his expression smug. Which could mean only one thing.

Gingerly Juliet opened her senses, not surprised by the unmistakable wall of magic that surrounded the mage. Justin might be an arrogant ass, as Victor claimed, but he was not stupid. He would never approach any vampire, let alone the powerful clan chief, without a spell of protection.

Not that it would keep a determined vampire from ripping out his throat.

"There will be no doubt if and when I desire to frighten you, devil spawn," Justin taunted.

A wave of icy power raced through the air, prickling painfully over Juliet's skin.

"Do not allow your ability to intimidate a few lesser demons to swell your head, Hawthorne," Victor drawled. "It would be a lethal mistake."

Taking advantage of Victor's brief distraction, Juliet slipped from his grasp and moved to the center of the terrace.

"Since my presence is obviously superfluous, I will leave you two to entertain each other," she muttered.

Justin stepped smoothly toward her, stretching out his hand. "Forgive me, Juliet—"

The words had barely left his mouth when he was abruptly slammed against the brick wall of the mansion, Victor's hand wrapped around his throat and a pair of vicious fangs a mere breath away from his jugular.

Shocked by the swift violence, not to mention Victor's ease in breaching Justin's considerable defensive spell, Juliet hurried to the vampire's side, laying a cautious hand on his shoulder.

"My lord, no," she said, her voice a mere whisper. The air was thick with danger. It did not seem particularly wise to startle the lethal vampire. "I will not tolerate you creating a scene."

There was a tense moment when Justin's life hung in the balance; then, with a low snarl, Victor tossed the larger man aside and turned to grab Juliet, his silver eyes flashing with a stark hunger.

"Take heed, little one. I have attempted to cultivate patience—you are very young, after all—but my desire for you is swiftly consuming me," he rasped. "I will not wait much longer."

Her heart slammed against her chest, but not in fear, despite the slender fingers digging into her shoulders and the savage glitter in the silver eyes. No. It was pure exhilaration racing through her blood.

"Are you threatening me?" she breathed.

He framed her face in his hands, staring deep into her eyes before lowering his head to cover her mouth with a harsh, shockingly possessive kiss.

"A promise, nothing more," he whispered against her lips; then, with a muttered curse, he abruptly released her and disappeared from the terrace with a terrifying speed.

Unconsciously Juliet pressed her fingers to her lips, feeling . . . shattered.

She had sensed the volatile emotions that lurked just below the surface when Victor was near. It was like standing in the middle of an alchemist's lab, acutely aware that the brewing concoctions might suddenly explode.

But she had never realized that his kiss, *any* kiss, could snatch the earth from beneath her feet.

Hearing a faint noise, she smoothed the shock from her face. The last thing she desired was for anyone to guess her unwelcome vulnerability to Victor.

She was prepared as Justin moved to her side, a scowl marring his handsome features and his dark eyes smoldering with hatred.

The man was accustomed to being the master of any situation. He was not only a powerful mage, but with Juliet's assistance, he had acquired a massive collection of magical weapons that would make anyone hesitate to challenge him.

Now Victor had effectively proven that he was capable of ripping out Justin's throat and leaving him another corpse in London's gutters. It was little wonder his hand was not quite steady as he patted the precise folds of his cravat.

"Damn the bastard," he bit out. "How did he slip back to London without my knowledge?"

Her lips twisted, her gaze skimming over the dark, seemingly empty garden.

"A demon does not survive a thousand years without acquiring the skills necessary to travel unnoticed," she pointed out dryly.

Justin was far from appeased. "Skills or not, I intend to have a word with my servants. They clearly have grown lax in their duties."

"Lax? Highly doubtful," she said. "They are terrified of you."

With a shake of his head, Justin made an effort to pretend that he had not just been tossed across the terrace by an infuriated vampire.

"And you, Juliet?" he demanded, his fingers trailing a suggestive path over her flushed cheek. "Are you terrified of me?"

She took an abrupt step backward. Justin was handsome and, when he made the effort, a charming companion, but she had no interest in becoming his mistress. As far as she was concerned, their relationship was strictly business.

"Not particularly."

"Hmm." He studied her with a rueful smile. "I wish I believed you, my dear."

With a restless shrug, Juliet turned to pace toward the edge of the terrace.

"Perhaps we should leave London."

"You have a sudden desire to travel?" There was a hint of surprise in his voice.

Perfectly understandable.

Juliet had never made a secret of her aversion to their constant touring from place to place. It was not that she didn't understand the need to avoid settling in one area for too long. Humans were not particularly perceptive, but eventually they did notice if their neighbors did not age. But it did not make the constant upheavals in her life any easier.

Now, however, she could not deny a cowardly urge to flee from Victor and the dangerous sensations he inspired.

"Why not?"

"For one thing, there is a pesky war being waged throughout Europe, if you will recall, my love," he drawled, "and while the winter months always put a damper on the generals' enthusiasm for battle, if my sources are not mistaken, the foolish Archduke Charles is planning a futile uprising in Austria, which of course will spark all sorts of nasty retaliations. We can only hope that Vienna is not damaged by his stupidity."

She shrugged. "The Continent is not the only place beyond England. We could visit India or the Americas or—"

"Juliet, you are well aware that I dislike the colonies," Justin interrupted, a hint of impatience entering his voice. "The society is tedious, the entertainments are rustic, and the natives little better than savages. Besides, my negotiations with the fey are not going as well as I would desire."

Her heart sank.

For all of Justin's magic, he was still human, and it was only with a potent mixture of rare herbs that he managed to hold back his mortality.

Herbs that could only be grown with fey magic.

Which meant that Justin would not dare to leave London until he was certain he had enough of the potion to last him for several weeks, if not months.

"What is wrong? You have never had trouble bartering for your potion before."

Justin grimaced. "The fey are . . . unsettled."

"That is hardly a shock. They are always flighty and unpredictable."

"It is worse than usual. For the past three months I have sought to meet with Yiant, offering him a number of my finest possessions for the privilege, only to be told the Prince is not receiving."

Juliet frowned in puzzlement. As she had said, the wood sprites were flighty creatures, but they were also cursed with an insatiable craving for magic. Nothing less than the threat of impending death would prevent a wood sprite from collecting a magical object.

"Did you offend him?"

"I would never be that foolish." Justin's jaw knotted with tension. "No. The Prince is either attempting to unnerve me in the hope of increasing the price of his goods, or he has gone into hiding."

"Why would a fairy go into hiding?"

"A good question."

A silence descended as they both considered the varied, and assuredly unpleasant, possibilities.

"So what do you intend to do?" she asked.

"Make him an offer so tempting that he cannot resist meeting with me." Justin shot her a searching gaze. "Speaking of which, have you managed to have a peek at Lord Treadwell's new collection, my dear?"

She waved a dismissive hand. It had taken less than a quarter hour to search through the Grecian collection that was currently being displayed in Lord Treadwell's Picture Gallery.

Not only were the badly chipped statues and pieces of pottery lacking any hint of magic, but she suspected they were outright frauds, without the least amount of historical or artistic value.

"Rubbish."

Justin cast a jaundiced glance toward the looming mansion. "Not entirely unexpected, but still a pity. Perhaps we shall have greater luck at the Stonevilles' soiree."

"Did Lord Stoneville purchase new artifacts?"

"No, but the rumor at the gentlemen's club is that he's recently taken on a young and very beautiful mistress."

She frowned in confusion. "What interest could we possibly have in his mistress?"

A knowing smile curved Justin's mouth. "The old goat must be eighty if he's a day. If he is managing to keep up with a female a quarter of his age, then he must have some magical trinket to—"

"Yes, I comprehend your meaning," Juliet interrupted, shuddering at the unfortunate image.

Far less squeamish, Justin held out his arm. "Shall we?"

Chapter Two

Two nights later, Juliet was seated on a Chippendale sofa with cabriole legs and threadbare brocade cushions that was tucked beneath the small window. God alone knew how long ago it had been relegated to the attics, but Levet had done his best to beat away the dust and cobwebs. He had also managed to clear enough space among the forgotten trunks and family portraits to place two wooden chairs around a small scrolled table in an appearance of a dining room.

The tiny gargoyle was astonishingly domesticated and complained bitterly (and far too often) at being forced to reside in the cramped, grimy attics.

As far as Levet was concerned, he should be inhabiting rooms at Versailles.

At the moment, however, amusement shimmered in the gray eyes and the delicate wings fluttered as he laughed at Juliet's tale of her daring burglary of the valuable crystal that held the tears of a fertility god, while Justin had kept the ancient Lord Stoneville distracted.

"You are certain it was a Damanica?" the gargoyle demanded, his French accent pronounced.

"Without a doubt." Juliet shrugged. "Justin is currently attempting to lure the wood sprites out of hiding with it."

Levet laughed again. "Pathetic. Do English wood sprites have no stamina? No manly vigor? *Sacre bleu.* They must be like fish left out of the water." He wiggled his hand. "Flop, flop, flop—"

"Levet," Juliet hastily interrupted.

"Ah, pardon, *ma belle.*" The sensitive gargoyle was instantly contrite. "I forget what a delicate flower you are."

"Delicate flower?" Juliet snorted. "Hardly that. I am a thief and a liar, and I sell my services to keep a roof over my head. Many would claim I am no better than a common whore."

"*Non*, do not say such terrible things. We all do what we must to survive."

Juliet heaved a sigh. She was painfully acquainted with the sacrifices that survival demanded.

"Yes, I suppose that is true enough."

Levet tilted his head to the side, regarding her with a narrowed gaze.

"There is something troubling you, *ma belle.*"

Juliet turned her head to glance out the window, more to hide her revealing expression than to admire the view of Hyde Park slumbering beneath the silver moonlight.

"Nothing more than ennui."

"Ennui? But only a few days ago you were telling me how delighted you were that the Season was at last under way."

Of course, she had been delighted. She had told herself that the restless dissatisfaction that had plagued her throughout the long winter would be cured by the return of society to the city.

It was only when Victor had strolled into Lord Treadwell's ballroom that she accepted her discontent had nothing to do with the lack of society and everything to do with the breathtakingly handsome demon.

The knowledge was galling.

And something she did not intend to share.

"I hoped that the return of society to London would provide a distraction," she said, her voice determinedly light. "Foolish, of course. 'Tis the same tedious balls, with the same tedious guests, with the same tedious gossip."

"But we adore gossip, do we not?"

"Only when it is interesting." Juliet turned back to her companion, her fingers fidgeting with a satin ribbon threaded through the bodice of her peach muslin gown. "Thus far I have heard nothing more fascinating than that Lord Maywood's youngest daughter was quietly removed from London after she attempted to elope with a blatant fortune hunter and that there has been an odd rash of lightning that people claim is coming from clear blue skies. One burned down a warehouse near the docks."

Levet's tail stiffened, as if startled by her inconsequential chatter.

"Lightning, you say? At the docks?"

"And why would you be interested in strange bolts of lightning?"

A smile touched the ugly gray face. "A nest of

pixies will often attract lightning. Perhaps they have settled near the Thames."

"You have a fondness for pixies?"

The gargoyle touched his fingers to his lips in a gesture of appreciation.

"But of course. The females are *très désireuses* and possess a remarkable ability to please a gargoyle."

With a sharp movement Juliet was on her feet, an odd ache clenching her heart.

"For heaven's sake, are all males so predictable?"

Levet gave a helpless lift of his hands. *"Oui."*

"Pathetic."

"Ma belle, please tell me what has upset you. I know it cannot be the lack of amusing scandal." Levet waddled forward, his gray eyes troubled. "Juliet?"

She sucked in a deep breath, knowing the tiny creature would not leave her in peace until she had confessed the truth.

"The Marquis DeRosa has returned to London."

"By my father's stone balls." Levet's wings snapped in agitation, the sudden breeze sending dust flying through the air. "Well, there is no need to ask why he is here. The cold-hearted sod will not be satisfied until he has made you one of his sycophants."

That was precisely what Juliet feared.

And why she fought so hard against her acute awareness of his sensuality.

"Hell will freeze over first," she muttered.

Levet reached up to grasp her hand, the blatant concern in his expression sending a chill down her spine.

"Be careful, *ma belle*. He is more dangerous than you could ever imagine."

"What would you have me do? I requested that Justin travel away from England, but he is too occupied with his negotiations with Yiant to leave London. I suppose I could go on my own, but . . ."

"*Non*, Juliet." Levet's tone was horrified. "For all of Hawthorne's failings, and they are varied and numerous, he does provide some protection from those creatures who would do whatever was necessary to claim you and your powers."

She paced the cramped space that had been cleared by the gargoyle, not for the first time resenting her dependency on the mage.

If only—

Juliet abruptly crushed the worthless yearning.

Her parents were dead. Nothing could alter that grim fact.

"I am not entirely helpless," she gritted.

"Not helpless, but you will never be ruthless enough to survive alone in the demon world, *remerciez un dieu*."

She ignored the painful truth of his words. "Perhaps Yiant will accept the Damanica as a proper token and offer Justin the herbs he needs. He will have no reason to linger in London once he has his potion."

"I would not be so certain."

Juliet halted her pacing to regard the gargoyle with a puzzled frown.

"What do you mean?"

"It is rumored that Hawthorne has at last convinced Madame Andreas to become his mistress."

Juliet snorted. "If you mean to shock me, Levet, you are wide of the mark. Justin always has one mistress or another. He will easily find another in the East Indies or Egypt or the Americas."

"Madame Andreas is not just another mistress, Juliet, she is considered the most beautiful woman in London," Levet corrected her. "Even DeRosa has been seen attempting to court her favors."

A sharp, savage pain jabbed through her heart at the mere thought of Victor being beguiled by the golden-haired, blue-eyed, voluptuous beauty. Which was utterly absurd. From the moment she had arrived in London she had heard whispers of the Marquis DeRosa's numerous mistresses, and had seen with her own eyes how the women flocked to be at his side.

Besides, it was common knowledge among the demon world that vampires were sexually insatiable. Until they mated it was not at all unusual for them to insist on a dozen or more lovers.

Damn Victor to the fiery pits of hell.

"Has he? Well, I hope . . ."

"*Oui?*"

"I hope he chokes on her," Juliet snapped.

Levet's lumpy brow furrowed as he regarded her in sudden dismay. "Did I make a middle of it?"

"Middle?" It took her a moment to realize what the gargoyle was saying. "Muddle. A muddle of it."

He gave a dismissive shrug. "Middle, muddle. Did I say something wrong?"

"Not at all." Juliet felt her brittle composure begin to falter. "If you will excuse me, I believe I will retire for the night."

"Are you not feeling well?"

"I seem to have developed a pain in my neck."

Without giving Levet time to halt her retreat,

Juliet left the attics, taking a direct route through the candlelit corridors to her private chambers.

Normally she found a sense of pleasure when she entered the sitting room decorated in shades of blue and ivory, with solid English furniture that had been designed for comfort rather than fashion. And most charming of all, the tall, arched windows that overlooked the cobblestone road. She adored spending her mornings sipping chocolate while seated on the cushioned window seat and watching the neighbors go about their business.

Tonight, however, she headed straight for the connected room, preparing for bed with stiff, angry movements.

She could call for a maid, of course. Justin had a full staff of servants, all of them of mixed demon blood so that Juliet had no need to pretend to be human. But she was in no mood to endure the curious gaze and inane chatter of her maid.

She only wished to crawl beneath her covers and pretend she was far away from London and the Marquis DeRosa.

Much to her surprise, Juliet managed to slip into a deep sleep, although it was marred with nightmares of being trapped in a small cellar while something—or someone—crept toward the door.

If she were a practicing witch, she might have attempted to discover the deeper meaning of her vivid dream and the choking fear that had seemed far too real. But with no genuine power beyond her ability to sense magic, she was willing to dismiss the vague premonition when Levet's voice echoed through her head.

"Juliet," the gargoyle called. "*Sacre bleu*, wake up."

"Levet?" Sitting up, Juliet glanced around the empty room, her father's demon blood giving her the ability to see no matter how dark it might be. "Levet, where are you?"

"I am speaking to you through your mind."

She frowned, lifting a hand to her temple. "I wish you would not. It is making me dizzy."

"*Non*, do not sever our bond. I need you, *ma belle*."

"Now?"

"*Oui*. I am in trouble."

Juliet's heart missed a beat at the unmistakable edge of panic in the gargoyle's voice.

"Dear God, are you hurt?"

"For now only my pride is injured, but I sense the future of my health is not at all certain. In truth, *ma belle*, it appears to be particularly dire."

Barely realizing she was moving, Juliet crawled from the bed and headed for the smaller of the two armoires. Her fey blood demanded that she occasionally escape the confines of the city and surround herself with nature. She always kept several sets of loose smocks and pants that were more fitting for a stable boy than a young lady of society. Perfect for her long afternoons in the woods.

"Where are you?"

"I am not entirely certain."

"Levet, you are not being excessively helpful," she said, swiftly exchanging her night shift for the pants and smock, as well as a pair of boys' boots. "I need to know where to begin my search if you desire to be rescued."

"And you think that has not occurred to me?" Levet barked. "Had I known I was to be attacked and held hostage I would have been clever enough to leave a trail of bread crumbs for you to follow."

Juliet moved to the dresser and began pinning her thick curls on top of her head.

"Do you wish my assistance or not?"

"Of course I do."

"Then tell me what happened."

"After you left me alone to entertain myself I decided to visit the docks."

"Why in heaven's name would you . . . ?" Juliet bit off her words as realization struck her. "The pixies. Really, Levet."

"I am a gargoyle, not a saint. And you were the one to tempt me with the promise of pixies."

Juliet stiffened at the ludicrous accusation. "I did no such thing."

"Juliet, something is coming," Levet hissed, his fear potent enough to spill through her. "Please, *ma petite*, I need you."

There was a painful wrench, and abruptly her connection to the gargoyle was severed.

"Damn."

Pausing only long enough to shove a knit hat over her curls, she clambered out her window and jumped the short distance to the nearby tree.

She might not possess Justin's terrifying magic or Victor's icy power, but she was willing to do whatever was necessary to rescue her one true friend.

No matter what the danger.

* * *

The estate of the Marquis DeRosa was less than a half-hour ride from London, but it provided all the space and privacy a vampire craved.

Built of white stone, it was designed along pure, classical lines with massive marble columns and tall windows that overlooked the manicured lawn and distant lake.

It was not the first manor house built on that precise spot. Victor had, after all, owned the property for several hundred years. But like all the others before, it was constructed as much for security as for luxury.

The vast grounds were guarded during the evening by his clan brothers, while the daylight hours were protected by poisonous Bguli demons who could defeat all but the most powerful enemies. The house itself was wrapped in hexes to keep out unwelcome intruders, including any overly forward humans.

Not that the elaborate defenses were actually necessary.

Only a demon or mortal anxious to seek his grave would be stupid enough to invade Victor's lair.

Not without invitation.

Sprawled in a massive wooden chair that had once belonged to a Roman general who had the misfortune to kill a human under clan protection, Victor surveyed the various guests who filled his elegant salon.

There was a combination of demons. Vampires, imps, several lovely nymphs, and a handful of human chattel, all of whom were extraordinarily beautiful, and all eager to capture Victor's brooding attention.

A pity he had no interest in the half-naked bodies that were deliberately poised on the chaise longues and large pillows tossed across the carpet. The tasty feast might be perfectly calculated to sate a hungry vampire, but Victor felt nothing more than cold apathy.

Waving away the silver-haired nymph attired in a thin gauze gown who knelt at his feet with her head tilted in silent invitation, he ruefully accepted that his once varied and exotic taste had now been reduced to one particular female.

A female whom he was still no closer to having in his bed.

His slender fingers were tapping a restless tattoo on the scrolled arm of the chair, his body aching for Miss Juliet Lawrence, when the far doors were thrust open to reveal a tall vampire with a halo of brown curls and large brown eyes.

Most people were deceived by the air of youth and innocence that clung to Uriel even after two centuries, but not Victor. Although the vampire would never possess Victor's own power, Uriel was a brutal killer when necessary and loyal beyond reason.

Which was precisely why Victor had demanded the demon maintain a constant guard on Juliet since she'd first captured his fancy.

With a lift of his brow, he gestured for the vampire to join him, knowing that Uriel would never have abandoned his post without a compelling reason.

Moving through the guests with fluid speed,

Uriel fell to his knees before Victor and bent his head.

"Master."

"Tell me."

"The female left her home."

"An odd hour." He frowned. It was because Juliet's maid had sent a note to say her mistress would be staying in for the evening that he had reluctantly agreed to this small gathering. His clan deserved a few entertainments even if their chief was preoccupied with a stubborn, unmanageable female. "She was with Hawthorne?"

"No, master, she was alone."

"Alone?"

"Alone and on foot."

"Damn." Victor's hands clenched the arms of his chair, the wood creaking as it threatened to shatter beneath the pressure. "I trust Johan is following her?"

"Of course."

He glanced toward the dark windows, judging the hours before sunrise.

"Juliet is impulsive, but she is not a fool. Why would she be traveling the London streets alone?" He returned his attention to his servant. "Did a messenger arrive?"

"No, master. No one approached the house."

Something perilously close to fury flared through Victor's cold heart as he flowed to his feet.

Where the devil would Juliet be headed to at such an hour? Although London was no doubt ablaze with parties, she would never attend one without a proper chaperon and certainly not on foot.

So that meant she was either conducting nefarious business or she was meeting a secret lover.

It was the latter thought that triggered his blast of icy power, sending the humans and lesser demons fleeing the room in fear and his brothers falling onto their knees.

"Where is Hawthorne?"

"He is in the Hampton Court gardens, still attempting to lure Yiant out of hiding."

Uriel's explanation reminded Victor of yet another mystery nagging at him.

"Have you discovered what has disturbed the sprites?"

"I fear not, master."

Victor flicked his finger, commanding Uriel to his feet.

"Perhaps my absence from London has allowed my clan to forget that my commands are not mere suggestions," he said, the frigid force of his voice wrapping around his servant and causing him to flinch in pain. "I do expect to be obeyed."

"Forgive us, master," the vampire pleaded, his voice tight with the knowledge that Victor could kill him with one blow. "We have sought to discover the truth, but the sprites refuse to speak."

"Refuse? How very bold of them," Victor drawled, his gaze skimming over his cringing clansmen. "And how very disappointing that my fine warriors have been bested by a handful of fey."

"We will discover the truth," Uriel pledged.

"Yes, you will." Victor narrowed his gaze, dismissing the trifling annoyance from his mind. He had far more important matters to command his attention. Not the least of which was putting an end to his delicate dance with Miss Juliet Lawrence.

He had struggled to be patient, but he would not tolerate having her in danger. And he most certainly would not tolerate her taking a lover. He would kill any man who dared to touch her. "Tonight, however, you will prepare chambers for Miss Lawrence and rid the lair of any undesirable guests before I return."

There was a brief flicker of surprise before Uriel managed to smooth his expression.

"Yes, master."

Victor headed across the room, pausing at the doorway. "Ah, and I will need the services of a chef."

"I . . ." Uriel blinked, then gave a hasty nod of his head. "Certainly."

Stepping into the antechamber, Victor pulled a satin cloak over his formal evening attire and glanced toward Madame Andreas, a lushly curved female who hovered with the rest of the humans.

With a tiny cry of pleasure, the blonde rushed forward, sinking into a deep curtsy that called attention to pearly mounds of breasts that overflowed the velvet gown.

"Francine."

"My lord?" she breathed.

"Hawthorne will be returning to his home within the next few hours. I want you to be waiting for him."

"Do you have any specific instructions?"

"Ensure that he remains unaware that Miss Lawrence is not in her bed. The more hours you can keep him distracted, the better."

She daringly lifted her gaze, regarding him with a stark sexual hunger.

"A foolish waste of my talents. Send one of your

other females to Hawthorne and I will make you forget the dowdy Miss Lawrence."

Victor's expression hardened with unmistakable warning. "Do not speak her name."

"What is so bloody special about her?" the woman demanded with a petulant jealousy.

"She is mine."

Chapter Three

Juliet was well aware of the dangers of traveling through London in the middle of the night.

Oh, not the usual dangers.

Any criminal or drunken lout who thought she was easy prey would soon discover the error of their ways, but there were predators that hunted the streets far more lethal than the human variety.

Mages, fey, demons . . .

All of whom could destroy her with embarrassing ease.

Which was why she had brought along her mother's amulet, which allowed her to focus the small amount of magic she possessed. In addition, she had grabbed a well-worn crystal that glowed with a soft power. It was the only possession she had from her father and it stirred her imp blood.

The objects would not save her from a full-blooded demon who wanted her dead, but they offered some protection.

Leaving behind the elegant neighborhoods, Juliet silently moved through the shadows, headed toward the cramped, narrow Rosemary Lane and onto Pennington Street, which eventually spilled onto the docks.

Once among the warren of warehouses and quays, Juliet halted, not at all certain where to begin her search.

Levet had said the docks, but they sprawled along the Thames from the medieval London docks to the East and West Indies docks that were still under construction. They were also crowded with sailors and dockhands even at this hour.

How the devil was she supposed to find a tiny gargoyle among the confusion?

Rubbing her nose at the potent stench that clogged the air, Juliet was considering the nearest warehouse when her skin abruptly prickled with warning, a chill wrapping around her.

A dark premonition crawled up her spine and with a gasp she whirled. Her heart lodged in her throat at the sight of the Marquis DeRosa, his raven hair pulled back to reveal the stark beauty of his face and his eyes shimmering pure silver in the moonlight.

"Now what, I wonder, would entice a young and innocent maiden to the docks at this hour?" he mocked softly.

She pressed a hand to her churning stomach, her brows drawing together in annoyance.

"My lord."

"Victor."

"I wish you would not sneak up on me."

The cape swirled around his powerful body as he stepped toward her, reaching out to cup her chin in his slender hand.

"You should be thanking whatever god you pray

to that I am the one sneaking up on you. It is beyond foolish to be wandering the streets alone."

With a shiver, she jerked from his touch.

How could a touch so cold send streaks of fire through her body?

"I am more likely to curse the evil spirit that crossed our paths. What are you doing here?"

"Attempting to keep you from an early grave."

Her eyes widened. "Did you follow me?"

His aquiline nose wrinkled in delicate distaste. "I can imagine no other reason to bring me to such a repugnant neighborhood."

Her hands clenched at her sides at his blatant confession. "Why, you . . ."

A raven brow flicked upward. "Yes?"

"You have no right to spy on me. I am not one of your concubines."

The silver eyes flashed with a ruthless intent as he framed her face in his hands, his intoxicating scent filling her senses.

"No, never my concubine," he agreed, lowering his head to stroke his lips down the curve of her cheek, halting to nuzzle the corner of her mouth.

"Halt that," she breathed, desperately attempting to fight the acute pleasure of his touch.

God Almighty, she craved this vampire. She logically comprehended that the beautiful demon would be a lethal addiction for any female stupid enough to fall victim to his seduction. Still, her body ached to be in his arms, the feel of his fangs feeding greedily at her neck as he plunged deep inside her.

Which was far more terrifying than any hidden dangers that lurked among the docks.

Closing her eyes, she poured her thoughts into

the amulet hung about her neck, feeling its heat prickle over her skin until Victor abruptly jerked his hands away.

He narrowed his eyes, astonishingly appearing more aroused than offended by her little parlor trick.

"Ah, you enjoy playing rough, little one?"

"I simply want you to go away."

"Juliet, be assured that hell will freeze over before I allow you to remain here alone," he said, the cold power of his voice sending the rats scurrying in fear and making the humans glance over their shoulders in unease. They would have no notion of why they were suddenly fidgety, only that they wished they were at a nearby pub. "Tell me why you are roaming these docks."

Her jaw tightened, but she was not entirely stupid. Beneath Victor's polished charm was a dangerous edge that warned he would not leave until he was satisfied.

"I am searching for a friend."

"Friend? Or lover?" he silkily demanded.

She blinked in shock at the abrupt question. "That is none of your concern."

"Do not pretend ignorance. You have known from our first encounter that I would not tolerate another man in your bed."

Her heart slammed against her ribs, her mouth dry. "You truly are an arrogant ass."

"Tell me." He grasped her shoulders, his eyes glittering with a fierce emotion. "Are you here to meet a lover?"

"No." Grimly she forced herself to meet his stark, possessive gaze, her chin tilting. "If you must know, I am searching for Levet."

"Levet?"

"The gargoyle. He is in trouble."

His fingers eased their grip on her shoulders, but his expression remained hard with warning in the wash of moonlight.

"Bloody hell. You risked your life for a deformed gargoyle who is not even worthy of being a part of his Guild?"

She stiffened. "There happen to be many of us who are unworthy to belong to a Guild or a clan or a coven, my lord. That does not mean we cannot possess friends who care for us."

"Juliet—"

Victor's words were brought to a sharp halt as a distinct sizzle flared through the air and then, without warning, Juliet felt herself being hauled to the ground. Victor covered her with his body just as a strike of lightning hit a building on the other side of the quay.

She heard the sound of distant shouts of alarm as humans rushed away from the unexpected shower of brick and glass, but with fluid speed, Victor was on his feet and scooping Juliet in his arms as he headed into the nearest warehouse.

There was the overwhelming stench of damp wool and smoke from the oil lanterns as Victor flowed past the stacked crates to the back of the long room, his movements silent and swift. Halting next to the heavy wooden doors, Victor set her gently on her feet and scanned their surroundings for potential threats.

"Is it pixies?" Juliet demanded, tugging down her loose shirt. Thank God she had possessed the sense to trade her corset and skirts for more suitable garments.

Victor tossed aside his cloak and removed his elegant jacket and waistcoat, carelessly dropping the expensive, but restrictive, clothing on the filthy floor.

"Why would you suspect pixies?" he demanded.

"Levet claimed that they attract lightning."

"It is true a nest might occasionally draw upon the energy of a storm to enhance their magic, but they are not capable of creating lightning from a clear sky."

Juliet grimaced. Of course, it could not be a nest of harmless pixies.

"Then what creature *is* capable?"

"A mage." He sent a questioning glance in her direction. "Or witch."

She paused, then gave a decisive shake of her head. "No. There have been no spells cast. At least none in this neighborhood."

"No magical objects?"

"Nothing with the power to—"

Again they were interrupted by that peculiar prickling in the air followed by a violent shake of the warehouse, as if the lightning had struck the slate roof.

Yanking her against his hard body, Victor wrapped his arms around her, his frigid energy pulsing through the warehouse.

"Damn. We must get out of here."

"I'm not leaving until I have found Levet."

He pulled back to glare at her in disbelief. "Do not be a fool. Whatever is creating such a violent disturbance in nature is beyond our ability to defeat."

"I am not asking for your assistance." She ignored the daunting implication that whatever was creating the lightning was more powerful than a vampire clan chief. "Indeed, I prefer to continue my search without your interference."

"Juliet, you can come with me willingly or I will take you by force. In either case, you will not be allowed to endanger yourself."

Jerking out of his arms, she glared at him with an unmistakable threat.

"Marquis DeRosa, if you attempt to force me to leave, I will never forgive you."

His brows snapped together at her mulish determination, and for a moment Juliet sensed he was poised to ignore her warning. Victor was a vampire accustomed to being in command. He gave an order and it was obeyed, without question and with a nauseating amount of groveling. His instinct would be to toss her over his shoulder and to hell with her own wishes.

But, even as Juliet was preparing for a futile battle to keep from being hauled away from the docks, Victor muttered a curse in a language that was long dead and, closing his eyes, tilted back his head.

"What are you doing?" she demanded suspiciously.

"Attempting to sense the gargoyle."

"Is he near?"

"Impossible to say."

"Impossible or inconvenient?"

"Both." Lifting his ridiculously lush fringe of lashes, the vampire stabbed her with an admonishing glare. "And before you condemn me to the netherworld, you are sensible enough to realize that there are hundreds of scents, most of them excessively unpleasant, that mask any particular trail." He paused, an unmistakable tension etched on his beautiful face. "Besides, there is a strange energy that is interfering with my senses."

Juliet studied the empty warehouse. "It cannot be a spell."

"No, it is the natural magic of a demon, but I cannot tell you the species. I only know that it is strong and very aggressive."

Perfect. Juliet unconsciously wrapped her arms around her waist.

"How can you know it is aggressive?"

"The hostility fills the air." The cold fingers lightly touched her cheek as Victor regarded her with a brooding frustration. "Juliet, this is no game. We have to leave."

With exquisite timing, another explosion rocked the warehouse, unexpectedly buckling the stone floor to reveal a gaping chasm.

A scream was wrenched from Juliet's throat as the earth crumbled beneath her feet, and with a sickening sense of helplessness she plunged into the darkness below.

Victor cursed as he grabbed for Juliet, only to have her snatched from his grasp as the floor collapsed.

He didn't hesitate.

For perhaps the first time in his very long existence, Victor leapt without considering the consequences, without seeking the potential dangers, his savage need to protect the vulnerable female simply overcoming his instinctive sense of self-preservation.

Astonishing.

Landing lightly on the balls of his feet, Victor moved silently to where Juliet sprawled on the packed-earth floor, her hand lifting to rub the back of her head.

"Ow." She struggled to sit upright. "Where are we?"

He crouched next to her, his hunter senses capable of determining that she had a small cut on the back of her head and a few bruises, but that she was essentially unharmed.

His fangs lengthened, aching with hunger at the intoxicating scent of warm peaches and blood that abruptly swirled around him. Damn. With an effort, he thrust aside his potent reaction, instead concentrating on their surroundings.

The small cavern appeared to be connected to a series of tunnels that ran beneath the docks, the smooth walls and carved ceiling proving they were not natural, nor the work of mere humans.

"I assume we have intruded into the lair of some demon."

"Lovely." With an effort, Juliet rose to her feet, glancing up at the opening far above them. "How are we—"

Her words ended in a small squeak as he shifted with blinding speed to stand directly behind her, one hand clamped across her mouth and his arm wrapping around her waist to tug her against his chest. Bending his head, he placed his mouth next to her ear.

"Ssh."

He felt her stiffen as she became aware of the

ominous foreboding that drenched the air above them.

"What is it?"

Her words were muffled and so low that only a vampire's heightened hearing could have heard them.

"Death," he whispered.

"I am desperately hoping that is a metaphor."

"Only if we are fortunate enough to avoid being caught."

Keeping his arm wrapped around her tiny waist, he lifted her off the ground and began backing toward the nearby tunnel, calling upon his powers to cloak them in shadows. It would not entirely disguise their scents, but it would hopefully mute them enough to avoid attracting unwanted attention.

Silently he moved away from the cavern, edging deeper into darkness until he at last halted where the tunnel split in two directions. He gently set Juliet back on her feet, but he kept his arm firmly around her, absurdly needing the tangible comfort of knowing she was unharmed.

Glancing over her shoulder, Juliet tilted her chin, refusing to reveal the fear he could feel trembling through her body. His lips twisted as he ruefully admitted that he admired her courage, even as it threatened to drive him insane. After all, if she were a bit more timid they might even now be at his lair, spending the evening in a far more satisfying manner.

Wickedly, intimately satisfying.

"What are we doing?" she demanded.

"Waiting and hoping the creature passes on without noticing our trail."

She nodded her head, then her brows tugged together as she noticed the thick scents that wafted from the far tunnel.

"Good lord, it smells of . . ."

"Humans."

"Terror," she softly corrected him.

His hand cupped her chin as he studied her delicate face. "And what would you know of such a thing, little one?"

"When I was young my parents and I were traveling through Africa. One night we entered a town where a slaver's ship was berthed." She shivered. "I will never forget the stench of desperation. It spread through the streets and tainted everything in its path."

"Your parents permitted you to be near such evil?"

"Actually, my mother used me to sneak aboard the ship and release the shackles that held the humans captive while she cast a spell that made the slavers believe they were being chased by hungry lions." A small smile of remembered satisfaction curved her lips. "The last we heard, they ran straight into a tribal village that happened to take a very dim view of their townsfolk being sold like cattle."

A cold fury clenched his stomach at the mere thought of what might have happened to her.

"Your mother sent you alone to release brutalized slaves?"

"She trusted that I was capable of performing

an important task as well as teaching me to care for others," she snapped, the raw wound of her parents' death suddenly visible in her eyes. "Something I have forgotten far too often since . . ."

His fingers softened their grip to trail over her cheek, oddly feeling her pain as if it were his own.

"How did you become Hawthorne's apprentice?"

"After my parents were murdered, I was determined to remain on my own." A tremor shook her body. "It did not take long before I learned that humans are not the only creatures capable of great evil."

"You were hurt?"

Her eyes clouded before she hastily lowered her lashes, as if she could hide her emotions from him.

"I was captured by trolls and sold to the highest bidder."

Victor made no effort to contain the eruption of frigid power that filled the tunnels.

"Their names."

She regarded him warily. "I beg your pardon?"

"Give me the names of the trolls."

"They did not bother to share their private information and it no longer matters." She gave a restless shrug. "I was fortunate that Lord Hawthorne was at the auction and purchased me."

"Hardly fortunate," he bit out. "The bastard has taken advantage of you and your talents for decades."

"We both know how much worse it could have been."

His jaw clenched. He wanted to deny the truth of her words. He detested the overly conceited bastard, and not just because he was a mage.

The man stood as a protector to this woman.

A position that belonged solely to Victor.

"Very well. I will concede there are worse fates than to be apprenticed to Hawthorne, but why do you continue to remain with him?" he growled. "The debt must be paid by now."

"I have nowhere else to go."

A dangerous emotion jolted through his heart at her soft words, his arm tightening in an unconsciously possessive motion.

"You are mistaken, little one. Your place is with me."

A bleak smile curved her lips. "And once you weary of me in your bed, my lord? Would I become a tasty meal for your clan?"

Unthinkable.

He growled low in his throat, knowing he would readily kill any of his brothers who tried to touch her.

"Perhaps I will never weary of you."

"I am no gullible mortal. A vampire's hunger is as varied as it is insatiable until he has mated."

His lips twisted in a humorless smile. "That is the common assumption."

"Ah, no doubt you are about to convince me that you are different from every other vampire?"

"But of course I am. I expected that went without mentioning."

"Arrogant—"

Victor swooped down to claim her lips in a kiss of naked, unrelenting need.

"My hunger remains insatiable, but it is no longer varied," he confessed. "I desire no woman but you."

"For the moment."

He pulled back to capture her wary gaze. "Since I first caught sight of you."

"Are you implying . . . ?" She sharply shook her head. "No, it is impossible."

"I can be deceitful when the occasion demands, but I will never lie to you, little one," he swore. "That you can depend on."

Chapter Four

Juliet's heart forgot to beat as she gazed into the silver eyes, mesmerized by the promise that shimmered in the beautiful depths.

Was it possible?

Could he truly have forsaken women since meeting her?

And if he had, why would he?

He had to have a potent reason to deny himself. It was, after all, unheard of for a vampire to go even a few nights without sating his sexual appetite.

So why . . .

It was the yearning ache deep inside her that abruptly shocked her out of her inane thoughts.

Good Lord, she had known for two years that she lusted after Victor. Hardly a shocking realization. What female in London did not desire the handsome beast?

But to long for something he could never, ever offer her was utter madness.

"This is hardly the time or place for such a discussion," she forced herself to say, spinning out of his hold and heading toward the far tunnel before he could guess her intent.

"Juliet. Damn." There was a stir of cold air before Victor was grasping her arm to bring her to an abrupt halt. "Where do you think you are going?"

"To see if we can help the humans." She squared her shoulders. "And then to find Levet."

"Do not be a fool."

"Fine. You remain here. I will go."

"Absolutely not."

She steadily met his smoldering silver gaze. "We have already been through this, my lord. You are not my keeper. In truth, you have no right to tell me what I can or cannot do."

His jaw tightened with frustration. "You have always possessed an independent spirit, but you have never willfully courted danger. Why are you being so stubborn?"

Her gaze dropped to where his slender fingers wrapped around her wrist, genuinely considering his question.

"Because I am weary of allowing my fears to isolate me from the world," she at last confessed.

"You are hardly isolated."

"Perhaps not physically, but I have avoided becoming emotionally involved." Her voice was soft, edged with regret. "I told myself that it would be illogical to become attached to others when I would eventually be forced to leave them behind. Spending time with Levet has made me realize I was simply being a coward."

He gave a short, humorless laugh. "You have readily defied the most dangerous demon in the entire British Empire. You consider that the behavior of a coward?"

"More like the behavior of a lunatic," she muttered, lifting her head to meet his glare. "But I was referring to my habit of avoiding relationships out of a fainthearted fear of experiencing the same pain I endured when I lost my parents. It has kept me in a prison of my own making."

"I would be the first to applaud your desire to share your life, so long as it is with me, but what does this newfound need have to do with recklessly endangering yourself?"

She shrugged, ignoring his frigid displeasure. Stupid, of course. Only a fool would willingly cross swords with a vampire.

But over the past months she had been plagued with a growing restless need to break free of the fear that had held her captive for far too long.

"Truly being a part of the world means taking risks, as my mother taught me. Whether it is with your heart or with your life." She sent him a challenging frown. "Do not try to convince me that you would not do whatever was necessary to rescue a vampire who had been kidnapped."

"It is my duty as clan chief."

"Well, this is my duty as a . . ."

"Yes?"

She yanked her arm from his grasp. "As a mongrel, I suppose."

His brows snapped together at her brittle tone, but before he could continue his lecture, she was moving down the tunnel, refusing to halt until she reached the heavy metal door that blocked the passage.

She pressed a hand to the wall of the tunnel,

knowing better than to actually touch the door until she was certain there were no nasty surprises. Her brow pleated with concentration. Unlike full-blooded demons, she did not possess finely tuned senses that allowed her to easily determine every nuance of her surroundings.

Which only meant she had to work harder, she grimly told herself.

Ignoring the annoyed vampire hovering protectively at her shoulder, Juliet pushed out with her senses, nearly going to her knees at the staggering odor of unwashed bodies and barely leashed panic.

Her every instinct urged her to turn around and flee, just as it had all those years ago when she had been in the bowels of the slave ship. Hardly unexpected. No creature with the least amount of sense would be eager to confront whatever was behind the door.

But now, as then, she called on the thought of her parents. Her fierce, fearless mother who defied her own coven to be with the imp she loved. Her impulsive, charming father with his ready laugh and open delight in his only child.

They believed in her, never allowing her to accept she was less because she was a mere mongrel.

Tonight she would make them proud.

"There are more than just humans," she muttered.

"Sprites," Victor determined with annoying ease. "A few nymphs."

"Gargoyle?"

"Not mixed among the others."

She snapped her gaze to his wary face. "But Levet is here?"

His lips thinned; he was no doubt regretting his promise he would never lie to her.

"Yes."

Relief surged through her. "Thank God."

"No god would be so cruel," he drawled.

She ignored Victor's callous indifference toward her friend. Vampires considered any demon not a vampire as a lesser demon. Even werewolves.

"First we must release the captives," she decided.

Victor scowled. "Juliet, you do realize this might very well be a trap?"

"Do you sense—"

"I do not need to sense danger to know it is there."

"I am doing this with or without you, Victor."

The silver eyes flashed with mocking amusement. "Ah, when you have need of me I am Victor, eh, little one?"

She clenched her teeth, belatedly realizing she had indeed allowed his name to slip out. It was a luxury she never indulged in. Not when she needed the formality to remind herself that Victor was a forbidden temptation. Just as she pretended she did not notice the manner in which his silk shirt clung to the chiseled muscles of his chest, or how precisely his pantaloons outlined the hard lines of his legs . . .

"I have several other names if you prefer," she muttered.

With an impatient sound, Victor captured her face in his hands and leaned down to steal a kiss that jolted through her with stunning force.

"Let us be done with this," he rasped against her

mouth. "I have a far better means to spend the evening."

She shivered, the image of the delicious vampire sprawled on satin sheets, his fangs latched onto the vulnerable throat of a woman, searing through her mind.

"I can imagine."

He pulled back, a wicked smile curving his lips at the thickness of her voice.

"Soon you will not have to imagine," he promised.

Annoyed with the indecent ease with which he could make her heart pound and her body ache, Juliet turned her attention to the heavy door blocking their path.

"Magic?" Victor softly demanded.

She held out a hand, lightly touching the dull metal of the door handle, stiffening when the door slid open with shocking ease.

"There are no hexes or curses."

"No silver," Victor deduced. Like most demons, vampires were lethally allergic to silver. "A spell?"

Juliet shook her head, ignoring the urge to gag at the putrid scent of unwashed bodies and human waste as she stepped to peer into the gloom of the cavern.

She expected the dozen or so people huddled against the far wall, and even their deplorable state of misery. Whether human or demon, being held as a prisoner was a ghastly fate.

No, but what did surprise her was the realization that none of them were bound in any way.

No cages, no shackles, no magic.

She turned to stab Victor with a puzzled frown. "What is keeping them in there?"

"Pure fear." His expression hardened. "There is nothing to be done, little one. So long as the prisoners are held captive by their terror, then nothing will induce them to leave."

"Could you glamour them?"

"I am powerful, but there is no vampire who could glamour so many at once."

She gnawed her bottom lip, considering their limited options.

"Then we must discover something that will convince them that it is more dangerous to remain than to flee."

His brows arched at her odd request. "I do not believe you would appreciate my means of convincing them just how dangerous I can be."

"No, I did not mean you," she hastily said, appalled at the mere thought of the poor creatures being tormented by a rampaging vampire. "I know a spell, but I have not attempted to use it for years."

The silver eyes flickered with a wary surprise. "I did not know you could perform magic."

She reached into her pocket to pull out her mother's amulet, ruefully wishing she possessed the sort of power that would frighten a vampire. Then perhaps she would have the courage to accept Victor as her lover.

"I have no talent for true magic, but I can perform a few small illusions."

"I do not like this."

She heaved an exaggerated sigh. "Is there anything you do like?"

His gaze flared over her with a blatant hunger. "You."

Good . . . Lord.

Juliet hurriedly bent down, using her finger to draw a circle in the dirt, and at the same time hiding the heat staining her cheeks.

"Stand back and do not break the circle."

Closing her eyes, Juliet rubbed her fingers over the amulet, using her mother's lingering powers to bolster her own as she filled her mind with the image of a Saulgon demon in full bloodlust. The actual demon had been extinct from this world for centuries, but the sight of the hulking creature with its gray, rotting flesh and double row of razor-sharp fangs was enough to break the nerve of the most courageous warrior.

At the same moment, she conjured the sensation of choking terror that had assailed her in the outer chamber.

Whispering the words of power, she sent the illusion spreading outward, touching the minds of the captives.

Engrossed with her spell, Juliet failed to notice the startled cries, and even the sudden pounding of footsteps. It was not until Victor snatched her into his arms and pressed her painfully against the wall of the tunnel that she realized she had very nearly been trampled by the fleeing prisoners.

"Damn," Victor snarled, keeping her wrapped tightly in his arms even after the last of the terrified humans had disappeared down the tunnel.

"It worked," she breathed, astonishment blending with relief as she sensed the prisoners continuing their frantic flight through the tunnels.

"Too bloody well," Victor growled next to her ear.

"What do you mean?"

"The escaping prisoners have attracted precisely the attention we hoped to avoid."

Shaking off the fog of her spell, Juliet stiffened as a violent wave of fury pulsed through the tunnel. Dear God. Something was charging toward them. And she did not have to be a full-blooded demon to know it intended harm.

Profound, agonizing harm.

The thought had barely flared through her mind when Victor scooped her off her feet and was bolting across the cavern to a narrow tunnel that Juliet hadn't noticed until that moment.

"Victor," she breathed, fear crawling over her skin.

"Just hold on, little one."

She did. Wrapping her arms around his neck, she unashamedly clung to him, knowing that without Victor she would still be stumbling across the cavern. Few things could match a vampire for speed.

Well, few things except for the creature chasing them, she realized with a stab of regret.

No matter how swiftly Victor sped through the tunnels, or how often he darted into side corridors, the menacing pursuer continued to grow closer.

"We will never be able to outrun it," she at last muttered.

"I fear you are right." Coming to a grudging halt, Victor placed her on her feet, his beautiful features grim. "It appears we must fight."

Juliet gave a sharp shake of her head. "No."

"No?"

"This is not your battle," she said, unconsciously pressing her hands to his chest. "You can escape. I will distract—"

He muttered an incoherent curse before grabbing her face and kissing her with a combination of frustration and yearning need.

"I will not leave you," he husked against her mouth. "I will never leave you."

"Victor—"

With a firm motion he thrust her back and turned to place himself between her and the approaching danger.

"Stay behind me."

She smacked him in the middle of the back, as aggravated with herself as with the stubborn vampire.

It was not that she regretted her decision to rescue Levet. Even if it meant facing her own death. She was done with hiding from the world. But she had not considered the unfortunate consequence that her decision would endanger Victor.

But then, why would she?

She had always known the Marquis DeRosa desired her in his bed, but it had never occurred to her that he would involve himself in her mad quest. He had not survived for so long by being reckless.

Now the thought that he might be hurt or even . . .

No, she could not even bear to imagine such a cruel fate.

"Damn you."

"I was damned many centuries ago," he assured her smoothly. "Let us hope it is enough to convince the Jinn to seek easier prey."

Juliet sucked in a startled breath, instantly distracted by his words.

"Jinn? Are you certain?"

"Regrettably."

"I thought they were a myth."

He shrugged, still turned to face the oncoming danger.

"The Commission has sought to keep them from mingling among the humans," he said, referring to the ruling council among the demon world. "But they occasionally flout the restrictions placed upon them and create chaos among the masses. Which explains why the wood sprites have gone into hiding."

Juliet unconsciously clutched her mother's amulet, a sensation of dread creeping down her spine.

"Lovely. How do we defeat it?"

"We don't," he managed to mutter before a dark shape abruptly lunged from the shadows.

Even though she was prepared, a scream was wrenched from Juliet's throat as the creature launched itself forward. Although it had taken the form of a human there was nothing reassuring about the beast. In fact, there was something highly unnerving about the delicately carved features and thick mane of golden blond hair that gave the Jinn its luminous beauty, when combined with the malignant lust for pain glowing in the large, lavender eyes.

Venomous beauty.

Clutching her mother's amulet in her hand, Juliet futilely wracked her brain for a spell. Not that she possessed the power to actually harm the Jinn, but she might be able to distract him long enough—

There was an unholy roar and Victor launched forward, his fangs fully extended and his frigid power blasting through the air.

Juliet instinctively stumbled backward, wise enough to give the two ferocious predators plenty of space. It was a common tragedy for harmless humans or lesser demons to be crushed when caught between more powerful species. Besides, she needed room to draw her circle if she was struck by a sudden inspiration.

A possibility that was increasingly unlikely as Victor and the Jinn collided with terrifying force.

In fascinated horror, she watched the massive battle, realizing that there was no means of casting a spell without risking Victor.

Her stomach clenched as the two warriors savagely fought, Victor's fangs ripping deep gouges in the Jinn's perfect skin as he shoved it against the wall. In return the Jinn filled the air with staccato jolts of energy that brought down showers of jagged stones smashing onto Victor's head.

Juliet bit her lip as she caught the exotic scent of Victor's blood. As a vampire he could not bleed to death, but the loss of blood would quickly drain his strength.

Victor again slammed the beast against the wall, his fangs striking over and over with sickening force. The Jinn, however, appeared indifferent to his vicious injuries. No, it was more than indifference.

The violet eyes sparkled with an unmistakable pleasure, as if the nasty creature relished the pain. Or perhaps he simply enjoyed the battle.

In either case, Juliet sensed that the Jinn was

merely toying with Victor, and that when he wearied of the game, something very bad was going to occur.

For both of them.

On the edge of panic, Juliet absurdly found herself searching her pockets, as if she might discover a hidden weapon. It was hardly shocking that she found nothing more than a bit of lint and the small crystal from her father. She had come to the docks to rescue Levet, not to wage war against a mythical demon.

Juliet cursed in frustration, gripping the crystal tightly in her palm.

She needed—

She gave a jump of surprise as the crystal abruptly flared with heat, almost as if it were feeding off her terrified emotions.

With a frown she opened her hand, realizing that the soft glow that always surrounded the crystal when she held it was decidedly brighter, the pulsing center seeming to echo her heartbeat.

For years she had attempted to call on the gifts of her imp blood with little more to show for her efforts than minor hexes and lingering headaches. Now she could actually feel the tingles of power darting through her body.

She stilled in shock. Was it truly possible?

Before she could consider whether it was all nothing more than a fluke, she heard a low rumbling from the Jinn.

Good lord, was that . . . laughter?

A sickening horror filled her as a familiar sensation of prickling electricity swirled through the air. She had suspected that bad things would happen when the bastard grew tired of playing. Now her fears were about to be confirmed beyond her wildest nightmare.

Instinctively she charged forward, but it was already too late.

With a massive shove, the Jinn freed himself from Victor's grasp and tossed the vampire against the far wall. Stunned by the brutal impact, Victor crumpled to the ground, his pale face marred with blood and his arm hanging at an odd angle. Without giving Victor the opportunity to recover, the Jinn raised his hand and a sizzling bolt of lightning erupted from the tip of his finger.

Juliet was blinded by the violent burst of light, her ears ringing as the solid rock wall shattered. She cried out as she dropped beside Victor's unmoving form, leaning over to wrap her arms around him in a protective motion.

"Victor . . ." she breathed, cruel pain wrenching her heart as she held him close, planting frantic kisses over his pale, beautiful face. "Please . . ."

She tasted his blood on her lips and felt the dampness of her tears falling down her cheeks, but her thoughts were consumed by the sense of the Jinn moving ever closer.

Did he intend to kill them both with his undoubted command of the elements?

Or was he plotting something even more hideous?

Squeezing shut her eyes, Juliet refused to accept failure. If she could not defeat the Jinn, then she must find the means to escape with Victor.

An easy enough task had she been a fullblooded imp.

Imps with any talent were capable of producing

portals that could move them from place to place in the blink of an eye. Her father had been particularly skilled with such magic.

But, of course, Juliet had never managed more than a weak gateway that collapsed the moment she attempted to enter it. And even that had left her exhausted for days.

Tonight, however, she did not allow herself to recall her innumerable failures.

Instead, she poured her thoughts and energy into the crystal still clutched in her hand, along with her mother's amulet. If she'd ever needed her parents' assistance, this was it.

Burying her face in the rich satin of Victor's hair, she willed the portal to form around them, sending up a silent prayer she did not kill them both.

Victor could feel Juliet wrap herself around him, obviously attempting to protect him from the advancing Jinn. With an ancient curse, he struggled to regain command of his battered body to push her aside.

By the gods, he would not allow Juliet to be harmed.

Not even if it meant—

His uncharacteristic flare of heroism was rudely interrupted as Juliet tightened her arms around him and the entire world shifted beneath him.

As a vampire, Victor was incapable of sensing magic, but he could not fail to notice the tunnel melting away to utter blackness before he landed with jarring force on a damp cobblestone street with the night breeze blowing in his face.

Briefly disconcerted, he held himself perfectly
still, absorbing the realization that he was lying flat
on his back in the middle of London with Juliet
sprawled on top of him.

He rolled to one side, carefully cradling the tiny,
unconscious woman in his arms as he scanned the
area around them.

Bloody hell.

Juliet must have created a portal to rescue the
both of them from certain death, but at what cost?

The stench filling the air warned him that they
were still dangerously near the docks, but thank-
fully there was no scent of the Jinn. Nor any other
predators besides those who owed their loyalty to
him.

Sensing one of his servants hurrying in their direction, Victor grimly rose to his feet, holding
Juliet against his chest. An unfamiliar torment
twisted his dead heart as he noted her unnatural
pallor and the pain that tightened her features
even in her deep state of slumber.

She had come perilously close to draining herself beyond the point of no return.

Too damnably close.

"Johan," he called softly, knowing the young
vampire would hear him despite being several
blocks away. "Find a carriage."

"Yes, master."

There was a short delay, then the sound of
horseshoes striking against cobblestones broke the
thick silence. Victor watched the elegant black carriage turn the corner and come to a halt in front
of him.

Leaping from the driver's bench, the massive

vampire was forced to calm the nervous horse before moving to offer Victor a deep bow.

"Master." Although attired in rough wool clothing with his blond hair pulled into a simple braid, there was no masking the brewing danger that shrouded Johan. He was a warrior poised to kill. Straightening, the younger vampire narrowed his gaze as he took in Victor's slowly healing wounds and the unconscious female draped across his arms. "You must feed, my lord. Shall I find a host?"

"Later." Victor easily dismissed his need for blood. At the moment his only thought was to get Juliet to the safety of his lair. "Return us to my estate."

"At once."

With a blur of motion, Johan pulled open the carriage door, waiting for Victor to settle on the leather cushion before slamming the door shut and returning to his seat atop the carriage. Then with a mental command he had the horse racing through the narrow streets with a reckless indifference to the occasional vehicles or even pedestrians that crossed their path.

Within a half hour they were wheeling up the long drive to his isolated mansion. As they pulled up to the wide veranda, Victor did not wait for the carriage to come to a halt, simply opening the door and leaping onto the flagstone courtyard. With the same impatience, he charged up the stairs, fully prepared for a uniformed servant to tug open the wide double doors.

"Uriel," he called, crossing the marble foyer and heading toward the private rooms at the back of the mansion.

With commendable speed the angelic vampire appeared at Victor's side, his brows arching as he caught sight of Juliet in his arms.

"Do you wish me to call for a human healer?"

Pausing before the door at the end of the corridor, Victor released a trickle of power to open the heavy locks. No one, not even his servants, was allowed in his personal lair without his permission.

"Not yet."

He glanced down at Juliet, a frustrated fury racing through him at the tumble of fiery curls that were in such contrast to her ashen face and the bruises already visible beneath her closed eyes. She looked like a crushed flower, he painfully acknowledged before viciously pushing the thought away.

No. She was merely exhausted. He would accept nothing else.

"You have food prepared?" he growled.

"Yes, the"—Uriel stumbled over the unfamiliar word. It had been several centuries since the vampire had eaten solid food—"chef was most uncooperative, complaining at being taken from his bed and then insisting the markets were closed and he could not discover the necessary ingredients to prepare a meal."

"I assume you managed to convince him to comply with your request?"

"Certainly. He promised a seven-course meal would be awaiting your approval."

"Ensure he keeps it warm until Juliet recovers."

Uriel gave a dip of the head. "The guests have been removed from the property and the upper chambers have been prepared for the female."

Victor's arms tightened. "The female will remain with me."

A rare shock rippled over Uriel's face. "But . . ."

"You have something to say, Uriel?"

"It will soon be dawn."

"I am well aware of the time."

Uriel's gaze shifted to the woman in his arms. "Then you are taking the woman to your lair? Your *private* lair?"

Victor's lips twisted; he did not entirely blame his young servant. He had never, in all his countless years, allowed a female to enter his lair.

"Your swift grasp of the situation is what I have always admired most about you, Uriel," he said dryly, stepping into the small, conspicuously plain room. "Be certain we are not disturbed."

Expecting his command to be obeyed, Victor slammed shut the door and crossed the floor to pull the lever hidden behind a particularly ugly oil portrait. Silently the paneling slid aside to reveal stone steps that led to the deep chambers beneath.

Passing through several more heavy doors, Victor at last reached his private resting place, crossing the barren room to lay Juliet on his bed.

On the point of covering her with a thick fur blanket to ward off the chill of being so deeply underground, Victor slowly froze, dumbfounded by the sensations that were quietly settling in the center of his heart. Sensations that he had barely noticed in his frantic haste to get Juliet to safety.

Now he couldn't deny the shocking truth.

He could actually *feel* Juliet.

Not just as a vampire conscious of another creature in his lair. Or with the awareness of a man near a beautiful woman.

But deep inside him.

Barely aware he was moving, Victor leaned down and with a jerk he had ripped open the sleeve of her loose linen smock.

"Bloody hell."

Victor allowed his gaze to study the intricate crimson tattoo that was forming beneath the inner skin of Juliet's forearm. A tattoo that was unmistakably the mark of his bonding.

He was mated.

To Juliet.

Irrevocably and eternally.

Chapter Five

Juliet opened her eyes. It was odd. One moment she had been deeply asleep, and the next she was wide awake, her heart pounding with fear.

With a small gasp she abruptly sat upright, anxiously glancing about the unfamiliar surroundings. She was not reassured by the stone walls that were covered by ancient tapestries or the heavy wooden furnishings that spoke of a splendid but barbaric past. Only the vast fireplace that was blazing with cheerful flames offered a hint of welcome.

"Victor?" she breathed.

There was a cool rush of air, then Victor was at her side, his raven hair left loose to frame his pale, perfect face and his muscular body covered by a brocade robe.

Juliet shivered, a strange yearning stirring in the pit of her stomach. Stripped of his elegant attire that added a layer of civilization, the vampire was savagely, irresistibly handsome.

"I am here." Settling next to her on the wide

bed, Victor held out a crystal glass. "Mulled wine, little one?"

"Thank you." She was relieved to discover her hand did not shake as she reached to take the goblet and sipped the warm wine. It was perfect. Spiced just as she liked it, with only the faintest hint of cinnamon. She cleared her throat. "Where are we?"

"My private lair." A smile curved his lips, but his eyes were watchful, predatory. "Dinner will be served whenever you wish."

Juliet blinked in surprise. Not only at the notion that Victor would consider she would be hungry when she awoke, but that he would bring her to his lair.

It was . . . inconceivable.

And strangely exciting.

She licked her dry lips, her heart leaping as his gaze dropped to watch the nervous gesture.

"How long have I been asleep?"

"Several hours." His brows drew together in a sudden frown. "You risked far too much by creating a portal. You might have killed yourself by calling on so much power with no training."

She drank her wine, ruefully accepting she was a fool if she'd expected gratitude for saving this vampire's life.

"It was not as if there was a lot of choice," she muttered.

He looked as if he intended to continue his lecture on her foolishness, only to give a faint shake of his head. No doubt accepting that she was beyond his ability to train.

"We will discuss this newfound desire to play with fire later." He reached to gently tuck a stray curl behind her ear, his slender fingers lingering to brush her cheek, his cool touch sending sparks of heated awareness through her blood. "There are more important matters we must address."

Feeling as if her mouth were suddenly as dry as the Sahara, Juliet took a large gulp of the wine, indifferent to the dangers of drinking on an empty stomach. Perhaps if her head was a bit fuzzy then she would not be so acutely aware that she was completely alone with Victor . . . in his lair . . . on his bed. . . .

"Of course," she managed to mutter. "We must consider what is to be done with the Jinn."

Easily sensing the rapid beat of her heart and the rush of her blood, Victor settled closer on the bed, his hand reaching to tug aside the heavy fur cover.

"Later."

"But Levet . . ."

"It is still daylight. The gargoyle will be in statue form for at least another three hours. There is no means to rescue him until he awakens."

Victor reached to pluck the empty glass from her fingers, leaning across her to set it on a low mahogany chest.

"Are you not going to have any wine?" she inanely demanded, shivering as he deliberately brushed against her body.

"Not tonight, I think. I prefer that my senses not be dulled when I am in your company. Your mere presence is quite intoxicating enough." His voice was husky with a thickening accent; the scent of sandalwood filled the air. "Have you fully recovered?"

"Yes, of course," she said, even as she wondered

if she were speaking the entire truth. It would be convenient to blame her giddy excitement on the events of the day, but she was not completely naive. "In fact, I should be returning home."

He laughed softly. Just a breath of sound but it flowed through her body, as potent as the mulled wine.

"You are home, little one."

Home.

With Victor.

Her heart clenched with a dangerous longing.

"Ridiculous," she whispered.

The smoldering silver gaze lowered to her unsteady lips. "It is perhaps lacking a feminine touch, but I assure you that it will be refurbished to suit your pleasure. Whatever you desire shall be yours."

It was a flamboyant promise but oddly she did not doubt him. "My lord . . ."

"What is it?"

Juliet spoke the confusion that had besieged her since the moment she had awoken.

"I did not think a vampire would allow others to enter his private lair."

He stilled, as if considering how best to answer her. Juliet watched in fascination as the firelight danced over his perfect features, adding a hint of mystery. Suddenly she possessed the most desperate urge to shove her fingers into the rich curtain of his raven hair and tug him down so she could drown in his kisses.

"A vampire will share his lair with one other," he said, at last breaking the silence. "His mate."

She abruptly tensed. "Mate?"

He moved to take her arm, laying it across his lap. Then, with a deliberate motion, he pushed aside the torn sleeve to reveal the crimson tattoo that shimmered beneath her skin.

"Mate."

Juliet forgot how to breathe as she stared at the unmistakable marking.

For two years she had struggled to keep Victor at a safe distance. She had sworn to herself that she would never become a mindless toy for the vampire.

But over the past hours she had been forced to admit that she had been far from successful in keeping the beautiful demon out of her heart. Why else would she have preferred to die than to watch Victor harmed?

But to become his mate. Good Lord.

"How did . . ." She lifted her head to meet Victor's unwavering gaze. "How is this possible? I thought that you must exchange blood to complete the bond."

He shrugged. "You must have taken some of my blood during our journey through the portal."

A heat stained her cheeks as Juliet belatedly recalled her frantic kisses over his bloody face.

"And now we are mated?"

"Not . . . precisely."

She frowned in confusion. "I do not understand."

"I am mated to you, but until you are prepared to accept the bond and offer your blood, it remains incomplete."

"So." She took a moment to consider the implications, a rather wicked smile slowly curving her lips. "You are bound to me, but I am at liberty to find another?"

"You are mine." He leaned forward, the silver

eyes shimmering with a dangerous purpose as she hastily pressed back against the pillows. He stretched his long length beside her, remaining raised on his elbow to study her pale face. "I was a fool not to have recognized the truth the moment I met you. There has never been another female who has fascinated me as you have. Even when you are at your most infuriating I still crave to be in your presence."

A shudder of anticipation wracked her body even as she narrowed her eyes.

"*I* am infuriating?"

"Admit it, little one. You do love to challenge me."

"Only because you are so insufferably arrogant, my lord—"

"Victor," he interrupted, his fingers running through her curls and spreading them across the pillows. "I want to hear my name upon your lips."

A delicious heat curled through the pit of her stomach, sending tiny tremors through her body. For once, however, Juliet made no effort to deny her scorching reaction to Victor's touch.

She was done fighting a battle she could not win.

"Victor. It suits you."

His hand moved to cup her cheek, his touch flowing through her until her toes curled in response.

"Just as Juliet suits you," he husked, his fingers drifting down the length of her throat. "You intrigued me from the moment I first caught sight of you. The candlelight shimmering like fire off your magnificent hair. Your features as pure as those of an angel. The elegance of your every movement. It stirred a hunger in me that haunts me no matter where I go."

Some deep part of her whispered that she should be frightened as his fingers briefly lingered upon the pulse at the base of her throat before gliding along the opening of her smock.

Not that he would physically harm her. That had never been her fear. And, of course, now he was bonded to her. A vampire would destroy the world to protect his mate.

No, he would not injure her, but she was not so foolish as to believe that she could give herself to Victor without consequences.

Fright, however, was the last thing Juliet was feeling as his fingers brushed over the curve of her bare breast. She arched upward as a jolt of pleasure burst through her.

"Victor."

"Look at me, little one," he whispered.

Allowing herself to become lost in the silver gaze, she made no demur as he tugged the smock over her head and tossed it aside. The remainder of her clothing swiftly followed until she was lying naked on the satin sheets.

The world had somehow slipped away. There was nothing but the dark eyes and the slender fingers that tenderly explored her body as if he were memorizing every angle and curve of her.

"This is madness," Juliet whispered.

The faintest smile curled the corner of his mouth. "This is fate."

"Fate?"

"Destiny." His head lowered, his lips brushing her mouth as he spoke. "I have waited an eternity to find you. I will never harm you."

Of their own will her hands lifted to grasp his shoulders. The brocade was smooth and delicious to the touch and she found her fingers stroking down the wide width of his back.

A low sigh hissed through his lips. His kiss became more demanding, his tongue dipping into her mouth with a sweep of wetness. At the same moment his hand cupped her breast and his thumb rubbed over the tight peak.

Juliet bucked against him as the shock of sensations jolted through her.

"Oh."

He pulled back enough that she could see herself reflected in his shimmering silver eyes. Or at least someone who looked vaguely like her.

Her curls were tumbled like a river of fire onto the pillows, her face flushed with pleasure, and her parted lips still damp from his kiss.

She looked like a decadent sacrifice offered up for some sensual beast.

"What has brought that frown to your beautiful brow?" he whispered.

Her attention returned to the man poised above her. Good heavens, he was so beautiful. Astonishingly beautiful. Unable to resist temptation, her fingers lifted to plunge into the heavy thickness of his hair.

Ah . . . yes. It was just as soft and silky as she had imagined.

"I have wanted you from the moment I saw you in the ballroom," she confessed in soft tones. "But that does not mean I intend to complete the mating bond."

His chuckle slithered down her spine. "You are my mate. You hold my heart and soul. We are one, whether you are too stubborn to admit the truth or not."

Holding her gaze, he pulled the brocade robe from his body. Her eyes widened at the sight of the hard, chiseled muscles that rippled beneath the ivory skin that was tattooed with a beautiful dragon. His shoulders were broad, his chest so pale and smooth the nipples appeared startlingly dark in contrast. Her gaze refused to lower beyond the contoured ripple of his stomach. Her body already felt as if it were burning from within.

Holding her gaze, he slid slowly downward. The rub of his skin against hers made her breath catch painfully in her throat.

His lips touched her collarbone, tracing the delicate line with the tip of his tongue before slowly traveling down the curve of her breast. Juliet shifted restlessly beneath the teasing mouth. Good Lord, nothing had ever felt so wondrous.

"You are so warm," he whispered against her skin, turning his head just enough to capture the tip of her nipple between his lips.

"Blessed Mother."

She arched off the bed and her hands slid to frame his face in silent encouragement. Whatever she had thought she knew of passion had never included the tender caresses that were sending a storm of sensations lashing through her body.

With obvious expertise he used his tongue and even his teeth to torment her nipple to a hard peak. Her eyes squeezed shut as she groaned low in her throat. He turned his attention to her other breast, his hands sliding down the curve of her waist.

Juliet was lost in the tide of building sensations

when his arms encircled her and without warning he had rolled onto his back. In one powerful motion she discovered herself perched on top of his hard frame. Her eyes widened as she regarded the fiercely handsome countenance.

"Victor?"

"Do not fear," he murmured as his hands smoothed down the curve of her back.

"What are you doing?"

His lips twitched in soft amusement. "If you have not noticed, I am a rather large vampire, while you, my beloved, are delectably tiny."

She smiled wryly. "Even if I had not noticed our size differences, your habit of calling me 'little one' would have given me a hint."

His expression settled in oddly somber lines even as his hands continued to send shocks of pleasure through her body.

"I have never made a secret of how desperately I want you, Juliet," he said, his voice husky with need. "But what happens, or does not happen, in this bed will be decided by you."

An unexpected thrill of power raced through her as she gazed down at the compelling man beneath her. She better than anyone understood the effort it took Victor to relinquish control. He was an ancient demon who had gained his position by brutal force.

Such a gesture revealed not only that he truly understood her freshly discovered need to take command of her life, but also a trust that was nothing less than astonishing.

Quite willing to prove her gratitude, Juliet leaned downward, outlining his sensuous lips with the tip of her tongue.

"Does this please you?" She nibbled a path down his clenched jaw and then the strong column of his neck, savoring his intoxicating taste.

He growled, his mouth parting to reveal his fully extended fangs, and a cool surge of power washed over her.

"*You* please me."

She slowly retraced her path, a heat pooling in the pit of her stomach.

"Are you certain?" she husked. "I fear I am not overly experienced in such matters."

"Allow me to show you."

Grasping her face in his hands, he lifted himself upward, capturing her mouth in a kiss of stark hunger. Juliet shivered with pleasure, her mouth parting to allow his tongue to tangle with hers.

Sinking into the bliss of his devouring kiss, she stroked restless hands over the satin smoothness of his chest. A delicious excitement swirled through her body as she felt the hard thrust of his arousal pressing against her lower stomach.

As if sensing the growing urgency of her desire, Victor pulled back, his body mesmerizing in the soft glow of the fire.

"Juliet, I need you," he said. "I need to be inside you."

His voice flowed over her skin like honey, flooding her body with liquid heat and making her fingers dig into the hard muscles of his chest with a flare of aching desire.

"Yes," she breathed, shuddering as his hands drifted over the curve of her hips.

With infinite care he explored the length of her thighs and then, with a small tug, he parted her legs until they fell on either side of his body. Juliet muttered her approval against his lips, but even prepared she gave a strangled cry when his clever fingers stroked through her damp heat.

"Sssh," he soothed softly. "Soon we shall be one. One soul. One flesh."

His low words seemed to echo deep inside her, but she ignored the dangerous warmth that settled in the center of her heart. Instead she concentrated on his finger that teased the tiny pulse of her pleasure.

"Not soon . . . now," she muttered.

His low growl filled the air, his erection pressing eagerly against her damp heat.

"You are certain?"

Certain? Her nails dug into his chest until she drew blood. She had never been more certain of anything in her entire life.

"Please, Victor."

"Yes."

Victor's hands were pressing at her lower back as his hips lifted and he was entering her in one sure stroke.

Her breath caught, but not from pain.

Searing pleasure rushed through her and she pressed her face onto his chest. She could feel him stroke into her before pulling out and returning with a slow, relentless pressure.

"Dear Lord."

"Mate," he whispered as his hips lifted over and over. "My mate."

"I did not know anything could feel so . . ."

"How does it feel, sweet Juliet?"

"Wondrous," she breathed, her body moving in perfect rhythm with his.

His soft chuckle filled the air with a thick satisfaction.

"You are mine," he vowed. "Mine for eternity."

She moaned as her body began to tighten with a shimmering anticipation. His steady, relentless pace was building a fire deep within her that threatened to burst out of control.

"My mate," he breathed, lifting his head to nuzzle at her neck.

His slight shift was enough to press him even deeper within her and with a force that caught her off guard the tension that coiled between her legs abruptly burst into a thousand pieces.

She cried out and squeezed shut her eyes, struggling not to swoon beneath the tide of sensations. It was overwhelming. A joy that edged perilously close to pain.

"Victor?"

With a moan, he laid his head on the pillows. For a moment she simply gazed into the handsome countenance, telling herself that what had just occurred was no more than incredible sex. Victor had, after all, near a thousand years and countless women to perfect his expertise, but something deep in her heart refused to accept the lie.

Staring into the silver eyes she knew she was bound closer to him than any other person in the entire world.

They were one.

One soul.

One flesh.

Mates.

Chapter Six

Seated across the table from his mate, Victor ruefully accepted that any hope that Juliet would be more compliant now that she was his lover was doomed to abysmal failure. Polishing off the last of the roasted duck, potatoes stewed in a delicate mushroom sauce, and freshly baked bread, Juliet sat back in her chair and offered him a stubborn glare.

"You can roar and bellow all you wish. I am not going to change my mind."

With an effort, Victor attempted to ignore the captivating sight of Juliet wearing nothing more than his brocade robe, her mane of fiery curls spilling down her back and her ivory features tinted with a delicate flush.

Not that he was particularly successful.

There would never be a moment that he would not desire his mate.

Even when she infuriated him.

"I do not comprehend why you must be so unreasonable."

"Me?" She arched a brow. "It was your decision to go on the hunt for the Jinn."

"Because he cannot be permitted to linger in London. Not only do his powers attract the attention of the humans, but his mere presence is a threat to my position among the demons."

She appeared remarkably unimpressed with his logic.

"So you are allowed to risk your life to remain clan chief, but I am forbidden from rescuing a friend from potential death?"

He paused, his vast experience with women warning him this was a trap with no escape.

"I would not use the word 'forbidden.' "

"Then what word would you use?"

"Strongly discouraged," he suggested.

She snorted. "I do not consider a threat to tie me to the bed as strong discouragement."

He growled, his fangs fully extended and aching with a hunger that would never be sated.

"Me either," he husked, leaving his chair and rounding the table with a slow smile of anticipation. "I consider that an invitation to paradise."

Juliet hastily rose to her feet, her expression stern although she could not disguise the heat simmering in her beautiful eyes as her gaze skimmed down his body, covered in nothing more than a loose pair of satin pants he had brought from his recent journey to China.

"Victor, you are not going to distract me."

Easily scooping her off her feet, Victor headed directly for the nearby bed, tumbling them both onto the silken sheets. With a swift roll he managed to end up on top.

"I will admit that was my original intent," he

murmured, burying his face in the curve of her neck. "But I believe I have been hoisted on my own petard. You are delectable."

Her arms circled his neck, her body instinctively arching beneath him.

"Victor."

The intoxicating scent of peaches filled his senses. "Hmmm?"

"This changes nothing," she muttered. "I am going with you to the docks."

Victor pulled back at her stubborn insistence, an unfamiliar pang twisting his gut.

"Why does this Levet mean so much to you?"

She blinked. "Are you . . . jealous?"

"Of a stunted, outcast gargoyle? Do not be absurd."

The emerald eyes narrowed. "Victor?"

"You belong here with me," he said before he could halt the revealing words. "Not with Hawthorne and that creature."

She studied him with an all too knowing gaze. "You believe if I rescue Levet I will return to Justin?"

Victor shied from the mere notion he was jealous of the mage, or the deformed gargoyle. He was a powerful vampire. A clan chief. The most honored creature in all the demon world.

"No, I believe it is a fool's errand and I will not let you deliberately put yourself in danger."

She smiled, not fooled for a moment.

"Justin has no claim on my affections," she assured him softly, her fingers threading through his hair. "He offered me protection and that is *all* I ever desired from him."

He studied her pale face, searching for . . . what?

Reassurance?

"You care for him?" he gritted.

"No."

"Then why do you remain with him?"

Her fingers continued to stroke through his hair, no doubt sensing his unnerving vulnerability. Perhaps in a century or two he would be accustomed to his overwhelming need for this woman, but for tonight he was still raw from the aching desire to complete the bonding.

"Our arrangement was mutually beneficial. My talents offered Justin the means to acquire his magical collection and I was given a roof over my head and security from all but the most persistent demons."

"I can offer you greater protection," he said, infuriated at the mere thought of Juliet depending on another man. "Nothing would be allowed to harm you while you are in my care."

She smiled wryly. "That I have never doubted."

"Then why do you hesitate?"

She shrugged, the movement causing the robe to gape, offering a tantalizing glimpse of her naked breasts. Victor swallowed a groan, his body fully aroused.

"At first I feared becoming another willing victim that you used and then tossed aside."

"And now?"

She met his gaze squarely. "Now I fear becoming your puppet."

Victor clenched his jaw, offended by her words despite the numerous women who had drifted in and out of his life. They had been mere dalliances.

Or dinner.

Juliet was the other half of his soul.

"Even if I wished such a ridiculous thing, I am not capable of enthralling you," he informed her, his voice edged with a distinct chill.

She gave a sharp tug on his hair, a rueful amusement shimmering in her emerald eyes.

"No, but you are capable of insisting upon others obeying your every command."

A portion of his pique was eased at her obvious teasing. "That is only because I know what is best for my people."

"And your mate?"

"Of course."

She rolled her eyes. "There, you have proven my point."

Victor shifted so he could cup her face in his hand, knowing that while his instinct would be to protect his mate, he would have to learn not to ride roughshod over her.

"Juliet, if you wish me to admit that I am an overbearing brute who is accustomed to being obeyed, I will do so," he said, giving a wry shake of his head. "I have been a clan chief for a number of centuries, while being a mate is all rather new."

She stilled, studying his face with wide eyes. "What are you saying?"

"That your happiness is more important than my need to control you."

"Then you will allow me to make my own decisions? Even if you do not agree with them?" She narrowed her eyes as he hesitated. "Victor?"

With a grim determination, Victor thrust aside centuries of absolute authority. To be mated meant compromise. Even if that compromise threatened to drive him to utter madness.

"Yes, but I hold the right to attempt to change your mind."

Knowing just how difficult his concession had been, Juliet readily smiled, her hands drifting down his bare back in a sweet promise.

"Agreed."

Shivering in ready response, he brushed his lips over the soft skin of her temple, sensing the rapid beat of her pulse. The hunger to taste her blood was near unbearable, but he ignored his ravaging thirst.

"I have conceded to your demands, little one. Now it is your turn."

"Does this compromise include removing my robe?" she husked.

He chuckled. "It is *my* robe, although what is mine is now yours, and it most certainly is going to be removed."

She allowed her nails to scrape lightly over his skin, the sensation sending pleasure jolting through him.

"So confident, my lord?"

He pressed a hard, hungry kiss on her lips before pulling back to regard her with a brooding gaze.

"Desperate. But that is not the compromise I speak of."

"Then what do you desire of me?"

"I want you to leave Hawthorne," he said, his voice revealing he was unwilling to bargain on this point. "Your place is in this lair with me."

"But our bonding is not yet complete," she said softly. "Would that not mean we were living in sin?"

He frowned at her foolish words. The connection between them was sacred.

"You are my mate."

"But you are not yet my mate."

A bleak, ruthless pain spread through his body. He had rarely given thought to taking a mate. Most vampires never encountered the one destined to make them whole. But on the few occasions he had considered the possibility, he had never envisioned binding himself to a woman who did not desire him in return.

"I see."

She bit her lower lip at his frigid tone, her expression rueful.

"I do not think that you do, Victor, and it's no wonder. I am making a complete muddle of this."

"Of your wish to return to Hawthorne?"

"Of my very awkward proposal."

"Proposal?"

She licked her lips, the nervous gesture astonishingly charming.

"Victor, would you be my mate?"

A wary hope replaced the icy chill of rejection, although he was careful to hide it behind a scowl. He might be mated, but that did not mean he had lost all pride.

"Juliet?"

Her breath caught, a hint of distress marring her beautiful face. "What? Did I do something wrong? Are women not allowed to—"

He captured her lips in a kiss of urgent longing, allowing her to feel just how desperately he wanted to complete their bonding.

"You are certain?" he muttered between frenzied kisses. "The mating is irrevocable."

Her hands moved in a restless path up and down his back, each caress sending sizzling sparks of heat through his body.

"This mating has been irrevocable from the beginning," she muttered.

"Thank the gods." Kissing a path along her jaw, he paused to revel in the poignant scent of peaches and willing woman. "I did not believe you would ever come to your senses."

She chuckled. "There are many who would claim I have lost them completely."

He pulled back, his fangs throbbing in protest. This was too important a moment to rush.

"And what of you, little one?"

"Me?"

"Does the thought of becoming my mate please you?"

Her expression was somber as she framed his face in her hands. "Victor, since my parents' death I have sought a place to call home."

He frowned at the tender ache he could feel blooming in the center of her heart. It bothered him that he was helpless to protect her from the wounds of the past.

"You have never revealed how your parents were killed," he said gently.

She winced, but she did not pull away. A victory, considering Juliet had never before trusted him enough to share her secrets.

"My father was considered beautiful, even among the fey," she said, her voice so low even his acute hearing struggled to catch the words.

His gaze skimmed over her delicate features, lingering on the wide emerald eyes that spoke of her fey blood.

"That I well believe."

A tremor shook her slender body, her nails unconsciously digging into his back. It was a pain Victor welcomed, wishing he could take away her wounds.

"Unfortunately, he attracted the attention of Morgana le Fey."

Victor was startled by the mention of the queen. It had been centuries since she had retreated behind her protective mists.

"I did not know she ever left Avalon."

"It was rumored she was hunting for some mystical weapon that is destined to kill her." The emerald eyes flashed with a long-brewing hatred. "Instead she found my father."

"And desired to take him as her lover."

"Yes."

Victor had heard rumors of the queen's insatiable lust for beautiful men, as well as her habit of treating them like pretty baubles that were inevitably destroyed when she grew bored.

Juliet's father had been destined for death from the moment he had caught the eye of the fickle Morgana le Fey.

"I presume your father declined her royal invitation?"

"He was not foolish enough to publicly reject her, but he attempted to flee with my mother and myself."

"Morgana was no doubt displeased."

"She commanded that we be hunted down and slaughtered."

Victor flinched as his bond with Juliet allowed him to feel the savage intensity of her loss.

"They died to protect you."

"Yes." Her gaze lowered, as if she could hide the tears that filled her eyes. "They died and I was alone."

"Never again," Victor swore, cupping her chin and lifting her face until he could capture her bruised gaze. "I will be at your side for all eternity."

Her hands swept up his back, the shadows lingering in her eyes.

"Victor."

"Yes, my love?"

"I want you to be my mate."

A fierce surge of savage hunger combined with pure joy in a potent explosion that left Victor reeling from the impact. Suddenly he felt as uncertain and awkward as a newly turned fledgling.

"Now?" he husked.

A smile of pure invitation curved her lips. "Now."

"Bloody hell."

Any hope of a slow, dignified mating that would reveal to Juliet just how much she meant to him was lost as he muttered a curse and swept her heavy curtain of hair to one side, exposing the vulnerable curve of her neck.

He had an eternity to prove just how much he adored her.

For now, he was desperate to make this woman his.

His lover, his partner, his mate.

With one smooth strike his fangs slid easily through her skin, the taste of her blood hitting his tongue with staggering force.

It was perfect.

She was perfect.

Juliet moaned as he fed from her throat, her

hands impatiently lowering to tug at his pants, her body arching in silent need. A need that Victor was quite eager to sate.

Reaching down, he ripped off the pants with one vicious jerk and tugged open her robe until there was nothing left between them. They were skin to skin, her delectable heat wrapping around him.

Allowing himself one precious moment to savor the anticipation, Victor chuckled softly as Juliet wrapped her legs around his hips with obvious impatience.

"Victor . . . please."

Victor reluctantly tugged his fangs from her neck, using his tongue to close the bleeding wounds. He could not afford to be greedy. Not when Juliet was determined to rescue the ridiculous gargoyle. Any loss of blood might weaken her.

Besides, there was more than one means of being a part of her.

"Yes, little one," he husked, settling between her spread legs and entering her with a slow, steady thrust.

Closing his eyes in pure bliss, Victor sent up a prayer of thanks to whatever god had seen fit to bless him with this beautiful, magnificent woman.

Chapter Seven

After a hot bath, Juliet pulled on a clean smock and pants that Victor had borrowed from the son of one of his vast stable of human servants. Like all vampires, he considered any sort of manual labor as being beneath him.

Unfortunately, he also possessed the vampire habit of forbidding any mirrors to be brought into their lair.

Brushing out her tangled curls, she awkwardly pulled her hair into a braid and tied it off with a thin strip of leather. No doubt she could have requested Victor to assist her, but she sensed that such an intimate act would soon have led them to the wide bed just behind her.

It was not that she wasn't eager to feel Victor's arms around her. Or to experience the intoxicating pleasure of having him feed from her vein. Good Lord, if she had a choice she would keep the delectable vampire in this private lair for the next century.

Unfortunately, the same bonds that allowed her to sense Victor's unwavering love and commitment for her also revealed his heavy sense of duty.

He was clan chief. And that meant ridding London of the Jinn before the powerful demon could bring harm to Victor's vampires.

"Juliet."

The sound of Levet's voice whispering through her head had Juliet on her feet, her heart slamming against her ribs in startled surprise.

"Levet," she breathed, ignoring his rude intrusion as a wave of relief rushed through her. "Oh, thank God. I have been so worried."

"Indeed?" the gargoyle said peevishly. "If you were so excessively worried then why have you not yet rescued me?"

"You might have mentioned that your captor is a full-blooded Jinn," she snapped, stung by his unfair accusation.

"Ah . . . well, I . . ." He coughed in embarrassment. "Does it truly matter?"

"Does it matter? I very nearly was skewered by a bolt of lightning. If it had not been for Victor I would not have survived to rescue you."

"*Sacre bleu.* Why would you tell the bloodsucker that I was captured?" Levet demanded in a horrified voice.

"It was not as if I had a choice. He followed me to the docks."

"That is no excuse for revealing my very private business. I thought our trust was sacred."

"Do you wish to be rescued or not, Levet?"

"*Oui,* but I do not desire to be made the source of mockery throughout London."

Juliet thrust aside her annoyance, reminding

herself that the tiny gargoyle was inordinately sensitive when it came to his manly reputation.

"I can promise you that Victor will tell no one you were captured by the Jinn," she soothed.

There was a moment of startled silence. "Since when do you speak for the vampires, *ma belle?*" Levet at last demanded.

"Just be patient. I am coming for you," she said, in no mood to endure her friend's outrage when he discovered her recent mating.

Levet detested vampires.

"Please hurry," he said, then without warning his scream of pain echoed through Juliet's mind.

"Levet?" She grasped her head, her ears ringing. "Levet?"

"That bastard just destroyed my wing," Levet panted, clearly in considerable agony. "When I get free I am going to turn him into a pile of steaming fairy dung. No . . . wait. Let us be reasonable—"

There was another scream and with an unpleasant wrench the sensation of the gargoyle was abruptly gone from her mind.

"Levet?"

She was distracted as the door to the lair was shoved open with enough force to make it snap off the heavy iron hinges, revealing Victor with his eyes glowing and his fangs fully extended.

"What has happened?" he growled. "I felt your distress."

Juliet shivered, caught between a terrified awe at Victor's power and a smug pleasure at the knowledge he would battle through the fires of hell to protect her.

"Levet," she said, forced to halt and clear her throat. "We have to find him."

Not surprisingly, Victor's brows snapped together at the mention of the gargoyle.

"I should have known the ridiculous creature
would be troubling you the moment the sun set."

"He has been hurt."

He planted his fists on his hips, the long caped
coat doing little to disguise the various swords and
daggers strapped to his lean body. With his hair
pulled back to reveal the elegant beauty of his pale
face and the lethal shimmer in the silver eyes, he
appeared to be an ancient god come to earth.

"I do not care."

She lifted a warning brow. "Victor."

His jaw tightened, but with a muttered curse he
turned to lead her down a narrow corridor to a
door hidden by a cleverly woven enchantment.

"The carriage is waiting for us."

Ignoring his cold disapproval, Juliet smiled
wryly and followed him through the narrow tunnels that crisscrossed beneath the vast estate. Despite their intense connection, they were both
strong-willed individuals who were destined to
quarrel on occasion. And while she might not
have much experience with being a mate, she did
know that Victor's natural arrogance would overwhelm a woman who did not have a stiff backbone.

"Good," she said. "I need to return to Justin's
house before we go to the docks."

"Why?"

"Because there is an amulet that might be helpful to us."

He turned into another tunnel, this one with a
flight of stairs at the end.

"What is its power?"

"It is capable of absorbing our scent."

He paused at the base of the stairs, glancing over his shoulder in puzzlement.

"Forgive my ignorance, but how would that be helpful?"

She shrugged. "It can be divided and left in several tunnels, ensuring our scents are in many places instead of just one."

The silver eyes flashed in appreciation. "Clever."

"We shall see." She grimaced. "First I must find the means to take the amulet without alerting Justin. It is one of his more valuable possessions."

He turned to smoothly climb the carved stairs, pushing open the trapdoor at the top.

"You have no need to fear Hawthorne."

Juliet gritted her teeth as she hurried to catch up with her aggravating mate, not surprised when she stepped directly into the stables. Vampires delighted in being able to travel from place to place without fear of sunlight.

"Victor?"

He inspected the sleek black carriage that was already attached to a pair of restless black steeds.

"Yes, little one?"

"You are feeling remarkably smug," she accused. "What have you done to Justin?"

He turned to meet her frown, casually leaning against the back of the carriage.

"Hawthorne arrived at the front door demanding to see you."

She shook her head, not surprised by Justin's brazen stupidity. Indeed, she had expected him to arrive hours ago. Not out of any love for her, but out of sheer greed. And, of course, a petty refusal to allow Victor to steal what he considered to be his personal property.

"Is he . . ."

"Dead? No, but he was foolish enough to threaten Uriel with a nasty spell." A cruel smile touched his lips. "My servant decided the intruder was in need of a lesson in manners."

A chill inched down her spine. "I do not think I want to know."

"He will survive." With a sudden motion, Victor straightened and opened the door to the carriage. "Which is more than he deserves."

Rolling her eyes, Juliet climbed into the carriage, waiting until Victor was settled at her side before offering her opinion on overly arrogant men.

"I am not certain who are more annoying, vampires or mages."

He flashed a smile that would have been a great deal more reassuring if it had not revealed his massive fangs.

"You shall have an eternity to decide, my love."

She settled back in the soft leather of the seat as she watched several vampires appear from the shadows, one climbing on the carriage to urge the horses into motion while the others ran silently at their side. It would be a waste of breath to continue the argument. Besides, Justin no doubt deserved a bit of punishment for being idiotic enough to enter a vampire's lair uninvited.

Leaving the estate, the vampires once again disappeared, no doubt headed directly for the docks while the carriage turned toward Mayfair. Their pace slowed as the streets became flooded with vehicles rushing from one glittering society event to another. Juliet smiled as their frantic gaiety filled the night breeze with the sound of laughter, for once not feeling the least pang of envy.

She at last had what she had always desired.

A home with a man she loved beyond all reason.

They halted just long enough for Juliet to dash into Justin's townhouse and retrieve the amulet she had discovered during their travels through Spain. Then, returning to the carriage, she used the short time during the drive to the docks to activate the amulet with her and Victor's scents before splitting it into several small pieces and handing half of them to Victor to spread through the tunnels.

All too soon they had reached the docks, and not giving herself the opportunity to consider just how insane it was to deliberately enter the lair of a Jinn, she shoved open the door and climbed out of the carriage.

In the blink of an eye, Victor was standing in front of her, his expression somber as he wrapped his arms around her in a protective motion.

"Juliet."

She tilted back her head to meet the fierce emotions smoldering in his silver eyes.

"Must we repeat the same arguments yet again?" she asked softly.

"If you are harmed it will destroy me, little one."

Her heart melted at the stark simplicity of his words. Lifting her hand, she pressed her palm against the cool skin of his cheek.

"I promise to take the greatest care."

"You free the gargoyle and leave the docks. Do you understand?"

"Very well, but if you do not return to me—"

He bent down to cover her lips in an achingly sweet kiss. "I have sworn to be at your side for all eternity. I love you, Juliet."

With a last kiss, he was turning and disappearing with a speed her eyes could not follow.

"I love you, Marquis DeRosa," she breathed before reluctantly making her own way to the nearby warehouse.

With none of Victor's talent for tracking his prey, she was forced to retrace her path from last eve and simply hope she stumbled across Levet. Not the best plan, but the only one she possessed.

Entering the warehouse, she crossed to the gaping hole in the floor and lightly dropped to the cavern beneath. Then, moving to the various openings that led to tunnels, she scattered the tiny pieces of the amulet before heading down the nearest passageway.

Her heart was thundering in her chest and her palms were sweating, but she took pride in the realization that the stench of human fear that had been prevalent hours before was beginning to fade. They had at least managed to save a number of prisoners.

She bypassed the tunnel where they had battled the Jinn, shivering at the memory. Victor had sensed Levet nearby. . . .

Juliet abruptly paused, tilting back her head. She might not possess Victor's vampire senses, but she was certain she could catch the faintest scent of gargoyle.

Hoping that she was on the track of Levet and not some other gargoyle, Juliet squeezed through a narrow opening, banging her head on the low ceiling as she struggled to follow the scent. Good Lord, another inch on her backside and she would never fit.

Her hands were scratched and her clothing was ripped in several places by the time she managed to reach the end of the tunnel, but her heart gave a leap at the sight of the entrance carved into the stone wall.

Bending low, she wiggled through the opening, cursing as she sacrificed several strands of hair and a small part of her scalp to a low-hanging rock. But at last she was in a cavern large enough for her to stand upright and even to drag in a deep breath.

Better yet, there was a tiny gargoyle only a few steps away, hung to the wall with silver manacles.

With a muttered prayer of thanks, Juliet rushed to tug on the cuffs. Her witch blood gave her immunity to the silver, while her imp blood gave her enough strength to loosen the metal and allow Levet to squirm free.

"At last," the gargoyle muttered with a distinct lack of gratitude. "I thought you had decided to leave me to rot in this godforsaken cave."

Juliet futilely tried to knock the dirt from her pants. "It is a notion with growing appeal. Are you hurt?"

"Of course I am hurt." Levet turned, wiggling his one remaining gossamer wing. "Can you not see I am missing a wing?"

She grimaced. "Are you able to walk on your own?"

Levet sniffed. "Gargoyles are renowned for their ability to overcome pain and perform heroic feats that stun and amaze the demon world."

"Yes, well, the only heroic feat I desire is getting out of here." She shivered. "As swiftly as possible."

"That is my specialty."

Expecting Levet to leave the same way she had entered, Juliet frowned as the gargoyle instead crawled between two large boulders and disappeared from sight.

With a shake of her head, Juliet bent downward, discovering a small tunnel.

"What are you doing?"

"Following the night."

"But . . ."

"Trust me."

Condemning the cramped tunnels and annoying gargoyles to the netherworld, Juliet crawled through the small space. Once she returned to Victor's lair, she intended to spend hours soaking in a hot bath.

At last reaching a connecting tunnel, Juliet straightened to find Levet waiting with an impatient expression.

"This way," he urged, waddling with surprising speed through the darkness.

"You are certain?" she demanded, only to sigh in resignation as he continued on without so much as a backward glance. Following in his wake, she ruefully reminded herself that she had willingly chosen to rescue the aggravating gargoyle, even if at the moment she longed to give him a good shake. "You have not yet explained how you were captured by the Jinn."

"He"—Levet halted to clear his throat—"caught me off guard."

"Hmmm. You are hiding something from me."

He hunched his shoulders, refusing to turn as he doggedly continued down the tunnel.

"It was not my fault."

"What was not your fault?"

"I thought there was a nest of pixies, so I decided to perform a bit of magic to impress them."

"Oh, Lord," Juliet muttered. She was familiar enough with Levet's dubious magic to presume that it had been nothing less than a disaster. "What happened?"

Levet paused, then turned down a side tunnel, his tail twitching behind him.

"There might have been the smallest of explosions."

Juliet frowned. Although she suspected that Levet's notion of a small explosion was a good deal more spectacular than her own, she knew there must be more to his tale than he was revealing.

"Did you wound the Jinn?"

"No, but a part of the tunnels were exposed."

"And?"

"And it happened to be the part where the Jinn had stored his treasure."

"And?"

Levet impatiently waved his stubby arms. "And I might have taken something he considered of value," he grudgingly admitted.

Ah. They at last were coming to the truth of the matter.

"Then why do you not simply return it?"

He turned into yet another tunnel. "I lost it trying to escape."

Juliet's stomach clenched with dread. She knew very little about the Jinn, but she did know a great deal about demons in general and there was not one species that did not consider the theft of its treasure a suitable reason to maim, torture, and kill.

"Maybe we should hurry," she suggested.

"My thoughts precisely," Levet agreed, his remaining wing fluttering and his tiny legs churning.

They rushed through the darkness in silence, both acutely aware of the heavy sense of dread that was beginning to crawl through the air. The Jinn was near.

Too near.

Intent on keeping pace with the gargoyle, Juliet nearly tumbled over the top of him when he came to an abrupt halt.

"*Mon Dieu.* I smell it."

Juliet regained her balance and glared at her companion. "What is it?"

"Continue north, *ma belle.* There is an opening less than a mile away."

"Levet?"

She watched in disbelief as the miniature demon scrambled up the side of the wall, pushing his small body through a crack that hardly appeared large enough for a bat.

Well.

She did not expect Levet to grovel at her feet with gratitude at her heroic rescue, but to actually abandon her?

She had thought they were friends.

Thoroughly vexed by the unexpected betrayal, Juliet stomped down the tunnel, dangerously distracted by her flare of anger.

Not that being on guard would have prevented the wall of the passageway from suddenly exploding inward as a body was thrown through it. Or her scream of fear as she recognized her mate lying in a pool of blood at her feet.

Falling to her knees, she reached to brush the raven hair from Victor's face, her heart contracting at the deep gash that marred the ivory skin of his forehead.

"Victor?"

His lashes slowly lifted to reveal remarkably clear silver eyes, his wounds already healing. She shook her head. Only a vampire could be shoved through four feet of pure rock and appear barely worse for the wear.

"I thought I told you to rescue the gargoyle and leave," he growled, flowing to his feet.

She straightened, glancing toward the gaping hole in the wall. "And I thought you intended to rid us of the Jinn."

There was a cloud of foreboding, then the booming voice of the Jinn echoed through the tunnel.

"Where is the gargoyle?"

Victor stepped in front of her as the Jinn slammed his way through the wall, the air crackling with electricity.

"If you have any other tricks, little one, now would be an appropriate moment to reveal them," Victor rasped, pulling a large sword from the scabbard on his hip.

"What of your warriors?"

"Dead or wounded."

Shaking off the clinging dust, the Jinn pointed a finger directly at Juliet, his eyes glowing with an eerie light and his hair floating as if caught on a breeze.

"Give me the gargoyle," he roared.

Drowning in the potent presence of the Jinn, Juliet was caught off guard when Levet abruptly appeared on a rock above the Jinn's head, his expression smug.

"I am here, you putrid saddlebag of rotting fungus," Levet taunted, holding up his hand to reveal a wooden box ornately decorated with gold and precious jewels, including a ruby the size of Juliet's fist. "And look what I discovered."

Wondering if her friend had taken complete leave of his senses, Juliet shook her head.

"What the devil is that?"

Victor stiffened with a tension that Juliet did not need to be a mate to sense.

"The Jinn's *tiglia*. It holds his anchor to this realm. Without it he will be forced to return to his own world," he whispered softly.

The demon's power surged through the tunnel, making the earth shake and the air so thick it was nearly impossible to breathe.

"Give that to me."

Without warning, Levet launched the box over the head of the Jinn, directly at Juliet.

"Catch."

Too stunned to think clearly, Juliet snatched the box from the air, her heart nearly halting at the malevolent magic that slammed into her.

Victor instinctively swept an arm around her, keeping her upright even as his wary gaze remained on the Jinn, who was already turning his fury toward Juliet.

"Can you destroy it?" he demanded.

Juliet's first instinct was to deny the necessary skill for such a task. After all, she had never been properly trained in magic. How could she possibly destroy such a powerful object? And in truth, she simply wanted to drop the vile thing and run as far away as possible. The mere touch of it seemed to taint her.

But, drawing on the bond with her powerful mate, she steadied her nerves and forced herself to actually study the box with her innate talent.

The magic was unfamiliar, but she ignored the complex weave and instead concentrated on the odd tentacles she could sense flowing from the box to the demon. It was almost as if the very essence of the Jinn was in the box while the physical body was allowed to move around the world.

So what if she severed the connection?

She sucked in a deep breath, lifting her head to meet Victor's steady gaze.

"I will need time."

His smile was filled with a savage determination. "I can give you that."

With a growl that made the hairs on her nape rise, Victor launched himself at the Jinn, the sword in his hand a blur of silver as he attacked. At the same moment, Levet jumped off the rock, directly onto the beast's head.

Momentarily paralyzed, Juliet watched in horror as Victor ignored the massive blows from the Jinn, striking the demon with enough force to halt his desperate attempt to reach his *tiglia*. She had never witnessed a battle between two such mighty foes. It was . . . terrifyingly beautiful.

It was only when Levet sent a fireball over her head that she came to her senses.

"*Sacre bleu*, Juliet, you must do something."

Juliet shook her head in sharp self-disgust, turning her rattled attention to the box she held in her hands.

She made no effort to destroy the actual *tiglia.* Such magic was beyond her skill. She doubted there was a witch in all of England who could perform such a spell. Instead she studied the tentacles that floated toward the Jinn like the strands of a web.

They were magical, but they did not draw their strength from the box or the demon. Instead she could feel the steady pull from their surroundings. The air. The earth. The water of the nearby river.

It was no wonder the Jinn could control lightning and earthquakes.

He was a creature of nature.

"Little one, you must hurry," Victor rasped, the chill of his power making her shiver.

"Do you think I am not trying?" she gritted, keeping her attention on the tentacles as she summoned her mother's magic.

She did not bother with a circle. She was not attempting to cast a spell, but rather to destroy an existing power. Ironically, it was a task that was easier for a half-breed than a full witch.

Needing a tangible means to focus her vision, she jerked off her loose shirt and wrapped it around the box, at the same time imagining she was smothering the tentacles. If they could not draw on the powers around them, they would die. And with them, hopefully the connection to the Jinn.

In the distance she could hear the sound of the vicious battle, smell the fresh blood spilling around her, feel the promise of death in the air, but she refused to be distracted. Not even when the Jinn's roar of agony sent a shower of stones falling on her head.

The end was close.

She could feel it.

Trembling from the effort of holding her vision in place, Juliet fell to her knees, her stomach heaving at the scent of burning flesh that suddenly filled the tunnel.

She had to persevere . . . she had to . . .

"Juliet."

Wearily lifting her head, she watched as Victor lunged toward her, abruptly covering her with his much heavier body. It was not until the ceiling collapsed, however, that she realized the Jinn was now no more than a smoking pile of charred flesh and they were about to be buried alive.

Not precisely the honeymoon she had been hoping for.

One week later

Seated at the small table he had situated before the fire in his lair, Victor sipped his aged brandy and watched Juliet absently nibble a piece of marzipan candy.

A frown touched his brow. She looked delectable, of course. Wearing an emerald satin nightgown that perfectly matched her eyes, and her fiery curls left loose to spill over her shoulders, she was the perfect image of Eve.

Feminine temptation at its very best.

But it was her obvious lack of hunger that caused a familiar stab of alarm to clench his heart.

"Shall I have the chef replaced, my love?" he demanded, his tone revealing he would happily go in search of a superior chef without hesitation.

"Good Lord, no. This food is heavenly." Juliet dropped the candy on the tray as she regarded him with astonishment. "Why would you ask such a thing?"

He waved a hand toward the table that was laden with lobster in butter, braised ham, creamed potatoes, steamed asparagus, and fresh pears from the hothouse.

"You have not eaten more than a few bites."

She gave a choked laugh. "Because I am still stuffed from the enormous meal you served when I first awoke. Are you attempting to fatten me like a Christmas goose?"

"You need food to regain your strength."

Leaning forward, she offered a slow, wicked smile that sent a predictable flare of hunger blazing through him. Juliet had only to be near for him to be hard and aching to be buried deep inside her heat.

"I would say that I effectively proved that I have fully regained my strength," she husked. "Or have you so easily forgotten?"

He reached to grasp her slender fingers, his gaze searing over her beautiful face.

"I will never forget a moment of our time together."

"Me either," she breathed, holding his gaze as she deliberately allowed him to sense her stirring arousal.

Over the past days they had rarely left the lair as they gloried in the explosive passion between them. Now he savored her ready response even as he glanced around the candlelit chamber, for the first time noting the hint of shabbiness.

"We shall need a larger bed," he abruptly decided.

"It seems just the perfect size to me," she murmured. "Besides, it is very old. You must have owned it for centuries."

He shrugged. "I have no sentimental attachment to the furnishings. In truth, I prefer they be disposed of so you can choose what pleases you. We can begin tonight if you are feeling strong enough."

Hoping to please his mate, Victor was disappointed when she pulled her fingers from his grasp and studied him with a wary expression.

"Victor, are you . . . perfectly well?"

"Why would I not be well?"

She shook her head in bewilderment. "Since we defeated the Jinn you have hovered and fluttered about as if I were as fragile as Venice glass. For God's sake, you even allowed Levet to visit when I said I wanted to see him."

He shuddered at the hideous memory. "Do not remind me."

"Is there something you are not telling me?" Rising to her feet, she circled the table and settled her hands on his shoulders, covered by his brocade robe. "Did my spell to break the Jinn's connection to this world do something horrible to me? Am I dying?"

He surged to his feet, shocked by her question. "No. You are perfect, Juliet."

She tilted back her head to meet his narrowed gaze. "Then why are you behaving so oddly?"

With a grimace he accepted there was nothing

to do but confess the truth. No matter how it might expose his vulnerable heart.

"I want you to be pleased with me and with this lair," he confessed, his voice raw with need. "I want you to feel as if this is your home."

Her eyes darkened with an unwavering love that instantly soothed his fears.

"Victor, this lair is merely a place where we are currently residing." She pressed a hand to his chest, a smile of satisfaction curving her lips. "My home is here . . . in your heart. And nothing, absolutely nothing, could please me more."

With a smooth motion, he swept her off her feet, headed for their bed. The cold emptiness that had claimed his soul centuries ago was melting beneath the tender heat of her gaze.

"You will never leave me?"

"I am yours, Marquis DeRosa," she promised, "until the end of time."

He tightened his arms around her. "Until the end of time and beyond."

Immortal Dreams

KAITLIN O'RILEY

Chapter One

London, England
Fall, 1870

Grace opened her eyes with a strangled gasp, staring blankly into the murky darkness surrounding her. Fear gripped her entire body and she lay motionless for some minutes before realization dawned. Sweaty and shaking, she sat up in bed, wiping the tears that had spilled down her cheeks as her wild heart rate slowly returned to a more normal pace. With a trembling hand she lit the lamp on her bedside table, allowing the warm glow to comfort her, and sighed heavily.

The dreams. Another of those haunting dreams had awakened her.

Now that her bedroom was lit, she instinctively glanced at the small ormolu clock resting on the fireplace mantel, not that she needed to look. She knew exactly what time it was. As expected, the elegant hands indicated a quarter past five o'clock in the morning. She always awakened from these strange dreams close to dawn.

Knowing she would not fall back to sleep now,

she rose from her four-poster bed and padded across the room to the large window. Lately she had been compelled to look out her window after one of those dreams, but she did not know why. Except she felt the answers to her questions lay somewhere beyond these walls. She pulled back the pretty rose toile curtains that reached to the polished wood floor.

The backyard of her London townhouse was shrouded in dark shadows, but she knew the grass was immaculately trimmed and the rose bushes and flower garden carefully tended. Her eyes scanned the lawn and moved upward above the trees. The last of the night stars were fading as soft fingers of light caressed the early morning sky. The world always seemed desolate and lonely to her at this hour, when the city was not yet awake and all was hushed and still. A sense of expectancy clung to her as she searched through the dimness, looking for a sign of movement. A sign of anything. She held her breath in anticipation. The eerie predawn light still held shadows but she could distinguish nothing out of the ordinary.

"Where is he?" she whispered impatiently to herself.

The question startled her, not only because she had said it aloud but also because of what it meant. She shook herself at her odd query, for she did not know whom she was looking for, but she could not get over the feeling that she was waiting for *someone*. A man. A certain man. The same man who haunted her strange recurring dreams. *Who was he?* She was quite positive she did not know anyone remotely like him. In her dreams she loved him. Even when she was married she had not loved

Henry with the same passion with which she loved the stranger in her dreams. This love was magical, intense, and wildly passionate.

Afterward the dreams always left her in a melancholy mood, and this one in particular had been more vivid and detailed than usual, and filled her with a sense of anguish and sorrow.

She had had the dreams for as long as she could remember, all her life, although they had occurred with more frequency in the past year. While they always left her with an overwhelming sense of loss and sadness, she could not deny the indescribable joy and deep love she experienced within the dreams. Nor the aching loneliness she felt when she awoke and faced her real life.

Grace shivered and dropped the rose toile curtain back into place. Moving back to her bed, she gathered her soft robe around her and donned her slippers. It was too early to ring for a servant, but she desperately wanted the warmth of the fireplace, for the first days of autumn chilled the air.

Grace walked to her elegant writing desk, unlocked a small drawer, and retrieved a familiar book, indulging in the memory of her dream for just a few more moments. She curled up on the overstuffed rose chintz armchair with her journal. Flipping through the pages, she noted that her last entry was dated less than a week earlier. The dreams were becoming more frequent, more intense. It was after Henry died that she first began recording in a journal the recollections of the strange dreams that had haunted her life. Never had she spoken to a soul about these dreams, not even to her husband.

For these dreams were special and quite unlike

ordinary dreams. She had often tried to find words to describe them and could only come up with "lifelike." These dreams were not flights of fancy, nor the vague processing of the daily events. These dreams did not fade as the day wore on. They did not become wisps of memory or flashing impressions of feelings as her other, more ordinary dreams did.

These dreams of him were lasting and vivid, as real as if the events happened while she was awake and living them in reality. In truth it was as if she were visiting another person's life during another era, yet somehow they were about her.

She had begun transcribing her dreams to keep track of them and over the years she had discovered that she lived another life when she slept. She could not shake the suspicion that it had been *her* life, if such a thing were possible. For the details were too intimate, too private, and too intense to belong to anyone but her.

Last night's dream in particular.

She had been naked with *him* in this dream last night again. Her cheeks growing warm, Grace closed her eyes, remembering the deliciously sensuous and passionate nature of the dream.

In the dreams she called him Phillip. He was tall with black, wavy hair, very fair skin, and deep dark brown eyes. His face was beautifully sculpted, his handsomeness almost startling in its perfection. He possessed a seductive voice, smooth and cultured. And he loved her. Or at least he loved the woman she was in the dreams. He called her by a strange name. *Gráinne.* His love for her was evident in every word he whispered to her, in the way he caressed her cheek, in the way he gazed adoringly at her. In the way he kissed her lips. Oh, the way he kissed her! The emotion and intensity between them was overpowering, all-consuming.

Never in her own life had Grace experienced anything like it.

Henry had kissed her, of course. Yet Henry's kisses never left her feeling the way she felt after Phillip kissed her.

A sharp rap on the bedroom door startled her, causing her to drop her journal on the floor. Before Grace could rise from her chair, the door opened and Mary Sutton stormed in.

"What in God's name are you doing up at this hour?" her sharp voice snapped.

"I . . . I couldn't sleep," Grace began to explain to her mother-in-law, her heartbeat increasing. With a furtive glance at her dream journal lying on the floor, she frantically wished she had had a chance to tuck her journal behind her before Mary entered.

With eyes like a hawk, Mary spied the journal and snatched it up. "What is this?"

Grace's cheeks flushed red and a sense of panic welled within her. She was always very careful to keep the journal well hidden. She would surely die of mortification if Mary read her journal now, knowing she would never be able to explain to Mary's satisfaction any of what was written within its pages. A tall, wide-girthed woman with steel-gray hair and permanent frown lines around her thin lips, Mary Sutton carried herself as a queen and expected others to treat her as such.

"It's nothing important. Just some thoughts."

Grace held out her hand. "Sometimes it helps me to sleep if I write down the thoughts in my head first."

"Your thoughts!" Mary ignored Grace's obvious request for the return of the book. With a disapproving frown, she thumbed through the hand-written pages. "Of course you can't sleep. How could anybody sleep when they are awake composing such drivel instead of in bed where they are supposed to be? Dream journal indeed!" She scoffed and flung the book back at Grace, who fumbled to catch it.

Grace breathed a sigh of relief, realizing that Mary could not read without her spectacles, so she could not see what Grace had written. She held the book close to her chest.

"God will be judging you on what you do, and I don't believe anything you've written in that book would be deemed as godly."

Grace remained silent. No, she doubted anything she had written was godly, but it *was* heavenly. She would not argue that point with her mother-in-law. She and Mary had always had differing views on God, and Mary's overzealous religious leanings had only become more intense since her son, Henry, had died.

"Honestly, Grace, I pray for your soul every day, but I worry that not even that is helping you," Mary admonished sharply, pulling the ties that secured her robe tighter over the girth of her stomach. She gave her a pointed look. "Well, have you decided to accept Lord Grayson's offer?"

Lord Grayson's offer! Grace's stomach clenched and she stared mutely at Mary.

She had completely forgotten Reginald Marks's

proposal to her last night! She'd been so consumed with her dream she had not given it another thought. After years of proper mourning and wearing black for Henry, Grace was finally socializing again. In the past months she had begun to attend balls, supper parties, and musicales. Last night Reginald Marks, Earl of Grayson, had made an offer of marriage to her. He was a wealthy widower with a grown son, and was a nice enough man. She had thanked Lord Grayson for his honor, declared herself overwhelmed, and begged for some time to think it over. Lord Grayson had not been discouraged by her hesitation and readily agreed to give her as much time as she needed to consider his offer of marriage.

Because Mary had been so instrumental in bringing this prospect to her, Grace could not summarily dismiss the man, as was her first impulse. She did not love Lord Grayson nor did she wish to marry him, but then again, she did not wish to marry anyone. After her husband's tragic death she did not believe she could love anyone again.

But then, love was not necessary for marriage. That she already knew.

But could she marry the Earl of Grayson? He was kind and gentle with her. He would take good care of her. Perhaps she would have a child this time. That would be lovely and was the main source of her regrets with Henry Sutton. She had always longed for a baby of her own.

She could do worse than the Earl of Grayson. Reginald Marks owned a great deal of property and was well respected in society. Although he was older than Grace by at least twenty years, judging from the amount of white taking over his brown hair, he was not unappealing. The promise of leaving Mary Sutton's home was also something to consider. Living with her mother-in-law had become more intolerable each year, as she had grown more intrusive and domineering in her ways.

With a mixture of fear and loathing, Grace stared at the large woman looming in front of her. Mary's blatant look of scorn and condescension was the usual expression she wore. Grace's relationship with Mary had been one of mutual dislike from the start, because Mary had not wanted her only son to marry Grace. When Henry died five years before, the only buffer between them had been removed and each year the friction between the two women only increased.

"Don't be a little idiot, Grace. I've worked tirelessly to cultivate this relationship for you with Lord Grayson, in spite of your efforts to deter him. You might not get another offer this good. You're thirty years old now and you are beginning to show your age. You've turned down every other offer you've received, but you would be a fool to refuse Lord Grayson."

It suddenly occurred to Grace that Mary was as eager to be rid of her as she was to be rid of Mary. She grinned at the irony. Yes, Grace would accept Reginald Marks's offer of marriage, if only to escape this woman.

Mary eyed her suspiciously. "You look like the cat that ate the canary, Grace. I don't like that smirk on your face. It's quite rude and disrespectful to me. Stop it this instant."

Grace ceased smiling, her eyes downcast.

"Did that smile mean you've finally come to your senses and have decided to be thankful for this opportunity the good Lord has generously bestowed upon you, however undeserving you may be?"

Grace merely nodded.

"Speak up, girl!" Mary commanded. "You will accept his offer this evening, will you not?"

She glared at Mary, thinking how wonderful it would be to finally be free of this woman's daily presence. "Yes, Mother, I shall accept Lord Grayson's offer."

Mary sniffed. "It's about time. Not since you married my Henry have I seen you make a good decision."

Grace said nothing. Henry was a sensitive subject between them, for she knew Mary blamed her for his death. And for the fact that she did not have a grandchild.

"Now that you are awake, you might as well get dressed and we shall begin prayers. Then you may help me sort through the linens to see which must be mended and pressed. Dolly made a terrible mess of that. But what did I expect, asking her to do something that required some actual thought?" Mary said, not waiting for Grace to respond. "Oh, we must call on Lady Dennis later today, so make sure you wear your dark blue dress. We shall leave for the Rutherfords' ball at eight o'clock sharp, for Lord Grayson will accompany us. You can tell him when he arrives that you have agreed to be his wife. Now you had better get dressed."

With that proclamation, Mary left the room. Grace stared at the door and released a breath, relieved to be free of her mother-in-law.

You have agreed to be Lord Grayson's wife. Grace hadn't told him yet. But she supposed she would.

A pang of regret filled her as again she thought of him. The man in her dreams. Phillip. Oh, if only she could feel a love like that in her real life.

It seemed, however, that a love like that was not in her destiny. For if it was, surely it would have happened by now.

Chapter Two

"Congratulations on your engagement, Mrs. Sutton!"

It was all Grace heard that evening while she stood in the crowded and overheated ballroom of Lady Rutherford's London townhouse. Grace wished she could simply slip away from it all. She had smiled falsely at everyone and was exhausted from the strain of pretending to be happy as well as spending the entire afternoon in Mary's company.

"Thank you very much," she managed to utter in wooden response.

She had danced and waltzed obligingly with her new fiancé, who beamed at her with delight and pride at her acceptance.

"We are going to be very happy together," Lord Grayson said as he escorted her from the dance floor, his hand possessively on her arm.

Grace stared at the whiteness of his hair, the lines around his blue eyes, and the tightness of his mouth. Somehow she did not think she would be happy with him, but she was quite certain that he would not make her as miserable as Mary Sutton did. She would bet money on that if she could. Her life would definitely be easier with Reginald Marks. He was a nice enough gentleman and she even liked him.

"Would you please excuse me?" she whispered softly, indicating subtly that she needed to visit the ladies' retiring rooms.

Lord Grayson nodded in understanding. "Of course. I shall eagerly await your return."

Grace made her way through the festive crowd and managed to step outside for a much-needed breath of air. The cool fall evening revived her sagging spirits and she stood outside until the chill finally forced her to rejoin the party. She made a quick visit to the retiring room so she could honestly say she had been there. She studied herself in the looking glass, smoothing her auburn hair and adjusting her bottle-green silk gown. Her cheeks looked flushed and her blue eyes seemed overly bright, but she could not bring herself to smile.

She exited the retiring room and wandered along the hallway of the Rutherfords' townhouse. Lingering, she strolled along another empty corridor and admired the gilt-framed paintings illuminated by beeswax candles in wrought-iron sconces.

She did not wish to return to Lord Grayson's and Mary Sutton's side just yet. Something drew her to this secluded area. A need to be alone? Perhaps, but she could not shake the feeling she was searching for something. Longing for something. She felt restless and out of sorts and not at all like her usual calm self. Last night's dream would not leave her in peace. It had haunted her all day. The sensual nature of it, the wild passion, filled her with an overwhelming desire for something she could not have. Her legs trembled as she moved slowly along the hallway.

Stopping before a portrait of some medieval-looking Rutherford ancestor, she sighed, pressing her hands together tightly. She wished . . . She wished she could live the life in her dreams.

"Good evening," a deep male voice stated from behind her.

The candles flickered and the hair on the back of Grace's neck stood on end. Her entire body began to tingle as the strangest sensation crept over her skin. Her mouth went dry. Slowly she turned around to see who had spoken to her, even though she knew instinctively who it would be. Her heart stopped at the sight of an extremely handsome man, dressed in black. *His eyes.* His intense eyes looked as if they could see right through her, see into her very soul. She suddenly felt as if she were stark naked in front of him.

It *was* him. *Him.* The man from her dreams. *Phillip.* The man she loved in the dreams that haunted her. The man she had kissed with a fierce passion in her dreams only last night. The image was still so vivid in her mind; she was mortified to face him.

For a long moment Grace could not breathe. She could not move. She could only stare at him in helpless fascination.

"Hello, Grace." He stood before her, his dark eyes penetrating hers. "Gráinne."

How did he know her name? And the name he called her in her dreams?

Her eyes fluttered with rapid movements. The world began to tilt and spin violently around her and then in an instant went completely black.

When Grace opened her eyes again, the man of her dreams was cradling her in his strong arms, while one hand gently caressed her cheek. Her heart pounded wildly as she glanced up at him. She still could not catch her breath. However, she could breathe well enough to notice how nice he smelled. Clean and spicy, but a spice she was unfamiliar with.

"I didn't anticipate that you might faint when you saw me, but I should have." He gave her a smile, warm and slightly suggestive. He had the straightest and whitest teeth she had ever seen. They were perfect. "It was lucky I caught you in time," he said, "or you might have hit your head on the marble floor. And we couldn't have that happen now, could we?"

She may as well have hit her head on the floor, for nothing made sense to her at all. She blinked helplessly at him, feeling as if she were wrapped in thick layers of cotton wool.

"Who are you?" she murmured low, noting how naturally he held her. As if she belonged in his arms. As if he were quite familiar with her. A surge of hot desire shot through her veins, surprising her with its intensity.

He stroked her arms with long, soothing motions. "You know who I am." His words were clear and calm.

The touch of his warm hands on her bare skin caused her to tremble. What did he mean? How could she know who he was when he was just a figment of her imagination? The man in her dreams was not *real*. Not a real person at all. And even if he were, how could he possibly know about her dreams?

She shook her head with a slow deliberateness. She wanted to say she had never seen him before, but that was not true. "I do not know you."

He smiled again and there was a hint of laughter in his dark eyes. "Yes, you do. I am Radcliffe."

The name meant nothing to her. Yet she could not deny the familiarity about him, how comfortable and at home she felt in his muscular arms. The soothing and rich timbre of his voice. The firm, possessive feel of his hands upon her. The look of warmth in his eyes. It was all eerily familiar. As if he had held her this way only last night.

And he had. In her dreams.

It was impossible. *Impossible*.

Suddenly a rush of panic welled within her and she had to get away. "Please . . . Please, let go of me," she pleaded as she struggled to release herself from his magnetic hold.

Without hesitation he set her free, a look of understanding on his handsome face. "Ah, my lovely Grace, do not be afraid of me."

Wobbling on her feet, she backed away from him, even though she longed to be in his arms once again. She cried, "How do you know my name?"

"Because, Grace, I know you." He paused and eyed her carefully. "I have always known you and I have waited a very, very long time for you."

She gasped at his words, which were tinged with a surprising sense of sadness. *How could he know her? How could he have been waiting for her?* She had not told him her name. The man was clearly insane. A sudden chill shuddered through her body.

What was he thinking, saying these things to her? He was a complete stranger. And yet, he wasn't.

"I must . . . I have to go now. . . ." She turned her back, suppressing a shiver, and began to walk on unsteady legs down the corridor to return to the ballroom.

He did not follow her, as she feared he would. She risked a glance back to be sure, but he remained standing there, his dark eyes fixed on her. As she hurried away, she heard him say, "You will not marry Grayson. He is not meant for you, Grace."

She practically flew to the ballroom, the richness of his voice haunting her. *He is not meant for you, Grace.* Then who was? She suppressed the urge to scream.

"Where have you been?" Mary Sutton snapped when Grace finally reached her side at the seating area near the ballroom. "You have been gone entirely too long. And look at you! You look as if you've seen a ghost."

"I . . . I went outside for some air," Grace murmured mindlessly, oddly comforted by the normalcy of her conversation with Mary. "I must have caught a chill."

"Well, that was quite foolish of you."

Lord Grayson eyed her kindly and, in a most thoughtful gesture, wrapped her black wool shawl around her shoulders. "You forgot to take your wrap with you."

"Thank you," she whispered, giving him a grateful smile. She eagerly pulled the warm garment tighter around herself. She still shivered.

"Would you care for some hot tea?" Lord Grayson asked with caring solicitation.

"Thank you, yes. That would be quite nice," she said, taking her seat along the wall. As she watched her new fiancé go off in search of her tea, it occurred to Grace that it would be lovely to have a man to watch over her again.

Mary sat beside her and whispered none too softly, "Lady Rutherford's daughter, Victoria, has the most deplorable manner. Look at her there, wearing that indecently low-cut gown and dancing with that no-account scoundrel, Lord Mayhew. She will cause her own ruin with her wildness one of these days. Her parents have been too lenient with that girl and now it is inevitable that she will come to a bad end, mark my words. And Lord Mayhew, well, everyone knows about him. He's gambled away his country estate! That is what comes of sin and wickedness. Why Lady Rutherford allowed that man into her home is beyond my understanding. . . ."

Grace ignored Mary's tirade of verbally attacking each of her friends and their offspring.

She could think of nothing but the strange meeting she had just had with the enigmatic Lord Radcliffe. Had she simply imagined it? Now, as she sat amidst the light, the noise, and the liveliness of the ballroom, it did seem as if her extraordinary encounter in the dimly lit hallway had not happened.

How had the man who had dominated her dreams for years suddenly appeared before her in flesh and blood?

A terrible thought occurred to her. Had she fallen asleep in the ladies' retiring room and dreamed the entire event? Were her dreams taking over more than her nights? *Was that possible?*

Her heart raced at the likelihood. Had she merely been dreaming again? Yet he had seemed so real. He had held her in his arms and she had felt him, right here in this very house. Yet he had always been real in all her dreams throughout the years.

What was happening to her?

Confounded by her situation, she pressed her fingernails sharply into her palms, making tight fists. Either she had a problem of dozing off in public places or the object of her dreams had suddenly materialized in front of her. Both explanations were more than a little disturbing.

"... in that tacky dress! She looks like an overripe tomato. Oh, and I heard it directly from Mrs. Fairwood that Lord Granger is thinking of marrying Helen Thatcher! Can you believe that he would stoop to ..."

Grace continued to ignore her mother-in-law, a skill she had become quite adept at over the years, focusing instead on the need to find a reasonable explanation.

How on earth could she account for what had just happened to her?

Lord Grayson returned then and handed her a white china teacup filled with hot black tea. As she thanked him, Grace hoped he had put some sugar in it. He smiled at her, satisfied that he had pleased her, and took his seat on the other side of her. Grateful for the steaming liquid to calm her racing nerves, with shaking hands she brought the cup to her lips.

Before she could take a single sip, that strange tingling sensation crept along the back of her neck again and she froze in place. The gaslights in the ballroom dimmed. *He was here.*

On pure instinct Grace slowly glanced up and, just as she knew she would, she met the eyes of the man who haunted her dreams. He stood casually against a long marble column across the room, staring at her. His dark eyes were focused on her alone. In his impeccable black suit and crisp white shirt, his form was tall and imposing. Every other man at the ball paled in comparison to his muscular and broad build. He was utterly handsome. He looked as if he were carved from marble, so perfect were his features. The tea forgotten, she lowered her hands with the china cup to her lap.

Could no one see him but she? Could no one see him staring at her?

Mesmerized, Grace could not look away from him. The intense longing and profound sadness he conveyed with his dark eyes stunned her. He seemed to speak to her through his eyes and she wanted to hear every word.

I know, he said to her without making a single sound. *I know everything.*

Her heart hammered wildly in her chest and she longed to answer him. She wanted to say, *I know that you know,* but other words sprang unbidden from the depths of her soul. *I love you.* She could not stop them from pouring from her, while the very outrageousness of her thoughts frightened her. His eyes widened slightly and he smiled at her with such deep understanding, her heart turned over in her chest. He knew her.

Suddenly people obscured her line of vision and she could no longer see him. Her view mo-

mentarily hidden by a dancing couple, Grace
craned her neck to find him again. But he was
gone and she felt his absence like a physical blow.
Her breath, which she had not realized that she
was holding, escaped her lungs with a long whoosh.

"Who was that gentleman?" Mary's voice demanded shrilly in her ear.

"Which—which gentleman?" Grace asked, nervousness settling in. Then he *was* real! Mary had
seen him. He was not a figment of her imagination!

"That black-haired man across the room. He
was staring at you quite intently not a moment
ago."

"I . . . I noticed him as well, but I have not the
faintest notion of who he is." Grace murmured. *He
was real. He was real. He was real. He had been staring
at her. He had!* Relief washed through her at the
confirmation that she had not completely lost her
mind.

"Well. I don't believe I care for the way he was
looking at you, Grace," Mary intoned with clear
disapproval. "I hope you gave him a properly dismissive glance."

Grace nodded absently, her eyes frantically
scanning the room for him, wondering where he
had gone. Her heart thumped an erratic rhythm
in her chest.

"Lord Grayson." Mary leaned across Grace's lap
toward Reginald Marks and tapped him lightly on
the shoulder. "Lord Grayson, do you know who
that gentleman is? That one. The tall one in the
corner over there conversing with Lord Mayhew."

Immediately Grace's eyes locked on to him as

he stood listening with polite interest to Lord Mayhew, a young man with blond hair. As if he knew Grace was staring at him, he lifted his gaze slowly to meet hers. Again she felt his presence physically. A surge of passion washed through every fiber of her body. Her cheeks warmed under his intense regard.

"Oh, that is Lord Radcliffe," Lord Grayson explained to Mary. "I believe he is a guest of Lord Rutherford from the country, if I am not mistaken. I was introduced to him earlier. Seems to be a nice enough fellow, although I do not know much about him or his family."

Grace watched him. Lord Radcliffe. He shook the other man's hand. He gave her one long glance, as if to say, *I will see you again.* And then he was gone.

She suddenly felt as if her world had turned upside down.

"Aren't you going to drink your tea?" Lord Grayson asked.

She blinked at him, realizing she still held the cup in her hands. "Oh, yes, of course."

As she finally sipped the tea, she puzzled to make sense of it all. He was real! An actual person. She had not dreamed their meeting in the hallway. But how did he know who she was? He could have learned her name from anyone at the ball. And he could easily have found out that she was engaged to Lord Grayson, for their engagement was the talk of the evening. It was merely a coincidence that this gentleman resembled the man in her dreams, and she had only imagined that he called her Gráinne and imagined the words he was saying with his eyes. Everything that had happened between them could be explained quite logically. Yes. It could. Quite logically.

Logic, however, played no part in the indescribable, hauntingly familiar feelings that swept over her in his presence. She knew this man from somewhere. . . .

Later that evening Lord Grayson escorted them home in his carriage. Once inside the townhouse, Mary pointedly excused herself and Grace found herself sitting alone with her new fiancé in the main parlor. A blaze crackled in the fireplace, warming the room.

"I know I said this to you earlier, but I am quite pleased that you have agreed to become my wife," he said pleasantly, standing before the white marble-topped mantel.

"I am happy that you are pleased," Grace responded from her seat upon the large damask sofa. And she was happy to please him, when she actually thought about it. He was a kind man and she knew he would be good to her. Her life with him would be peaceful. If she had a child with him, that would make her happy, although he already had an heir. His grown son attended Oxford.

Lord Grayson moved from the mantel and sat beside her, his face beaming.

"I hope we shall be very happy together, Grace," he said, taking her hand in his. He gave it a gentle squeeze. "Have you given any thought to when?"

"When?" Grace echoed, her heart still reeling with all that had happened this evening with Lord Radcliffe.

"When you would like to get married, sweet

girl!" He chuckled at her obtuseness and continued lightly. "I was thinking perhaps just before Christmas. We could do something quite small, just our families and a few close friends. There's no need for a grand wedding, since this is not the first for either of us."

Christmas? Why, that was only a month away! She could be out of Mary's house in a month. "Yes . . . Of course."

He smiled at her, obviously delighted with her acquiescence. "I knew you would be reasonable about this. But with some women, you never know for certain. They set such a store by weddings and the like."

He leaned in to kiss her. Grace instinctively recoiled from him.

Good heavens! Grace was no innocent maiden. She had been a wife and knew what her duties entailed. And she was not averse to kissing Lord Grayson. He was attractive and smelled clean. But somehow, after seeing Lord Radcliffe this evening, it seemed wrong to have Lord Grayson kiss her. She dared a glance at his pale blue eyes. He looked embarrassed. She knew she had insulted him.

"I am sorry," she murmured, feeling contrite. "You surprised me."

"No, no. Forgive my impulsiveness." He shook his head and squeezed her hand again. "I admit I am a bit carried away with you. I should have asked your permission first."

She smiled at him.

"May I?"

She nodded. This time she did not pull away from him, but sat perfectly still while he placed a light kiss upon her lips. It was not unpleasant. He simply did not inspire within her the same passion she felt merely thinking of Phillip.

Satisfied, he released her hand and rose from the sofa. "I shall begin first thing tomorrow to make arrangements for our wedding."

Relieved that he had not pressured her for more, she sighed. "That sounds lovely."

"Good night, Grace."

"Good night, Lord Grayson."

He flashed her an indulgent grin. "You must call me Reginald now, my darling."

"I shall . . . Reginald."

With that, he left the house and Grace continued to sit there for some time, staring at the golden flames flickering in the fireplace.

She was now officially engaged to be married to Reginald Marks.

How different this wedding would be compared to her first wedding to Henry Sutton ten years ago. She had been in love and excited to marry her handsome young beau, filled with hope and excitement for the future. But about her upcoming marriage to Lord Grayson she felt nothing but . . . indifference.

Her heart was filled with an indescribable longing for something, someone she dared not name.

Chapter Three

"Gráinne! Wait for me!"

She laughed at him, her red hair blowing wildly about her face, her horse racing across the green fields. Let Phillip catch her if he could! She urged her horse to go faster, leaning into him and whispering in his ear. Midnight leapt gracefully across a small stream, landing with ease upon thick grass on the other side. Excited that she had such a lead over Phillip, who usually bested her in everything, she smiled in triumph. He would not catch her now.

She guided Midnight up the small hill in eagerness, imagining Phillip straining to reach her. Savoring the victory that she knew was within her grasp, she moved farther up the hill. Just as she crested the top, Gráinne screamed in frustration.

Phillip sat astride his large gray stallion, waiting patiently for her at the top of the hill. Not even out of breath. He smiled winningly, his handsome face a picture of absolute superiority.

Furious beyond words, she flung her riding crop at

him. It missed his head and sailed to the ground behind him.

He laughed loudly as he leapt from his horse and was at her side, reaching up to pull her with ease from her saddle.

"How could you possibly arrive before me?" she cried with undisguised irritation.

"Because, my darling, I have powers beyond your wildest dreams." He grinned at her, revealing his perfectly white teeth. He wrapped his muscular arms around her shoulders, pressing her to his broad chest.

Gráinne's anger melted at his very touch, as it always did. He had that effect upon her senses. She turned her face toward his and he leaned in and kissed her, as she had wanted him to.

"Why don't you ever let me win?" she pouted when his lips left hers.

"Because you are so beautiful when you are angry." He laughed again. "And you kiss better too."

She shoved at his chest, but it was like shoving a brick wall. He pulled her tighter against him, bringing his mouth down over hers in a rough and hungry kiss. Gráinne felt that familiar rush of desire pour through her veins and kissed him back with an eagerness that matched his own. His lighthearted laughter and her petulant anger dissipated instantly, replaced by the heated passion that they could barely conceal when around others. Their mouths devoured each other, lips and tongues meeting in a frantic and erotic dance.

His hands moved along her spine, to her neck, splaying through her long, silky red curls. He cupped her face with his hands and stopped kissing her long enough to whisper, "I love you more than is humanly possible, Gráinne."

"I love you even more," she murmured before he lifted

her in his strong arms and carried her to the small, whitewashed cottage with the thatched roof. It was to this refuge they were racing. It was to this little cottage, tucked away in the woods, where they met in secret, where her parents could not find her. Her parents not only disapproved of Phillip, they outright detested him. They had forbidden Gráinne to see him, but that had not stopped her. For she had fallen madly in love with the handsome stranger, who had arrived mysteriously one day in their small Irish village a few months earlier. Everyone was wary of Phillip Stuart and disliked his blatant wealth and polished manner. Gráinne's father was a landowner and her family was the wealthiest in the county, so Phillip's money meant nothing to Gráinne. It was everything else about him that fascinated her.

He was so different from any of the other men she knew. The worldly and sophisticated way in which he spoke, the air of mystery that clung to him, and the devil-may-care attitude had lured her restless spirit from the moment she laid eyes on him. She knew she was meant for him. And he knew it too.

Once they were inside the cottage, Gráinne could not remove her clothes fast enough. Phillip obliged by hastily undoing the rows of buttons down the back of her gown. The soft kisses he pressed upon the sensitive skin along her spine sent shivers of delight through her entire body. Oh, there were people in town who would tear her to shreds if they knew what she had been doing in this little cottage with Phillip, but she did not care. Their scornful looks were worth even one of his kisses. Her parents were ready to send her to a convent, but Gráinne only laughed at them. She was marrying Phillip and that was that. She loved him and wanted to be with him. Forever.

She pressed her naked body against his and they fell into the large feather bed together. His body was perfect *and she ran her hands across his chest, moving over the smooth, taut planes. His warm skin was like velvet. Her mouth found his and that was all that mattered. Being here in his arms was all that mattered to her anymore. All except one thing.*

"When?" she begged him. "Please tell me when."

He moved over her, settling himself firmly between her legs. She sighed.

"Soon," he breathed into her ear, her body shivering in response. "Very, very soon, my love."

She arched her hips hard against him, her heart hammering. "You said you wanted to marry me. My parents are becoming more and more anxious about us. What are we waiting for?"

His dark eyes bored into her, desire flaming within their depths. "I want to marry you, Gráinne. I want it with all my heart. I just don't know if you truly wish to marry someone like me."

Her fingers clawed into the smooth skin of his back, pulling his weight down upon her. She couldn't get close enough to him. She wanted him with a desperate need. "I do. I do want to be your wife. I want to be with you always."

"You have no idea what that means."

"Then tell me." *She began to cry, even though she tried to fight it. The hot tears sprang unbidden. It had come to this argument last time they were together and he had not given her a satisfactory answer.* "Tell me . . ."

"Oh, Gráinne," *he whispered, a tortured expression on his face. He pressed kisses to the tears that spilled from her eyes.* "I wish I could. I want to give you everything. I want to give you the world and spend eternity with you."

"I want that too!" *she cried, through her sobs. Through her desire for him.*

"The cost for that is too high."

"No cost is too high to be with you, Phillip."

She maneuvered herself beneath him, feeling the hardness of his body and wanting him with an urgency that terrified her. Thrilled her. He responded willingly, driving into her with a force that startled them both. She met him stroke for stroke. They moved with increased rhythm. Their bodies and eyes locked with each other.

"Make me what you are, Phillip, please. . . . Make me what you are."

An anguished cry sprang from his lips as he lowered his head to her neck. . . .

Grace awoke with a strangled gasp, her body soaked with sweat and her heart pounding. She could not think where she was. Her body throbbed with a familiar, aching need.

Another dream. Another quite intimate dream. About him.

Trembling, Grace sat up, her damp flannel nightgown clinging to her breasts. She covered her heated cheeks with her hands and breathed deeply, willing her heart to return to a more normal pace. Although she shook with the unfulfilled ache of desire, she fought the urge to cry.

The dreams were becoming more intense, more passionate and fraught with an impending sense of loss. There was some secret, some sort of mystery, to these dreams and Grace could not unravel it. Something did not make sense. Something she was not sure she wanted to know.

After a moment more she lit the lamp next to her bed. Again, the pretty ormolu clock read quarter past five. Following her usual pattern, she left the warmth of her bed, wrapped herself in her robe, and moved silently to the window, seeking she knew not what. With trepidation she drew back the rose toile curtain to peer out at the dark enshrouded garden.

Her eyes scanned the lawn, searching for him as she always did. Wondering why she did this after every dream, she stared intently, almost willing him to appear. The clock ticked. She waited and watched, standing perfectly still. A wild hope in her heart, she held her breath. And then, there he was, stepping from the shadows along the garden wall. He wore a black top hat and a long cape flowed behind him. He walked with an elegant grace, his tall form moving with purpose toward the house. Stopping just below her second-story window, he looked up at her.

Her fingers gripped the curtain tightly, almost tearing the fabric. They stared at each other in the dim morning light. She could make out his pale skin and perfect features, could see the edge of his black hair beneath his hat. He looked exactly the same as he had in her dreams. Exactly the same as he had when she met him in the hallway last night. The dark eyes in his handsome face bored into her and she fought the impulse to throw open the window and jump out. She knew with an instinctive certainty that he would catch her in his arms quite easily. As if he could read her thoughts, he held out his hand to her in invitation to do just that.

Then what? She asked him, but he did not answer. He merely raised a dark winged eyebrow.

Make me what you are. The words she had uttered to him in her dream flooded her consciousness, even though she had no idea what they meant.

Make me what you are. What was the significance of that?

He was inviting her to be with him. Whatever that entailed, she knew that if she went to him now, her life would change irrevocably. What *would* happen if she ran off with him? The ensuing scandal would be beyond repair. In spite of the wave of desire and longing that overcame her at the sight of him, blind fear kept her rooted to the relative safety of her bedroom.

She could not go.

They continued to gaze wordlessly at each other until the pale glow of an overcast sunrise began to illuminate the sky. By taking a step backward, he suddenly broke the odd spell between them. He raised his hand and tipped his hat to her before he fled silently into the shadows.

As if he had disappeared before her very eyes, Grace gasped and pressed her fingers against the cool windowpane. If she pushed any harder she could shatter the glass. She stood motionless, staring at the place she had last seen him, hoping he would return to her.

It was all too much. The dream. His appearance just as she woke. Their wordless exchange. Finally she turned from the window, not knowing what she feared more. That she had imagined his presence outside her window. Or that she hadn't.

She wrapped her arms tightly around herself to ward off the chill that crept through her bones and sank to her knees on the wooden floor.

Chapter Four

The young lady at the piano played beautifully, the haunting strains of Chopin's "Nocturne in E-Flat Major" filling the room. Grateful not to be subjected to an off-key recital, Grace enjoyed the evening's musicale at the Forsythes' home more than she had enjoyed one in quite some time. This piano piece in particular affected her strangely. Lord Grayson sat to her right; however, Mary Sutton had remained at home, nursing one of her terrible headaches. Happy to be free of her mother-in-law's negativity for the evening, Grace smiled warmly at Lord Grayson. He placed a possessive hand on her arm.

Comforted by his touch, Grace relaxed. She was glad to be with people. Glad to have real, living beings talk to her and touch her. These were not figments of her imagination. And she did not want the evening to end. She did not want to go to sleep and drown in another life in her dreams. It was all becoming too real, too frightening. She had almost jumped out of her bedroom window this morning. To what end?

No. It was good to be in the company of others, without Mary hovering over her, listening to the lovely strains of music and having Lord Grayson beside her. She gave him a shy glance and he grinned sweetly at her. It took so little to please him. All she had to do was give him a smile. Marriage to him would not be such a bad compromise after all.

When young Elizabeth Rutan finished playing her piece, everyone removed to the salon for refreshments. Grace allowed Lord Grayson to lead her to a small table, where he promised to bring her some cake. Grace sat with Mr. and Mrs. Whitaker, a couple she had been friendly with for a number of years, for she and Henry had married only a month after the Whitakers. The two couples had spent a great deal of time together before Henry died.

"It's wonderful news that you and Lord Grayson are to be married," Lucy Whitaker commented brightly. She was a pert blonde with an easy smile and an upturned nose. "Have you set a date yet?"

"Well, it is not definite, but we think we shall marry in a quiet ceremony before Christmas," Grace explained. Lucy and her husband, Daniel, had been very supportive of her after Henry died. But not even they knew the true circumstances surrounding Henry's death. Mary had made quite sure no one knew.

"We're so happy for you, Grace," Daniel said. "Reginald Marks is a good man."

"Yes, I know," she agreed. He was a good man who would take good care of her.

"Oh, Grace, I would like you to meet a friend of mine. Here he comes now," Daniel began.

The hair on Grace's neck stood on end and her stomach lurched. Even before she turned around she knew. He was here.

"Hello, Radcliffe! You remember my wife, Lucy, but I would like you to meet a very dear friend of ours," Daniel said with warm enthusiasm. "Grace, this is Lord Radcliffe. Lord Radcliffe, may I present Mrs. Grace Sutton."

"Good evening, Mrs. Sutton," a rich and achingly familiar voice said as she lifted her gaze to lose herself in the dark pools of his eyes. The urge to reach out and touch him caused her to tremble. "It is a pleasure to meet you," he continued.

"Good evening," Grace managed to whisper. Her pulse quickened and her cheeks flamed.

For years she had thought of him as a fantasy, as an unattainable vision or apparition in her life. Last night he had held her in his strong arms. Then he had made love to her in her dreams while she begged him to marry her. This morning he had appeared below her bedroom window, inviting her to leave with him. Now here he stood before her, as real as day. And familiar with her closest friends on top of it all!

"Lord Radcliffe just arrived from Ireland," Daniel Whitaker went on. "He has an estate there near my cousin's and he's in town for the month."

Grace's heartbeat increased at the mention of Ireland, but she was not surprised. Not truly. Of course, he was from Ireland! In her dreams she and Phillip were in Ireland, riding horses along the misty seashore, rocky cliffs above them. She could see quite clearly the endless green fields dotted with limestone walls and the quaint little cottage where they met in secret, even though Grace had never been there. She'd never been more than a few hours from London in her life. But how could her dreams be so vivid and lifelike? And how could she have dreamed up someone like Lord Radcliffe? Something strange was happening to her.

Lord Grayson returned with dessert and Grace forced herself to look away from Lord Radcliffe's mesmerizing gaze and focused on her lemon cake instead. But she could not swallow a single bite. Not with Lord Radcliffe's possessive eyes on her. Nor could she follow the conversation going on around her. Words were spoken. Laughter ensued. Heads nodded. Yet Grace had no idea what anyone said and if they had spoken to her, there was no way she could answer. She kept her eyes down, for she dared not meet his with Lord Grayson beside her.

At some point, Lord Grayson put his hand on her shoulder and announced it was time that they took their leave. Grace finally glanced up from her untouched plate. As she expected, Radcliffe's eyes were on her. She willed herself to look away.

"It's time for me to go as well," Lord Radcliffe said casually to Lord Grayson. "I shall walk out with you, if you don't mind."

"Of course not," Lord Grayson said before saying goodnight to the Whitakers and leading Grace over to their hostess. They thanked Lady Forsythe for a lovely evening and made their way outside to await their carriage. Nervously, Grace pulled her merino wool wrap tighter around her shoulders at the cool air.

Lord Radcliffe stood waiting for his carriage to

be brought around as well. His eyes never left Grace. She could feel his stare.

"Lord Grayson! Lord Grayson!" A young manservant wearing the Grayson livery came racing over to them. "May I speak to you a moment please, my lord?"

Surprised, Lord Grayson excused himself to step away to speak privately with the young man. Grace was left standing alone with Lord Radcliffe. She dared a glance at him. He smiled knowingly at her. A moment later his carriage pulled up.

"Lord Radcliffe," Lord Grayson said in an urgent voice, "it seems there is a bit of a family emergency that I must attend to personally. Would you mind seeing Mrs. Sutton home safely for me?"

Radcliffe's eyes flickered briefly to Grace. "It would be my pleasure."

"Reginald, what is the matter? Can I be of any help?" Grace asked, filled with worry, and not just for her fiancé but for the idea of being alone in a carriage with the man of her dreams. Literally.

"I'm afraid not, my dear. I shall explain everything to you later," he whispered in a tense voice. He patted her arm. "Please let Lord Radcliffe escort you home now. It would ease my mind greatly."

Grace nodded her head, watching Lord Grayson hurry down the street with the manservant. Slowly she turned back and faced Lord Radcliffe. He held open the door to his gleaming black lacquered carriage and extended one hand to her.

Taking a deep breath, she took his hand and allowed him to help her into the luxurious carriage and settled on the seat facing forward. He followed quickly behind her, and his entire being seemed to fill the small space. She had expected him to sit across from her on the opposite seat, but he sat right beside her. She inched herself as far from him as she could, but still his thigh pressed against her leg. An unexpected heat flooded through her.

Grace took a deep breath, filled with the wonderfully clean and oddly spicy scent of him. He rapped on the roof and the driver set the carriage in motion. Easing back into his seat, he turned and smiled at her, revealing his straight white teeth. A sudden thought occurred to her.

"Did you plan this?" she asked with mounting suspicion and a sense of panic.

"How else could I get you alone with me, Grace?" He held up his hands in mock helplessness.

The confirmation of her suspicions did little to allay her nervousness. "What was this emergency Reginald had to attend to? Nothing serious, then?"

"It depends if you consider his son in a drunken stupor and losing his shirt at a card game serious or not."

Grace pursed her lips. Somehow Lord Radcliffe had arranged for Reginald to learn of his son's exploits. Reginald would be quite angry with his son but at least the boy was not permanently injured in any way. Perhaps it was better she did not know the details of Lord Radcliffe's ruse. "Why did you do this?" she questioned with a shaky voice.

"You know why." He placed his hand under her chin, tilting her face toward his. "Besides, I can hardly continue to skulk around your bedroom window before dawn, now can I?"

Her heart turned over in her chest as she gazed up at him, his dark eyes mesmerizing her. He *had* been outside her window this morning. She had not imagined it. She had not dreamt it. He was real and here with her now. He had her alone with him in a darkened carriage. She did not know what to think.

She whispered, "You are not taking me home, are you?"

"Do you want me to take you home?" His voice melted her.

In all honesty she did not want to go home. A part of her longed for this man to take her wherever he wanted and to do with her whatever he wished. Lost in his eyes, a heated desire washed through her, making her slightly dizzy. "I . . . I do not know what to do," she murmured.

His voice was hoarse. "I do."

Before she knew what was happening, he lowered his head, his mouth slanting over hers in a possessive and searing kiss. He continued to kiss her passionately, his tongue searing her own with its heat. Grace clung to him in a breathtaking frenzy. This was a dangerous kiss, a kiss that would lead to much more, and she was powerless to stop it. Never had Grace experienced a kiss such as this. At least not while she was awake.

He consumed her with his passion and she let him. His mouth moved over hers expertly, and she savored the exquisite taste of his lips, his tongue, his breath. The intoxicating scent of him enveloped her. His tongue plundered and ravaged her. His hands gripped her so tightly she thought she would faint. She didn't want him to let go and held on to him desperately, for it was familiar and new and frightening and exciting all at once. And, oh so much better than her dreams, for this kiss was real! This kiss was happening now. To her. She was kissing him back just as passionately.

Suddenly he released her and Grace opened her eyes wide in surprise. His smile sent shivers to the tips of her toes. She should be outraged. She ought to slap him for kissing her in such a way. Instead, she felt ridiculously happy.

"Who *are* you?" she whispered through her kiss-swollen lips.

"I am Stuart Phillips, the Earl of Radcliffe."

"Stuart Phillips?" The name jarred her senses. It was more than a coincidence. Phillip Stuart was his name, the man in her dreams.

"Yes." Again he spoke in that calm, seductive voice.

"Who are you? How do you know me? Where did you come from? What are you doing here?"

"Why so many questions, Grace"—his eyes flickered over her—"when you already know the answers?"

"I . . . I have had . . . I have had dreams. About you." The words came out before she could stop them.

"Have you now?"

She nodded. He seemed almost amused by her confession and she felt inordinately foolish. How could she possibly explain this to anyone, let alone the man about whom she dreamed? And after she had just allowed him to kiss her!

"Why are you here?" Her voice trembled.

"Ah, my love, have you not guessed?"

She shook her head. She didn't want to guess. She wanted answers.

He took her hand in his. Very slowly, he began to remove her glove. With great care he inched the fabric away from each finger, until her fingers were bare. She shivered at the contact of her bare skin against his. He brought her hand to his lips and pressed a kiss into her palm. He turned her hand over and kissed each finger. He continued to place soft, sensuous kisses all over her hand. The desire that pooled within her intensified with every kiss until she thought she would expire from the anticipation of what he would do next.

"I could not stay away from you any longer, Grace."

"You barely even know me . . . ," she breathed. He still held her hand in his, his thumb stroking her palm. She could not focus on anything but the feel of him caressing her hand.

"Ah, but you see, my love, I do know you."

She held her breath. "How?"

"We have met before."

"When? Where?" she whimpered, while her heart raced in her chest. Yet she knew what he would say.

"Ireland."

"I have never been to Ireland. In fact, I have never set foot outside of England in my life."

He looked at her intently and squeezed her hand. "Grace."

"Yes?"

"Let's talk about the dreams you have."

Her mouth went dry. It was so foolish. How could she possibly describe her dreams to him? Such passionate and intimate dreams. Her cheeks warmed at the memory of last night. She said nothing.

"I am in your dreams, am I not?"

Grace nodded, unable to speak.

"You call me Phillip in your dreams," he stated as if it were quite ordinary.

Again she nodded her head. She held her breath.

"And in these dreams you and I are in Ireland, are we not?"

She stared at him with fear and wonder. How could he know such things?

"And I call you Gráinne."

She gasped at the sound of her name. It was impossible. It was completely impossible for him to know that. Had he somehow gotten ahold of her dream journal? Had he paid a servant to read it and report to him? But for what reason? Nothing made sense.

She choked out the words. "You called me Gráinne last night in the hallway, didn't you? I thought I imagined it."

"I could not help but call you that. Do you know that in Irish the name Gráinne means Grace?"

No, she did not know that. It still did not explain how he knew about her dreams.

"We kiss in your dreams, don't we, Grace? We do more than kiss." His silky voice whispered in her ear. "It's why you allowed me to kiss you just now."

For a moment Grace thought she would faint, as she had when they first met in the hallway. Suddenly she found the words she needed. "How . . . How do you know such things?" she practically begged him. "How can you know my dreams?"

He cupped her face in his hands, forcing her to look at him once again. "Because I have the same dreams, Grace."

If he had suddenly sprouted wings and begun to fly she couldn't have been more surprised. "No!" she cried. "Is such a thing even possible?" She reached up and touched his face, running her fingers along his strong jaw, his perfect aquiline nose.

"I have dreamed about you for more years than I care to give a number to, Grace. When I saw you at the ball, I could not believe my eyes."

"But what does it mean? Why do we share the same dreams?"

"Because we have loved each other once before."

She certainly loved this man in her dreams. And he loved her. She could not deny that fact. What he said made sense. "A long time ago?"

He nodded. "Another life."

Nervous laughter bubbled within her, but she suppressed it. "Another life?" she questioned.

"Yes." He stated it matter-of-factly, as if people discussed their past lives at the supper table on an ordinary basis. "You see the truth of what I am saying?"

No, she did not quite see and at this point she was not sure she wanted to see.

She whispered, "It cannot be."

"Then how do I know about your dreams? How we hid from your parents by running off to the cottage? How do I know I made love to you, wanted to make you my wife?"

He knew! It defied all logic and sense of reason but he knew all her dreams.

With a sure movement, he leaned in and kissed her again. Grace thought she would explode from the fire he stoked within her. Good heavens! She could not help but kiss him back again. He felt too good, tasted too good. And she wanted him too much. She had been alone for five years. It had been five years since she had experienced a man's touch on her body and she relished his hands on her now. Craved his hands on her naked skin.

They kissed and kissed and kissed, as the heat grew between them. Their tongues swirled together. His arms circled her waist and pulled her tighter against him. She did not protest but pressed herself against his broad chest, filled with a wanting too strong to resist. His hat fell from his head as she ran her fingers through his thick black hair. His hand followed the curve of her hip, up to her breast. He removed her wool wrap and began to undo the buttons of her gown.

Grace suddenly froze. She was kissing a stranger in his carriage when she was engaged to another man. It was wrong. Everything about this situation was wrong. In fact, it was terrifying. She pulled away from him, panting heavily. He still had his arms around her.

"Please . . . Take me home," she murmured mindlessly.

"Gráinne." His voice was filled with anguish. "Grace."

"Please," she begged. "Take me home now."

"You belong to me."

She stared at him, not knowing what to say. "I . . . I need to go home."

"If that is what you wish." He released her and opened the small window to give instructions to the driver. He turned back to her. "But we are far from finished, Grace."

No, she did not doubt that. But at the moment it was all she could do to hold herself together. She needed to be alone. She needed to make sense of all of this.

"Where were you planning to take me tonight?" she suddenly asked.

"To my house." He inclined his head. "You belong with me. In my bed."

In spite of the blatant intent of his words, her body quivered at the prospect he presented. She had dreamed of being in this man's bed in such intimate detail for so long, she almost felt he had the right to say such things to her now. To do such things to her. The temptation to allow him to do so was powerful. But rampant fear overwhelmed her. She busied herself by righting her appearance.

They rode in silence, while a thousand questions raced through her mind. All of which went unspoken and unanswered.

When the carriage came to a halt in front of her house, Lord Radcliffe opened the door and leapt to the ground. He turned and extended his arm to her. She allowed him to help her down. He followed her up the steps of the townhouse and stopped at the front door.

"Grace," he whispered to her, taking both her hands in his, "I know you are overwhelmed by this and I will give you time. We have much more to say, more than I can explain to you in this short carriage ride. We will see each other again."

His words brooked no argument. He clearly meant what he said. Part of her longed to jump back into the carriage with him right then and there. Part of her wanted to run inside and lock the door. "Yes, I know," she murmured, accepting the inevitable.

"You must break your engagement with Grayson. The sooner the better."

"What?"

"I cannot keep contriving to speak to you alone by getting rid of him. It only complicates our situation. You don't belong with him, Grace."

"I accepted his proposal only last night. I cannot just—"

The door opened and Mary Sutton stood before them. Her eyes narrowed and her mouth formed a tight frown. Grace groaned inwardly, as he dropped her hands.

"What in God's name is going on out here?" she demanded, her eyes darting suspiciously between Lord Radcliffe and Grace.

Before Grace could answer, he did it for her. "Good evening, Mrs. Sutton. I don't believe I have had the honor of meeting you before. I am Stuart Phillips, Lord Radcliffe. It seems there was some unexpected family matter that needed Lord Grayson's immediate attention, and he asked me to see your daughter-in-law home safely."

Mary was completely taken aback by his smooth manner. "I see," she said through pursed lips. She was clearly not happy with the situation but could do nothing but scowl at the both of them. "Well, thank you, Lord Radcliffe. Now it's time for Grace to come inside."

"Yes, of course. It is rather late," he said blithely, a charming smile lighting his face. "Good evening."

Grace paused and said, "Thank you, Lord Radcliffe." She tried to avoid his eyes but could not help but seek them out. He gave her a look so full of longing and desire that she almost gasped aloud. Only Mary's tugging on her arm broke the spell as she stumbled through the entrance of the house. The door slammed shut behind her with a loud thud.

"Well, I have never witnessed such a spectacle in all my life and never hope to see the likes of that again!" Mary cried, placing her hands on her wide hips in indignation. "And to think I witnessed it with my sainted son's widow!"

"I don't know what you are making such a fuss about," Grace declared. She turned to head up the stairs to her bedroom, longing to be alone.

Mary took hold of her arm once again and spun her around. Mary's fingers dug into the flesh of Grace's upper arm. "What is going on with you and that man? I demand to know."

"Nothing is going on, Mother." Grace stared at the woman she hated to call "mother." "Lord Grayson asked him to take me home and Lord Radcliffe was kind enough to do so. I had no choice in the matter."

"I am not blind, nor am I stupid, so do not think to pull the wool over my eyes, miss. I saw the way that Radcliffe man was ogling you last night. And here he is taking you alone in his carriage at night and whispering and holding hands with you on my front doorstep. There is a certain look about you now. It all adds up to wickedness and sin in my book."

Everything added up to wickedness and sin in Mary's book, which always left Grace wondering just what book Mary had been reading. But in this instance, she could not deny that Mary's suspicions were well founded if not completely justified. Lord Radcliffe had been ogling her, had arranged to get her alone, had kissed her in his carriage, and made it clear he would be seeing more of her. The matter was fraught with all kinds of complications when she was engaged to another man. Filled with shame at her behavior, Grace had no defense except for the fact she had no idea what was happening to her and it all seemed quite beyond her control. She had not intended for any of it to happen.

"I shall ignore your comments and go to my room now," Grace stated, pulling her arm free of Mary's grasp. She made it as far as the first step.

"You had better stay away from that Radcliffe man, if you know what is good for you. He is nothing but trouble, mark my words. Lord Grayson has seen fit to make you his wife and does not deserve to be humiliated by the likes of you parading about with that wicked gentleman."

Grace did not turn around. She straightened her spine and took another step.

"You may walk away from me now, but we will continue this discussion in the morning. I am telling you now that I absolutely forbid you to see that man again. Do you understand me, Grace?" Mary demanded, her voice like ice.

Without looking back at Mary, Grace nodded her head very slowly and continued to walk up the stairs.

Chapter Five

Gráinne paced impatiently within the small, cramped cabin of the ship. Where was he? He simply had to get to her before the ship sailed. He had to stop them from taking her away. How long would it take him to figure out where she was when he arrived at the cottage and found her gone? Her parents were determined to get her as far away from Phillip as they could.

Oh, such a scene they had had last night!

Somehow they had learned of her secret visits to the cottage with Phillip. Her mother had screamed at her and called her terrible, filthy names. Her father declared that she had shamed the family with her behavior. Gráinne had cried and begged them to simply let her marry Phillip. Her father refused, deciding to send her to a convent in France immediately.

Phillip had to get to the ship and free her before it sailed. If he did not, then Gráinne would escape at the first opportunity that presented itself in France, for there was nothing she could do now. Her father was taking no chances when he locked her in the windowless cabin.

A sudden scream escaped her when she felt the lurch

*and sway of the small ship as it left the dock. She could
not even look out the window, for there wasn't one, but
she knew. They were leaving. And Phillip had not reached
her in time.*

*"Oh, Phillip!" her heart cried. "Why didn't you listen
to me? Why didn't we marry sooner? They couldn't send
me to a convent if I were married to you! If you made me
like you, I would not be in this position!" Great sobs
wracked her body. She ached to be with him. He was her
life. She needed him and now she did not know when she
would see him again. She threw herself on the narrow
bed and cried herself to sleep.*

*She awoke some time later when she was tossed to the
floor by the wild rocking of the ship. The room was in
complete darkness. Terrified, she could hardly stand because of the violent pitching of the ship. The cabin door
burst open and she could tell from the dim light in the
hallway that her father stood there.*

"Gráinne!" he called frantically. "Are you there?"

*"Papa?! What's happening?" She reached for her fa-
ther and he held tightly to her hand.*

*"There's a storm. We're taking on water. We must get
above deck."*

*Panic set in, for she glimpsed the abject fear on her fa-
ther's face. Quickly, she followed him out of the cabin.
The ship rolled to one side and they were both flung
against the wall. Icy-cold water rushed through the corridor as high as their waists. She and her father desperately
fought their way against the surging sea, struggling to
get above deck. Gráinne could barely move her legs and
she was so terribly cold.*

*"Phillip!" No one could hear her cries above the din of
the waves and the screams of the other passengers. Great
sobs racked her body, but still she screamed for him.
"Phillip! Phillip!"*

Gráinne knew then she was going to die. Here in the cold, dark sea. Alone. Without him. If only Phillip had changed her. She had been so willing. She wanted to be with him at any price and was willing to pay it. If only he had listened to her, she would not be in this terrible situation. If only he had made her immortal then, she would not be dying now. . . . "Phillip!"

"Phillip! Phillip!"

Grace lurched up in her bed, gasping for air. Her frantic cries for Phillip had awakened her. Shivering uncontrollably with the bedclothes twisted around her legs, she could barely move. Filled with panic, she took deep breaths. She could still feel the icy water filling her lungs, but the air felt so good now. Air, she needed air.

Overcome with fear and sadness, tears sprang to her eyes and she sobbed in the darkness of her room. Sobbed for herself, sobbed for wanting to be with Phillip. The pain and loss were unbearable. Had she died in her dream? What was happening to her? Why was she having these torturous dreams? It had to stop. It had to. She simply could not endure any more.

She reached out and lit the lamp on her bedside table. Although she tried to resist the need, she could not help but look at the clock. Quarter past five. Grace shook her head. Why did she always wake at this time? What did any of it mean? She rose and straightened the bedclothes, which she had so entangled. Craving warmth, she reached for her thick robe. She folded her arms across her chest and she stood still, struggling against the magnetic force that pulled her to the window.

She could not keep doing this to herself. She would not go and look for him again. Perhaps once she was married to Reginald and no longer in this house, the dreams about Gráinne and Phillip would finally cease to torment her.

Perhaps if she spoke to Lord Radcliffe about it, she wouldn't have the dreams anymore.

Last night he said he shared the same dreams. He knew details of those dreams that were impossible for anyone to know. Unless he had read her dream journal. She crossed the room to her desk and unlocked the small drawer that held the journal. The leather-bound volume was still in its place. She knew she would not be able to bring herself to write about the drowning she experienced in her most recent dream. She shivered at the memory.

There was no possible way Lord Radcliffe could be reading her journal.

Then how did he know? How had he called her Gráinne? Could it be possible for them to be dreaming the same dreams? Her head hurt from trying to sort it all out. She had asked herself all these questions before she finally fell asleep last night and had no answers then either. She locked her journal back in the drawer and returned the key to its secret hiding spot, inside the locket her father had given her, which she placed in her jewelry box.

She turned to stare at the window. Would he be there, as he was yesterday morning? What would she do if he was there? What would she do if he wasn't? She longed desperately to see him. Needed to ask him countless questions. But she also feared the answers.

Unable to resist the temptation any longer, she made her way across the room and stood beside the window. With a shaking hand she pulled back the rose toile curtain. It had been raining during the night and the pane was spotted with droplets of water. Her eyes scanned the dark garden and her heart began to race.

And there he was, waiting for her beside the garden wall. His tall figure loomed above the shadows. His eyes sought hers through the misty predawn light and again, he held out his hand to her. Beckoning her to join him.

With a deliberate slowness, Grace nodded to him before letting the curtain fall back into place. Acting on pure instinct, she rushed silently about her room, dressing as quickly and warmly as she could. As he had said last night, he did not know when they would get a chance to be alone again. She needed to speak with him. She needed answers or she would lose her mind if the dreams continued. Maybe together they could make sense of what was happening to them.

Once she was dressed in her warmest gown, her wool pelisse and hat, and sturdy walking boots, she scribbled a quick note to Mary, explaining that she had gone for an early morning walk and would return soon. She raced to the window again. Lifting the curtain she could see that the shadows had begun to disappear as the sun rose behind a thick blanket of gray clouds and mist. Lord Radcliffe smiled when he saw her and she could not help but smile back at him. As fearful as she was, something drew her to him and she could not stay away. She nodded to let him know she was coming.

As she left her bedroom, she realized there

would be hell to pay with Mary later if she discovered what she was doing. She had no choice but to see Lord Radcliffe. Tiptoeing silently along the corridor, she prayed Mary would not hear her leaving. Grace moved like a wraith through the quiet house. Sounds from the kitchen alerted her that the servants were up and readying the fires. She slipped into the parlor and out the side door unnoticed. The patio was slick with rain, which was beginning to fall again. The sky had lightened but the heavy mist shrouded the garden, as she made her way to where she had seen Lord Radcliffe standing.

His hand grabbed hers and pulled her to him. Without a word she followed him through the garden gate and into the narrow alleyway behind the townhouse. They scurried along the cobblestones to where his warm and waiting carriage stood at the end of the alley. He helped her up and was beside her in an instant as the driver urged the horses into motion.

Alone with him now, she suddenly realized how reckless her behavior was. Not a soul knew where she was. Even she didn't know where she was going. She had just run off with a complete stranger! Slowly she faced him. When she looked in his eyes, she knew he was not a complete stranger at all.

"I did not know if you would come with me today," he whispered.

She sensed how relieved he felt that she had come with him. "I did not think I would either."

"Why did you change your mind?" He took her gloved hand in his.

"I need to know what is happening to me. To us. Can you tell me?" she asked.

"I can try." He squeezed her hand. And oddly enough, this reassured her.

As the carriage made its way through the rainy London streets, she had no need to ask where they were going. She was not in any danger. She rested her head against the leather seat and closed her eyes with a sigh.

"You are even more beautiful than I remember, Grace."

Her eyes flew open at the sound of his voice. She found him staring at her, his hand still holding hers. No one had ever called her beautiful before. She could pass as pretty perhaps, but not beautiful. Her cheeks warmed and her heart skipped a beat.

"What do you remember, then?" she asked him, full of wonder.

"Your hair is a softer red now, more of an auburn, and not the fiery red that Gráinne possessed. Your facial structure is similar to hers." He lifted his other hand to caress her cheek. His touch sent a spark of desire through her. "Same translucent skin, same high cheekbones. But it's your eyes that are so striking. You have the most incredible blue eyes, exactly the same shade as Gráinne's. I recognized them the moment I saw you."

Grace held her breath. If what he said was true, she had been this other person, this Irish girl Gráinne, in another life. She could almost believe it because it explained so much. It was what she had suspected all along and written about in her dream journal. She *had* been this other woman. But what worried her more than anything was Lord Radcliffe. He was exactly the same.

"But you have not changed," she began slowly. Fear trickled up her spine. "You are still the same person, are you not?"

He said nothing. But he did not deny it. He stared at her, the dark pools of his eyes drawing her in. He leaned closer, as if to kiss her. His lips were so close.

She whispered, "You have not changed at all, yet I have. You look exactly the same. If we are dreaming of a past life, wouldn't you have changed too? As I have?"

"You are right. I have not changed." His sensuous lips hovered close to hers. She longed for him to kiss her.

She barely breathed. "Why?"

His mouth sought hers then, his lips searing hot. He possessed her mouth so completely that all thought, all desire to speak, was obliterated at his touch. Her tongue met his and she lost herself in his hot and hungry kiss. She brought her arms up around his shoulders, feeling the strength of his muscles through the material of his black cape.

She was lost to him then. There was no resistance, no regrets. Unlike last night, she was completely willing to follow him to the ends of the earth. What had changed? She did not know. She only knew she needed him. And wanted him with a desire she could not fight.

When the carriage stopped, he finally released her with great reluctance on both their parts. Very gently, he carried her from the carriage, through the pouring rain, and up the steps into his townhouse. If there were servants in his house, she did not see them. While clinging to him, she had brief impressions of a dark and elegant residence. He continued right up the main staircase and along a dimly lit hallway before opening the double doors of a grand bedroom.

The luxurious room was shrouded in shadows. The thick, burgundy velvet drapes hanging at the windows allowed not a ray of light into the room. A fire blazed in the hearth and a few candles flickered in sconces on the walls. It could have been midnight in his chamber and not dawn. In a smooth movement he placed her gently in the middle of a very large bed draped with more velvet curtains. She watched him remove his hat and cape.

He was so handsome it almost hurt to look at him. His black hair, pale skin, and dark brown eyes, his beautiful smile, his lush lips, his perfect teeth, his straight nose. It was all too much. He came to her side and divested her of her coat and hat as well. He bent over her feet and unlaced her black boots, tossing them to the floor. He looked as if he were about to devour her.

And she was going to let him.

Yes, she would have to face the wrath of Mary and the disappointment of Lord Grayson later. But for now . . . For now, she simply did not care. The questions, the dreams. Everything could wait until later. All that mattered was the two of them in this room, in this bed. For the first time in her life, Grace felt as if she were really alive.

She began to unfasten the buttons that lined the front of her green plaid gown, lifting her eyes to his as she did so. He watched her in fascination and a thrill went through her, knowing that she excited him. She stilled her trembling fingers and focused on shrugging out of her gown. When she was down to her corset and chemise, he slowly began to remove his white shirt, the rest of his clothes following quickly. They could not disrobe fast enough. In a matter of seconds they were both naked in his massive bed. He covered her body with his and she clung to him.

His kisses melted her as they rained down upon her. He kissed her face, her cheeks, her lips. He moved his head lower to her neck, breathing in deeply and stroking his hot tongue along the length of her throat. She shivered at his touch, aching for more. Inch by inch he made his way across her chest to her breasts, kissing and licking her sensitive nipples.

Combing her fingers through his thick head of hair, Grace pulled lightly. She wanted him so desperately and his slow, deliberate movements drove her mad as she burned with need for him.

He made love to her slowly, carefully, as if cherishing each and every second.

Afterward he wrapped his arms around her, pressing kisses into her hair. She breathed in the scent of him, content and secure.

"I love you, Grace."

"I love you . . ." She paused and gave him a quizzical glance. "I don't know what to call you."

"Call me what's in your heart."

"Phillip. It's how I think of you."

His dark eyes locked on her. "You belong with me."

"Yes." She kissed him on the cheek. She belonged to Phillip and Phillip alone. She loved him and never wanted to be without him again. "Will you tell me now?"

He hesitated, his expression guarded. "I do not know where to begin."

"You have the same dreams as I do?" she questioned.

"Not quite."

"Then how can you possibly know what I have been dreaming?"

"Because I lived it with you."

Grace blinked. "What do you mean?"

"They are not dreams for me. They are memories. Memories that have been tormenting me for over one hundred years. Beautiful, cherished memories of how much you and I loved each other."

Incredulous, Grace could hardly get her mouth to form the word. *"Memories?"*

He continued as if she had not spoken. "We loved each other so much, Grace. I told you everything about me and you loved me anyway. I didn't deserve you and could not believe that you could love . . . someone like me. But I lost you before we could marry, before I could make you mine."

"I drowned, didn't I?"

Pain wracked his features. Grace placed her hand against his cheek.

"Yes. Your parents tried to keep us apart. They were taking you to France to place you in a convent. Your ship sank in a terrible storm."

"I know," she whispered in awe. "I had that dream last night. I kept calling for you. . . ."

"I wished I had died when you died."

Grace held her breath. "But you didn't."

"No, I didn't."

"You kept on living."

He nodded, not breaking his gaze with her.

"As you live now?" she whispered.

"Yes."

"How is that possible, Phillip?"

"I've waited and searched for you for a hundred years, Grace."

"How is that *possible*, Phillip?" Her voice rose an octave as she repeated the question.

"I could only hope that I would find you again. That your soul would find a way back to me in another body. And that I would be able to find you when you did. I've lived a century in heartache and grief. Searching for you."

"How. Is. That. Possible?" she asked quite deliberately. Fear began to grow within her. His words defied all logic, all reason. She could accept that she had lived another life before. On some level that made sense to her. But what Phillip was suggesting . . . How could he still be living and look exactly the same after one hundred years? It was impossible. Either he was stark raving mad or she was.

He grabbed her closer to him, pressing his fingers into the naked flesh of her arms. "Look at me."

She blinked.

"Do you believe I love you?"

"Yes." There was not a doubt in her mind that this man loved her.

"And you love me?"

"Yes, Phillip, I love you." And she did love him. The power of her love for this man overwhelmed her. He had become the center of her world, her life. She would do anything for him.

"Then listen to me very carefully, for I am about to tell you something that may make you hate me."

She shook her head. "I could never hate you."

"This might change your mind." The line of his mouth tightened and he looked disgusted with himself.

"Tell me." A feeling of dread crept up her spine.

"Telling you what I am does not negate how I feel about you, Grace. Do not fear me, because I would never hurt you. Never. I promise you."

The dream. In her dream. *Make me what you are*, Gráinne had begged him. *Make me what you are.* Good heavens, what *was* he? What was he that he could still be living over one hundred years and not have aged a day? What did Gráinne know that she did not? Her breath came in shallow gasps. "What are you?"

He grimaced and stared into her eyes, clearly dreading what he was about to say. "Vampire. I'm a vampire."

Chapter Six

Phillip stared at her, watching her blink in confusion. Was she afraid? Did she loathe him for the beast that he was, as she lay naked in bed next to him after he had just made love to her? Now he had confessed that he was a monster.

"What does that mean?" she questioned.

"You have never heard of vampires?" he asked, incredulous.

She shook her head. "Should I have?"

He shrugged. "I just assumed you knew what they were. What I am." Had she not read of them? Had her life with Mary Sutton kept her so sheltered?

"What is a vampire?" she asked, her face puzzled.

This was worse than if she already knew. Now he would have to explain. "A vampire is a monster."

Grace smiled. "Be serious, Phillip."

"I am serious." He kissed her lips as he moved over her, covering her naked body with his once again. "I am a monster."

She was an angel. A beautiful angel. Could an angel love a monster? She had before, when she was Gráinne. He could only hope.

Her delicate brows drew together in a charming way. "What kind of monster?"

"You have no idea what a vampire is?"

"No." She shook her head, her long auburn hair spilling around her. "I have a vague idea of gothic stories but other than that, no. I do not, and Gráinne did not, see you as a monster. At least not in the dreams I had. That is why I am asking you to explain to me . . . Explain how you can have lived over one hundred years . . ."

He hated this part. "Because I am a vampire and vampires are immortal. I am over three hundred years old, Grace."

She stared at him in disbelief and whispered, "*If only you had made me immortal,* I cried in my dream last night."

"I will live forever," he confessed.

She took a deep breath. "Go on."

"Vampires are creatures of the night. We feed on human blood and we live forever."

"Human blood?" she echoed woodenly.

Phillip cringed, not wanting to see the revulsion in her eyes. "Yes. We bite humans and drink their blood and they die. It is how we survive." He looked at her steadily. "I was made a vampire when I was thirty years old. I was bitten by a female vampire in 1570. I have been a vampire ever since."

That day so long ago haunted him as if it were yesterday. Lady Anna Barlow had seduced him with her beauty and cursed him by making him a monster. And he had loathed every day of his endless existence until Gráinne came into his life.

Grace said, "It sounds like a strange sort of twisted fairy tale."

He shook his head. "The happily ever after is rather unlikely."

Her beautiful blue eyes met his and he saw the fear in them. "Do you want my blood?"

He wanted so much more than her blood. He wanted her love, her companionship, and her constant presence. He wanted her with him always, for he had lived too long without her. Every ounce of his self-control was centered on not harming her. "You are not in any danger. I've long since learned to control my . . . baser urges. I would never hurt you, Grace. I love you too much."

He sensed her unease and only wished to calm her. He leaned in and kissed her silky cheek.

Grace began to tremble nervously. "I don't know what to think."

He held her tightly to calm her. "If nothing else, Grace, know that I love you more than life itself and I will never let you go again."

"You are not going to kill me for my blood?" she asked, a strange light in her blue eyes.

"I have not searched for you for a century only to kill you now."

She touched her hand to his face, her fingers caressing his full lips. He stilled, allowing her to explore him, wanting her to feel utterly safe. He could not help but kiss her fingertips. Spreading his lips slightly, he allowed her to feel the smoothness of his perfect, white teeth. He opened his mouth and she sank her finger deeper inside, until she ran against a very long, very sharp tooth along his upper jaw and found a matching one on the other side. Two very sharp teeth used for ripping flesh, like a wolf. Yes, now she could understand why he would call himself a monster. He expected her to recoil from him in disgust, but she did not. Her blue eyes glittered with passion.

He bit down on her finger, locking it in place, and their eyes met. He could feel her arousal as she began to breathe heavily. He loosened his hold on her finger, sucking gently on it instead. Grace slowly pulled it from his mouth and arched her hips against him.

With a low growl he lowered his head and covered her mouth with his. He kissed her roughly as desire for her washed over him in a tidal wave. He knew she wanted him as much as he wanted her and it thrilled him. He entered her in one swift stroke.

It was only the beginning.

They made love over and over in his massive bed until she was exhausted and he had to let her rest. She slept peacefully in his arms and he watched her, breathing deeply of her sweet scent.

She finally opened her eyes and yawned sleepily. She smiled at him and murmured, "I'm hungry."

"You've worked up an appetite." He admired the color that suffused her soft cheeks. "I'll ring for the servants and have some food sent up for you."

"What about you?"

He laughed ruefully.

She smiled at him. "Why are you laughing?"

He shook his head. "Because I don't eat food."

"You feed only on human blood?" she asked, her eyes huge.

"Yes."

"But not mine?"

His face became very serious. "You think I am jesting?"

"No . . . You have two very sharp teeth. . . . Yet . . . it all seems . . . I don't know what to believe," she admitted.

"Well, believe me, for I am telling you the truth."

Grace sat up in bed, pulling the sheet over her luscious breasts. "Prove it, Phillip. You keep telling me you are this kind of monster, this vampire. I don't believe you. I don't believe you are a monster. Prove it to me."

Dread filled his heart at her words. "Do not ask me to do that."

"How can I not? You claim to be over three hundred years old, a creature that lives on human blood. An immortal being, who loved me in another lifetime. You say these things and just expect me to believe you with no proof? I am not a fool, Phillip."

His eyes narrowed. "I never said you were."

"Then do not treat me as such," she said coldly.

He pulled her to him. She wrapped herself around him and he held her close. He loved the feel of her in his arms.

"Vampires have some special gifts, special strengths."

"Such as?" she prompted.

"Some vampires can read people's thoughts. Some have extraordinary hearing and can hear even the faintest of noises. Some are incredibly strong or can see things miles away."

She cupped his face in her hands. "And you, Phillip? What special gift do you have?"

"Well, for one, I can read people's dreams."

Grace froze.

"That is how I found you, Grace."

"How?" Her voice was barely a whisper.

"I've waited for you for years. I've traveled all over the world searching for you. Somehow, I sensed your dreams about Gráinne. They brought me closer and closer to you. As you dreamed about your other life and learned how much I loved you, the dreams called to me. Very faintly at first. About ten years ago I was in China and I realized I needed to come to England."

"That was when I first started to record my dreams," she confessed, "just before I married Henry. I wrote them down in a special journal."

"Writing them down made them stronger, making it easier for me to find you. Most people forget their dreams upon awakening," he explained. "When you write them down, you help preserve their memory, making them stronger. Every time you had a dream about your life, Gráinne's life, and recorded it, you left a clear path for me to find you. Your dreams were so vivid, so clear, I was reliving our life together with you. But once you saw me, you stopped writing about them, didn't you?"

"Yes," Grace admitted, spellbound by his confession. "But how could you know that?"

"Because I know you, Grace. I know everything about you, because I can see all of your dreams, not just your dreams about Gráinne. I know you were devastated by your parents' death when you were sixteen. I know you thought you loved Henry and were happy enough in your marriage with him. I know you hate your overbearing mother-in-law and I can't say I blame you. I know you want to marry Lord Grayson simply to escape her. And you are correct in your assumptions of him. He does love you and would be good to you." He paused before looking at her knowingly. "And I know you blame yourself for Henry's suicide, but you shouldn't."

Grace's eyes grew round and she pulled away from him. "There is no way you could know those things."

He drew her back into his arms, placing a kiss on her lips. "I've seen your dreams, Grace. All of them. I know how you were the one to find Henry's body that morning, hanging from the rafters in the attic. I know about the nightmares. I know how Mary took care of everything. How she and the doctor had agreed to keep the suicide a secret to avoid a scandal and the official story that was told was that Henry died of an unexpected heart ailment. That doctor passed away the following year, so that left only you and Mary guarding the truth. And you have never spoken to a soul about losing Henry in such a way."

Tears spilled from her blue eyes as he spoke and he was wrenched with guilt for bringing up the topic of her deceased husband. He whispered, "His death was his choice, Grace, and you are not to blame."

She hid her face in his chest, the warmth from her tears heating his skin. "You can't know these things about me," she sobbed.

"But I do," he answered softly in her ear. "And I know you love me."

"How? How do you know these things?"

"You asked me for proof, Grace. I just gave it to you. I know these things about you because I can see your dreams. While you were sleeping a little while ago, you were so exhausted and so peaceful, you didn't dream at all."

She said nothing.

"The reason I can know these things is that I am a vampire."

Grace slowly nodded her head. "And I knew about this, Gráinne knew."

"Yes."

"I wanted you to make me what you are. . . ." Her voice trailed off as the significance of those words occurred to her.

"Yes, you wanted me to make you a vampire all those years ago. I had misgivings and did not want to turn you into the monster I was—"

"You are not a monster," she protested.

He hated what he was and not once in three hundred years had he gotten used to it. He cupped her sweet face in his hands. "Yes, I am, Grace. Do not doubt that for a second."

"Why didn't you make me a vampire then? I wouldn't have drowned. We could have stayed together—"

An anguished groan tore from his throat. "Don't think I have not tortured myself with that regret every minute of the past one hundred years. If I had done what you asked, I never would have lost you." He closed his eyes at the memory. "When I learned your father had taken you to France, I was immediately on a ship on my way after you. I was caught in the same storm, but when it ended, there was no sign of your ship. All aboard were lost before dawn."

"Quarter past five," Grace murmured softly.

He glanced at her and said, "Perhaps." After a moment, he began again. "I cannot say for sure what I did for decades after that. I was so consumed with grief and rage over losing you, I truly became a monster. I killed indiscriminately, with no mercy. I am ashamed now of the terrible things I did during that time."

Instead of recoiling from him, she placed a kiss on his cheek.

Her touch warmed him. Phillip went on, "I existed in a murky haze, drifting from place to place, country to country, continent to continent. Living forever is a torturous existence when you have no wish to live. Until one day I woke up and everything changed. That aching, endless pain of losing you was gone. I felt I suddenly had a reason to live. I felt there was hope. It was such an astonishing change that I marked the day. It was February 17, 1840."

"That's my birthday!" she cried in astonishment.

"I know." He smiled at her. "But I didn't know it at the time. All I knew then was that I wanted to change how I was. I wanted to live. It was a few years later I sensed that you were alive. I knew you were living somewhere and I had to find you. Your dreams called out to me, I suppose, as you grew older."

Grace explained, "They've just always been with me, so different from regular dreams. I could never rid myself of the feeling that they were important. Sometimes I would have the same dream over and over. The dream of when we first met, by the little stone fence. Do you remember that?"

"Like it was yesterday." He placed a kiss on her lips. "You were the most beautiful woman I had ever seen."

She smiled at him. "I had that dream for years.

Then I would dream about other meetings, other times of us together. They became more frequent and more intense in this past year."

"You dreamed more as I got closer to you."

"But if Gráinne knew you were a vampire, why didn't I dream about your being a vampire? Why didn't I know that? That part was so vague."

"Because I didn't want you to know that until I saw you first, because I assumed you knew what a vampire was. I didn't want you to be frightened of me."

"You influenced my dreams?"

He shrugged sheepishly. "To a certain extent. Being a vampire is a highly guarded secret and I can control what you know about me. I wanted to tell you myself. I wanted to explain."

Grace stayed quiet.

As he held her warm, naked body in his arms, he had revealed many secrets to her. As ugly as those secrets were, she did not seem to be repulsed by him as he feared she might have been. Uncertain how much she had changed from being Gráinne to Grace, he did not know how she would react to his secret. Gráinne had not feared him, but he did not know what to expect from Grace.

"So what happens now?" she finally asked.

"That is up to you."

"I am not marrying Lord Grayson."

He laughed, filled with satisfaction at her words. "I should hope not! Not after what we've done in this bed all day."

"Phillip?" she asked hesitantly.

"What is it?"

"Are you going to make me a vampire?"

A long silence ensued. His eyes focused on her.

"I want you with me always, Grace, because I know what it is like to live without you. But as before, I would hate to take your humanity from you. I would hate to make you a monster."

"But would you if I asked you to?"

He hesitated, just as he had done when Gráinne asked him a century ago. "Yes."

Her pretty blue eyes widened.

"But only if you have had time to think about what you are committing to, what it really means, and how the world as you know it will change completely. Once you become a vampire, it cannot be undone. It is nothing to take lightly."

She kissed him and he felt as if the sun had warmed him. "Will you explain more of the details to me?"

"If you promise to take some time, a few days at least, to consider the impact of becoming a vampire with me. When you are quite sure, then I will make you a vampire."

"Do you know how to make a vampire? Have you made one before?" Her blue eyes glanced at him in uncertainty.

"Yes. And no." He certainly knew how to make one, but he had never bestowed that horror on a human being and he had huge reservations about doing so to Grace. However, he had lived the alternative and knew, once having found her again, there was no way he could exist without her in his life. He had to make her a vampire. But he wanted her to have more time to think about the gravity of the choice she was making. "You need to go home and decide you want to be a vampire when you are not naked in my bed and under my influence. I won't take no for an answer on this."

Grace suddenly sat up, panic on her face. "Good heavens! Home! What must they be thinking? What time is it? How long have I been here?"

"It's almost six o'clock in the evening."

"I've been with you all day!" she cried in anguish. "I left a note that I'd only gone for a walk. They must be frantic looking for me by now."

He sought to calm her. "Get dressed and I will take you home."

"What can I tell them? They won't believe I was out walking in the rain all day."

"Most likely not, but you can say you were with a friend."

She gave him a wry look and then hurried to dress as Phillip watched her. She was beautiful and sweet, just as she had been as Gráinne. He could not believe his good fortune in finding her for a second time. He had been lucky to even meet someone as wonderful as her a century ago. To have her in his life once again brought him more happiness than he had a right to have.

Chapter Seven

Every lamp was lit and the house was practically glowing from the street. Filled with dread, Grace entered the house. As much as she hated leaving Phillip and had toyed with the idea of simply staying with him forever, she knew he was right. She had to make a clean break with her human life before she joined him in his vampire world.

As was always her way, she needed to wrap matters up neatly and say her goodbyes. She had to face Mary one last time. She had to end her engagement with Lord Grayson in person. He had been nothing but kind to her and she owed him at least that much respect.

Grace squared her shoulders and opened the door. The household was in an uproar and her sudden entrance only made it worse. A chorus of shouts and cries greeted her as the servants gathered around her in the foyer.

"She's home!"

"She's safe!"

"Oh, Miss Grace, we have been looking for you everywhere!"

Mary loomed in the doorway of the parlor, her round face pinched in a tight frown and her eyes narrowed with mistrust. Lord Grayson stood behind her. Grace felt a twinge of guilt when she saw the worry and concern on his features. He rushed to her side, placing an arm around her shoulder and guiding her into the warm parlor.

"My dear, are you all right? We have been searching for you all afternoon. I came right over as soon as Mrs. Sutton sent a note around telling me you had not returned from your walk."

Mary waved the servants away and followed Grace into the parlor. Grace sensed her mother-in-law's anger boring into her spine, but knew Mary would say nothing in front of Lord Grayson. She'd save her wrath for when they were alone.

Lord Grayson escorted Grace to a seat on the sofa, where he helped her take off her coat. As she removed her hat and gloves, he sat beside her, clearly worried, his face appearing older than she remembered.

Mary did not sit, but said in a clipped tone, "I can see that you are unharmed and quite well, Grace, so I can assume you were not in any danger all day. You left this house before dawn, without a word to anyone, sending everyone into a panic over your whereabouts and safety. Now you return over twelve hours later as if nothing were amiss. I think you owe us the decency of an explanation."

Lord Grayson gave her a puzzled look. "Are you sure you are unhurt, my dear?"

"I am fine," Grace assured him. Her life had

turned completely upside down in the past day, but she could divulge only so much information.

He patted her shoulder. "I am relieved to know you are well, but I must admit to my curiosity. Where have you been all day, Grace?"

She avoided Mary's eyes and focused on Lord Grayson. "I was with a friend."

"What friend?" Mary demanded, her voice rising in anger.

Grace placed her hand over his. "May I speak with you privately, Reginald?"

"Yes, of course." He turned pointedly to Mary. "If you would please excuse us, Mrs. Sutton."

Mary huffed in indignation and stalked from the room.

He turned back to her with a questioning expression and squeezed her hand. "I have the most dreadful feeling I am not going to like what I am about to hear."

Grace took a deep breath. "I fear you are correct, Reginald." Pausing, she gazed into his kind eyes. As nice as he was, she might have found a kind of peace with him. They might have led a very pleasant life together. Had she not met Phillip. Again. After the day she had spent in his bed, there was no possibility of her settling for Reginald. It would spell misery for both of them, for in her heart she would always want to be with the man she loved. Phillip.

Grace took a deep breath before the words spilled out. "I am very sorry, but I cannot marry you after all."

He looked away from her, as if he could not bear to see her face. Grace felt sick, even though she knew she was making the right decision. As much as she longed to be with Phillip, Reginald needed to be with a woman who loved him in return.

"That is what I feared." He turned back to face her. "May I ask why you have changed your mind about becoming my wife? Has it anything to do with who you were with today?"

"Yes," she paused, considering just how much to share with him. "I have discovered that I am in love with someone else."

The expression on his face looked as if someone had punched him in the stomach and his lips made a tight line. "I see." He pulled his hand away from hers.

Grace could not meet his eyes. "I am sorry."

"Is it Lord Radcliffe?" he asked.

She nodded her head. "How did you know?"

"Your mother-in-law mentioned that you were . . . lingering with him on the steps last night. How can this be, Grace? You only just met the man." His words were tinged with a hint of anger.

"Yes, I know," Grace attempted to explain. "It seems rather sudden, but I assure that our feelings are true and that—"

"Your feelings?" Lord Grayson rose from the sofa and began to pace back and forth in front of her. "It seems you have not considered anyone's feelings in this situation but your own, Grace. My feelings were not something you thought of. We announced our engagement to everyone. You have now publicly humiliated me with this Radcliffe man. I am the seventh Earl of Grayson. How can I face anyone, knowing my fiancée has jilted me for another man? How can I hold up my head?"

Tears stung behind her eyes and she blinked. Oh, he was taking this much worse than she had expected. "I am very sorry, Reginald. I did not intend to hurt you or humiliate you—"

"Did you not spend the entire day with this man, unchaperoned?"

She opened her mouth but nothing came out.

"Did you not sit here in this very room two nights ago and promise to become my wife?" His angry words echoed through the parlor.

"I—" she began again, but he would not let her speak.

"Did you not kiss me and plan a December wedding while sitting exactly where you are now?"

"Yes, I did, but—"

"You break your promises too easily, Grace. You have humiliated me and proven yourself to be a woman of loose morals and low character. I am well rid of you. Goodnight." He turned and stalked from the parlor.

Grace covered her face with her hands. No, he had not taken it well at all. But at least it was done now. Her heart ached for him and she felt wretched about breaking her promise. But how could she explain that she had met the vampire she loved one hundred years ago and was now going to become one herself so they could be together forever? She shook her head and a hysterical laugh bubbled within her. No, he was quite right. He was well rid of her.

She rose and wrung her hands together. She still had Mary to deal with. But not now. It had been an overwhelming and exhausting day and Mary could wait until morning. Grateful that her mother-in-law was nowhere to be seen, she made her way up the main staircase to her bedroom, longing for a hot bath and some quiet and solitude. Grace opened the door of her bedroom and froze at the sight.

Good heavens! Her neat and orderly room was a shambles! Everything had been searched. Her wardrobe was wide open and articles of her clothing were strewn about the floor. Every drawer was open and upended. Her elegant writing desk had been turned upside down. Every memento and keepsake of her life had been touched, moved, pawed through.

And worst of all, Mary Sutton sat in the overstuffed armchair in the middle of her room with her wire spectacles perched on her nose. Grace's dream journal was in her hands.

Mary sneered, her round face a study in disgust. She held up the leather-bound journal as if it contained all the world's sins. "It is no wonder my poor son hung himself to get away from you."

Covering her chest with her hands, Grace gasped, not only at the outrageous invasion of her privacy, but also at the pure venom in the woman's words.

"How dare you say such a thing to me!" Grace cried, furious at being blamed for Henry's death.

Ever since that horrific day, Mary had not so subtly been hinting that Grace was the reason Henry had taken his life. Not that Grace needed more cause for grief, for she had tortured herself many a night worrying that she had inadvertently done something to make her young husband end his life. A good enough reason never surfaced, whether real or perceived, to rationalize what he had done, not only to himself, but also to her and their life together. After burying herself in sorrow for years and allowing her mother-in-law to punish her for something she had not done, Grace had finally begun to grow angry over the situation.

She was angry with Henry for being utterly selfish and for leaving her alone. Angry at Mary for forcing her to lie to everyone about how Henry had died and for making her feel responsible for his death. And most of all, angry with herself for allowing the situation to come to this.

Now to have Mary fling such hateful words at her and to see her private, intimate dreams and thoughts in the hands of her mother-in-law was more than Grace could bear. She wasn't sure if the change in her was due to spending the day with Phillip or knowing that she was about to permanently remove herself from this life that she could finally stand up for herself.

"Oh," Mary hissed coldly, "I have every right to dare, since what you do in my house reflects on me!"

Something in Grace finally snapped. "This is *my* house. Henry left it to *me*. What I do in my house is my business. It is only by my generosity that I allow you to stay here!"

Mary's face turned almost purple with outrage and a rush of triumph flooded through Grace. It wasn't often she left Mary speechless. They had never discussed the fact that the house belonged to Grace, because Grace had been too considerate and never wanted Henry's mother to feel that she had to leave her home. But Grace wanted her to leave now. She never wanted to lay eyes on the woman again.

Mary sputtered some incoherent words before

rising from the armchair and taking a step toward Grace. She still clutched the journal tightly in her hand. "I suppose this ugly behavior of yours has something to do with your disappearance today. You were with *him* all day, weren't you?"

Grace did not care anymore. "As a matter of fact, I was."

"After I expressly forbade you to see him?"

"Yes." Grace folded her arms across her chest. "I am going to marry him."

"That's what he says now, you stupid little fool, to get you into his bed. He's not going to marry you. You just met him, for God's sake! And you now have ruined your engagement with Lord Grayson."

"I broke off my engagement with him before he left. I am marrying Lord Radcliffe within the week," Grace declared boldly, surprising herself with her newfound assertiveness with Mary.

Mary nodded her head slowly as if she knew better. "Well, it is quite obvious to me what has happened to you. It is a good thing I have already sent for Doctor Vickers."

Grace's brows drew together in confusion. "Doctor Vickers?"

He was the family physician, but she had no idea why Mary would summon him here tonight. Grace had never liked the man. He always looked at her in a leering way that made her uncomfortable. She was thankful she was healthy and had no cause for his services, unlike Mary, who called on him several times a month for her various and vague illnesses.

"Yes. It is apparent that you are in need of professional help, Grace."

Grace laughed at the absurdity of her assertion.

"I have been worried about you for some time," Mary continued. "Your sleeplessness and waking at odd hours. Your ravings about wicked dreams and past lives in this journal. Your reckless behavior in disappearing today and spending time alone with Lord Radcliffe, a man you hardly know. And, of course, breaking an engagement to a well-respected and wealthy earl is clearly the action of an unbalanced mind."

"An unbalanced mind?" Grace echoed in disbelief.

"Ah, Doctor Vickers." Mary's eyes moved behind Grace. "It was good of you to come right over. I've been so worried."

Grace spun around to see the rather tall, broad-shouldered, bearded, and bespectacled doctor standing in the doorway of her bedroom. He held a black leather medical bag in his hand. A chill of unease crept through her.

"Good evening, Mrs. Sutton." He nodded his head in her direction, his eyes flickering over her. "Miss Grace."

"It's worse than I first thought, Doctor. Just look at her. Look at this room." Mary waved her hand, indicating that Grace had created the terrible mess. "Grace has become completely irrational and her behavior quite reckless. She ran off in the pouring rain before dawn this morning, without telling a soul where she had gone. And as I suspected, she spent the entire day being seduced by an evil man she barely knows. Then this evening she broke her engagement with Lord Grayson. If that weren't proof enough, there is this journal, full of lurid descriptions of sinful dreams and desires of another life she claims to have had."

"The situation does seem rather worrisome." His sharp eyes raked over Grace and she could not help but shiver. "It is most fortunate that you sent for me, Mrs. Sutton."

Grace stared between the two of them. They thought she was insane. Suppressing a nervous laugh, she began to speak. "Doctor Vickers, please let me explain—"

"Now, now, Miss Grace. There is nothing to get upset about." He stepped toward her more quickly than she thought a man of his size could move and placed his hand quite forcefully on her arm, compelling her to step backward. "Why don't you have a seat in this chair and rest for a while?"

She stumbled and he practically pushed her into the armchair where Mary had first been seated.

"There is nothing wrong with me," Grace protested, as panic began to grow within her. Something was happening and Mary had planned it.

Doctor Vickers loomed over her, peering closely. "Her eyes are quite dilated." He set his black bag upon the small end table next to the chair and began rummaging through it. "Mrs. Sutton, may I ask you to leave us for a moment while I examine her?"

Mary smiled triumphantly at Grace. "Of course, Doctor." She hurried from the room, closing the door behind her.

"Now, now, Miss Grace, there is nothing for you to worry your pretty little head about. I can take care of you." He uncorked a small amber glass bottle filled with a dark liquid. "If you drink this, my dear, you will sleep tonight without those dreams troubling you."

"I don't wish to drink that. And I am not having troubling dreams." She attempted to stand, but he easily pressed her back into the chair.

"You mean you deny all that Mrs. Sutton has claimed to be true?"

"Yes, I deny it!" she cried in indignation. "I am perfectly sane!"

He set the glass bottle upon the table next to his bag and took hold of her wrist. "Then you did not break your engagement with Lord Grayson this evening?" he asked in a calm tone, as he felt for her pulse.

Grace shook her head. "No, I did break it off with him, but—"

"Then you did not spend the day with another man when you know such an action would destroy your reputation forever?" he questioned, his eyes glittering shrewdly.

Grace felt her cheeks turn scarlet at the memory of all she had done that day with Phillip. She could not answer.

"I see from your lack of response that that accusation is also true." Doctor Vickers flashed a sly grin, revealing crooked front teeth. "Your pulse is racing. And what about the erotic dreams, Grace? Do you deny writing about them as well?"

"I . . . I . . ." Mortification engulfed her completely and she regretted ever writing her private, intimate dreams in that blasted journal. "No, I do not deny it," she murmured so low she barely heard her own voice.

"Do you believe you have lived another life?"

The ridiculousness of the statement sounded so

glaring when he said it. Grace knew it to be true from the deepest depths of her soul, but did not know how to explain it in a rational way. She *had* lived and loved Phillip in another life, but she knew no one would believe her. She said nothing.

"I thought so," he whispered.

His hand moved with deliberate slowness up the length of her arm and brushed lightly across her breasts, lingering there before placing his hand over her heart. She recoiled from his touch, pressing herself into the back of the chair.

"Yours are not the actions of a sane woman, Grace."

No, perhaps they were not after all, she thought. Maybe she *had* gone insane. It would explain why she had agreed to let Lord Radcliffe change her into a vampire. All of what had happened to her in the past few days was crazy. Perhaps she had gone stark raving mad?

Releasing her, Doctor Vickers reached into his bag to grab some sort of instrument with a long wooden tube. "I'll need you to unbutton your dress, Grace, so I can listen to your heart properly. Loosen the corset also," he commanded coolly.

"There is no need for this," she began. "I assure you, I am perfectly fine."

"You are not fine," he stated in a harsh tone, startling her. "Your pulse is rapid, your eyes are dilated, your cheeks are flushed, and you are overwrought. Now I insist upon listening to your heart. Would you rather I have Mrs. Sutton join us?"

Grace preferred to be humiliated without Mary looking on. The sooner she got the examination over with, the sooner the doctor would leave. Reluctantly she began to unfasten the buttons down the front of her green plaid gown, recalling that she had done the same thing in front of Phillip earlier today. Shame flooded her now, where it had not this morning when she had undressed for Phillip. Feeling Doctor Vickers's eyes on her, she unbuttoned her gown to just below her chest, just enough to loosen the ties on her corset. She kept her hands poised to shove him away.

Without saying a word, the doctor leaned his head closer to her, placing the long wooden instrument against her chest and the other end of it to his ear. His face was entirely too close to her breasts as he listened for some time. His hot breath warmed her skin, yet made her shiver in disgust. She concentrated on the sound of the rain slapping against the window.

He raised his head and removed the medical instrument, yet kept his eyes on her. His expression was puzzled. "You have a most irregular heartbeat."

"What does that mean?" she asked, hurrying to button up her dress.

"It could mean a variety of things, but we would need more tests done in my surgery. I can examine you properly there. However, that is not what worries me now."

"What is it?"

"Your behavior is not rational."

"That is not for you to decide," she said as she fastened the last button.

Suddenly the door opened and Mary entered, her sharp eyes taking in the situation. Grace was shocked to see Lord Grayson following behind her mother-in-law's large figure.

"Reginald!" Grace exclaimed. He would not

meet her eyes. Why had he come back? His departure earlier had seemed so final.

"Well, Doctor Vickers?" Mary questioned eagerly. "What is your professional opinion?"

"I think you were quite right in your assessment, Mrs. Sutton."

Mary nodded her head in grim satisfaction. "As much as I hate to admit such a thing, I was afraid that might be the case. Lord Grayson has returned and would like to weigh in on the matter."

Grace stared at the three of them. *Weigh in on the matter?* What was going on here? "There is nothing the matter. I am fine," she stated yet again.

Lord Grayson focused all of his attention on Doctor Vickers, ignoring Grace completely. "I don't know what to think, quite frankly. She seemed perfectly rational when she agreed to be my wife. I did not suspect her of being the flighty, impetuous type or I would not have asked her to marry me in the first place. You can imagine my surprise to learn of her scandalous behavior today, running around after a man she hardly knows, and my greater shock when she confessed to me that she is in love with this man and needed to break our engagement. After Mrs. Sutton revealed to me just now the lurid contents of her dream journal, I am terribly worried for Grace's mental state. I care for her a great deal and I would hate to see her come to any harm. The change in her is dramatic and her behavior is not that of a sane woman."

Doctor Vickers nodded his head. "Those were my thoughts exactly."

"You are already aware of my position," Mary chimed in. "This is a sad day for me. To see the woman I thought of as my own daughter for ten years, come to this."

"Come to what?" Grace shouted in frustration.

"She is not even aware of how extreme her behavior is," Doctor Vickers said to them. "Yet she does not deny any of it."

Mary made a "tsk, tsk" sound and frowned sadly. "I never would have expected such from her, but she even threatened to force me out of my home this evening."

Grace tightened her hands into fists. "I did no such thing!"

"Look at her," Mary said, shaking her head with pity. "May God have mercy on her poor soul."

Lord Grayson stayed mute, still avoiding her eyes, but looked appalled.

Doctor Vickers cleared his throat. "There is only one thing to do then and I believe we are all in agreement."

Panic laced with fear welled within Grace's chest. It was as if they had come to some kind of prearranged consensus about her. She took a deep breath and tried to speak calmly, knowing that if she became upset they would only use it against her. "There is nothing wrong with my mental state. I am perfectly sane and I know exactly what I am doing. The three of you can leave my room, and my house, immediately."

They simply ignored her and acted as if she had not spoken at all.

"It is rather late to take her this evening, but I can make an exception," Doctor Vickers said. He gazed at Grace with unmasked lust and she unconsciously wrapped her arms around herself.

"You are not taking me anywhere," she stated firmly.

"There is no need to go to all the trouble to proceed there tonight, especially with the rain," Mary said, again ignoring Grace. "It can wait until the morning."

"We can give her this." The doctor held up the small amber-colored bottle. "It will calm her and help her sleep through the night."

"I am not going anywhere," Grace stated again in a louder voice, "and I am not taking anything this man gives me."

Lord Grayson had a pained expression on his face as he asked, "Will she be safe there?"

"She shall be perfectly safe, for I shall see to her personally," Doctor Vickers said, his eyes glittering. "I give you my word on that."

"This is ridiculous!" Grace exclaimed. "I am not insane simply because I broke off an engagement because I fell in love with someone else. I am not insane for writing about my dreams!"

Doctor Vickers handed the bottle to Mary. "We will try to give this to her later. Perhaps I should stay here this evening just in case?"

Mary took the bottle and nodded her head. "Yes, that would be best." She moved toward the door.

Lord Grayson gave her a cold and distant look and Grace wondered how she had ever thought she could marry the man. He left the room hurriedly.

Doctor Vickers said, "Good evening, Grace. I shall see you in the morning. You need only ring for me and I shall come."

"That is highly unlikely," she snapped at him.

He smiled at her and exited the room. Mary's eyes narrowed. "I shall pray for you all night, Grace." She too left the room, closing the door behind her.

And Grace was left alone.

It wasn't until she heard the key in the lock on the other side of the door that she realized they had locked her in her own bedroom.

Chapter Eight

Something was wrong. Lord Radcliffe paced back and forth in his bedroom. It was almost four in the morning and he knew Grace was not sleeping, for he could not read her dreams. He could not sense anything from her.

When she left, he had said he would give her time, at least three days, before he came for her, so she could consider on her own all sides of what she would become. To be sure. Yes, they loved each other, but what he was asking of her was beyond the realm of love.

As soon as she left he had misgivings about releasing her. He should have kept her with him. Should never have let her out of his sight again.

When she drowned that day a hundred years ago, Phillip had not known how to bear the pain of losing her. Nor the guilt he suffered over not giving her what she so desperately wanted. But Gráinne had had plenty of time to know what she was doing.

It was Phillip who was unsure.

He had never made a vampire before and he was terrified something would go wrong and he would lose her. Oh, he knew what to do, and he had seen it done, but it was a dangerous business. And through his fear and hesitation he lost her anyway.

He was determined not to do that again.

Was Grace that tortured over what she was about to become that she could not sleep? Was she terrified? Was she alone?

Becoming a vampire was not an easy decision to make.

Of course, he had not made the decision for himself. That had been made for him.

When he was thirty years old, he had lived a comfortable life. He was raised by an aristocratic family and experienced a happy childhood. He was an economic advisor to Queen Elizabeth I and held a position at court as the Earl of Radcliffe. He had a pretty young wife, Sara, who had just given birth to their daughter. Phillip had named her Jane, after his mother, and hoped for a son for the next go-round. Yes, he was prosperous and successful and life was good for him. Aside from the death of his father when he was twenty, Phillip had not experienced any hardships and his existence had been pleasant and peaceful.

Until the night he met her.

She had stepped out of the shadows of the castle one evening and he was dumbfounded by her allure. Never had he seen anyone so exquisitely beautiful, so achingly tempting. Her silky black hair fell in waves to her waist and her lush, over-ripe breasts spilled over the top of her red velvet gown. Long black eyelashes lined the most gorgeous, startlingly green eyes. They mesmerized him. She spoke in a sultry whisper, luring him with her erotic words. Helplessly he took her hand and followed her up the stone steps to her chamber.

Straying from his marriage vows was something he had never had any intention of doing. He loved his wife. He loved his baby daughter. But this woman bewitched him.

This woman destroyed him.

The passionate and highly erotic night spent in her bed had been an incredible mix of pleasure and pain.

When dawn broke the following morning, she revealed the horrific creature she was and what she was going to do to him. Before Phillip could escape the evil woman, she bit his neck, slicing two razor-sharp fangs into his flesh and changing him forever.

When he awoke, shivering and sweating, she was beside him. Lady Anna Barlow instructed him on his new, terrifying existence—the ways of vampires. He could never see his wife and daughter again, for fear he might attack them, so overpowering was his thirst for human blood. Overwhelmed with pain and grief, he let his family think he had disappeared. With Anna by his side and filled with an indescribable anger and self-loathing, Phillip at first killed indiscriminately, caring only to satisfy the endless, torturous thirst within him. And that is what he did. Eventually, Anna left him and he was on his own, which he did not necessarily mind. Losing his wife and daughter had filled him with an aching sadness.

Over many decades, he learned to control his bloodlust and roamed the fetid London streets, searching only for victims who would not be readily missed and whose sad lives would be nothing but a mercy to end. He traveled the world, moving from city to city, country to country, slaking his desires and his thirst in an anonymous haze.

Until the day he met Gráinne.

His entire existence changed the day he saw her beautiful soul and fell helplessly in love. With Gráinne he felt almost human again. He didn't want to be alone anymore. He only wanted to be with her.

That same soul, the exquisite soul that redeemed and saved him, now inhabited the body of Grace Sutton. He would do anything to make her life easier. Now that he had found her again he would never let her go. He had not sensed any danger from her home environment. Tension yes, but danger no. Her mother-in-law was a tyrant and that Grayson man was not for her. But the fact that she was not sleeping made him anxious. A great unease crept along his spine.

He had fed earlier that evening, along the London docks. It was fertile ground for the refuse of human life. He could dump the bodies in the Thames and no one would suspect a thing. Keeping a low profile was an unbroken code in the secretive and mysterious vampire world.

Slipping on his cape and hat, he made his way through the misty London night to Grace Sutton's townhouse. He knew the way like the back of his hand, for he had stood beneath her bedroom window for many a night before Grace saw him, reading her dreams.

How he loved and cherished her. This beautiful woman who altered his whole existence . . .

Phillip moved on silent feet down the alley behind her house, until he passed through the garden gate that led into the Suttons' yard. With his keen night vision he scanned the grounds and then observed the stately stone house. Immediately, he noted that two windows were aglow with lights. How odd for close to five in the morning. He had observed this household for some time now and he knew the servants did not wake this early. The one window he focused on in particular was Grace's.

The light glowed from within. He saw her at the window and his body froze at the sight of her.

Something was definitely wrong.

It was still so dark outside she could not see him, or she would have signaled to him. Her beautiful face was distraught and creased with worry. Long auburn hair cascaded about her delicate shoulders. He could see she was still wearing the same green plaid dress she had on yesterday. Her hands pressed against the rain-splattered glass as if she were in pain and his body convulsed in response. Sensing danger, his eyes intuitively peered through the other window, in the room next to Grace's.

This window in particular held his attention, for he did not recognize the large, dark-haired man with spectacles. His hulking form paced the room, walking back and forth in front of the tall window. Who was he and what was his purpose in the Sutton household?

Emitting a low snarl, Phillip clenched his fists. He began to crave blood, even though he had already fed earlier that evening. An unexplainable desire to kill the lumbering man standing in the window coursed through his body. The sheer pleasure of tearing the dark-haired human to shreds and leaving nothing for them to find afterward would be quite intoxicating.

The thought startled him, for he had not felt that unbridled urge of bloodlust in thirty years, since Grace was born and the compulsion to kill for killing's sake had eased. The man, whoever he was, must have threatened her or had intentions to harm her in some way. It was the only explanation that made sense. And one thing Phillip had learned over the years to never doubt was his senses.

Without hesitating an instant, he quietly unlatched the kitchen door and ascended the servants' staircase on silent feet. Moving along the upper hallway, he judged which bedroom belonged to Grace from the positioning of the windows. The soft glow of light illuminating her doorway confirmed what he already knew. Her heavenly scent was discernable by then. He reached for the handle but found it locked. Unsurprised, he removed a slender metal key from his pocket. It worked for most any door. The lock clicked and the door opened.

Grace still stood by the window but turned her head at the sound of the door. Fear was etched in her features. Her beautiful blue eyes widened in surprise upon seeing him. They stared for a moment and then she fairly flew into his arms, but he reached her first.

He grabbed her tightly to him, breathing deeply. It felt like days had passed since he had touched her, when it had been merely hours. She rested her head against his chest and he stroked her hair, weaving his fingers through the soft tresses.

"You came," she murmured against his chest.

"Grace," he whispered, pressing kisses to the top of her head. "Something is wrong, isn't it? You haven't slept all night."

"Mary brought a doctor here to examine me, to confirm that I'm insane. They found my dream journal and are using it as proof. They want to take me to the asylum in the morning."

"And they locked you in?"

"Yes," a deep voice said from behind the doorway. "To keep her from running to you." He chuckled, the slight sound incongruous from a man that large. "But it seems we erred in not anticipating that you would come to her rescue."

The large hulking figure he had spied from the window stood in Grace's bedroom. Phillip would have attacked him before he even finished speaking if he did not have Grace in his arms. But he did. Her entire body tensed with fear due to this man's presence and she clung to him. Phillip knew nothing could harm her while he was there, but Grace did not know that. Yet.

"You erred on more than one account, then," Phillip stated in a commanding voice.

The man ignored Phillip's comment. His eyes glittered as he stared at Grace. "I gather you are the Lord Radcliffe everyone has been referring to this evening. Permit me to introduce myself. I am Doctor Neville Vickers and I can assure you with all medical authority that this woman is a danger to herself and needs proper psychiatric attention. Consider yourself fortunate that you discovered the truth of her mental instability before you rushed into a marriage with her. She is now under my personal care."

"Like hell she is."

Doctor Vickers took a small step back at Phillip's words. Clearly affronted, he took a moment to reassess the situation.

Phillip grinned. The man had no idea what he was up against.

"You need to leave this house now," Doctor Vickers declared with indignation. "And Grace stays here."

"No. Grace is leaving with me." Phillip moved Grace protectively behind his body, holding her hand. She squeezed tightly.

Doctor Vickers shook his head. "I'm afraid I cannot let you do that."

"If you wish to live past dawn, then I suggest you turn around and go back to your room and lock yourself in," Phillip threatened calmly.

"How dare you come into this house and threaten me?" His eyes narrowed through the wire-framed spectacles.

"Get out of my way," Phillip commanded.

Doctor Vickers squared his shoulders, blocking the doorway with his bulky body.

Phillip clenched and unclenched his hand. They needed to get out of the house soon. His body thrummed with the urge to rip into the one who endangered Grace's safety. If he fought with the idiot doctor, the noise would rouse the entire house. On the other hand, he could silence the man permanently without making a sound. He hated to do that in front of Grace, but perhaps she was better off seeing him for what he truly was. A killer. A creature of the night.

A vampire.

Phillip faced her. She looked up at him with worry in her eyes. He kissed her cheek and whispered in her ear, "I'm sorry." He forced her to take some steps back and released her hand. He turned his full attention to the doctor.

"I must insist you leave the premises. Without Grace," the doctor commanded. Again he gazed at Grace as if she were a tasty morsel he couldn't wait to devour.

This was going to be a pleasure for Phillip. In an instant, Phillip was behind the doctor and closed the door. The bulky man spun around, but it was already too late. With his back to Grace, Phillip had bared his teeth. As usual, his movements were so fleeting, so skilled, there was no chance for his victim to struggle. Centuries of honing his lethal moves had made him an efficient killer.

The doctor's eyes widened in horror but he had no time to scream before Phillip grabbed his thick neck and sank his fangs deep within the white flesh.

The hot rush of blood slowly began to slake the thirst in his throat. Soon, too soon, the doctor's body slackened and slumped to the carpet, completely drained of its life's blood.

It took but a few silent moments and it was over. Doctor Neville Vickers was dead. With a shaking hand, Phillip wiped his mouth. Slowly he turned back to face the woman he loved, dreading the expression of horror in her eyes he was certain to see when he did so.

Chapter Nine

Grace could not control the wild hammering of her heart and the rush of noise in her ears. Her whole body trembled, but not with fear. Phillip had just killed Doctor Vickers in front of her very eyes. Thrilled that the vile doctor was gone for good, she felt no remorse at all at his passing. She had no doubt what he intended by having her under his "personal care." Grace was only shocked by the quickness of the act. Perhaps Mary was right. Maybe Grace *was* full of sin and doomed to hell.

But that was only if she remained mortal.

She sought Phillip's warm brown eyes. She smiled at him.

He came to her side, pulling her close. There was incredulous relief in his voice. "You don't loathe me?"

Grace shook her head and touched his smooth cheek with her fingers. How could she hate the man who had spent a century searching for her? Who had killed to protect her? Who loved her enough for two lifetimes? She had loved him for longer than she could remember, for it had always been him. "I love you."

He covered her mouth in a searing kiss, before grabbing her hand firmly in his. "We have to leave here now, Grace. There is no more time."

Without hesitation she nodded and followed him. She would follow him anywhere. Her parents had died when she was young. Her husband had left her in a selfish act of cowardice. Her only other relation had just tried to have her sent to an asylum for the insane.

No, Grace had no one left whom she cared for anymore. Her life was with Phillip now.

They fled her bedroom, closing the door on the lifeless body that lay on the floor. On quiet feet they exited the still-sleeping house. Once again the predawn light was shrouded in thick gray mist. Grace realized she had forgotten her coat. Indeed, she had taken nothing with her. Shivering, she held tight to Phillip's hand. As if he read her mind, Philip removed his black cape and wrapped it snugly around her shoulders. Grace breathed in the warmth of him. They hurried through the garden gate and into the narrow alley.

By the time they reached his plush carriage, the rain was falling in a torrential downpour. The carriage took off quickly.

"You know we must leave London immediately," he said calmly. "They will be searching for us both."

"I have never lived anywhere but here, so I don't care where we go, as long as we are together." And truly, all that mattered to her was being with the man she loved. Even if he was a vampire.

The smile that lit his handsome face made her heart turn over in her chest.

"We shall make a quick stop at my house, for papers and money, and we'll be on our way."

"To where?"

"Paris?" he suggested.

"Why not?" She laughed at the outrageousness of it all.

He kissed her mouth and her blood raced.

"There is one thing we must do first," she said. "Today."

Phillip stared at her.

She looked into his dark eyes, wanting nothing more than to be with this man for all eternity. No matter what the cost. She leaned back into the crook of his arm, her auburn curls falling to the side, exposing the soft, white skin of her neck.

"Please," Grace whispered softly, echoing the words Gráinne had uttered to him a century ago. "Make me what you are."

More by Bestselling Author
Hannah Howell

Books by Bestselling Author
Fern Michaels

_2/2_

___The Jury	0-8217-7878-1	$6.99US/$9.99CAN
___Sweet Revenge	0-8217-7879-X	$6.99US/$9.99CAN
___Lethal Justice	0-8217-7880-3	$6.99US/$9.99CAN
___Free Fall	0-8217-7881-1	$6.99US/$9.99CAN
___Fool Me Once	0-8217-8071-9	$7.99US/$10.99CAN
___Vegas Rich	0-8217-8112-X	$7.99US/$10.99CAN
___Hide and Seek	1-4201-0184-6	$6.99US/$9.99CAN
___Hokus Pokus	1-4201-0185-4	$6.99US/$9.99CAN
___Fast Track	1-4201-0186-2	$6.99US/$9.99CAN
___Collateral Damage	1-4201-0187-0	$6.99US/$9.99CAN
___Final Justice	1-4201-0188-9	$6.99US/$9.99CAN
___Up Close and Personal	0-8217-7956-7	$7.99US/$9.99CAN
___Under the Radar	1-4201-0683-X	$6.99US/$9.99CAN
___Razor Sharp	1-4201-0684-8	$7.99US/$10.99CAN
___Yesterday	1-4201-1494-8	$5.99US/$6.99CAN
___Vanishing Act	1-4201-0685-6	$7.99US/$10.99CAN
___Sara's Song	1-4201-1493-X	$5.99US/$6.99CAN
___Deadly Deals	1-4201-0686-4	$7.99US/$10.99CAN
___Game Over	1-4201-0687-2	$7.99US/$10.99CAN
___Sins of Omission	1-4201-1153-1	$7.99US/$10.99CAN
___Sins of the Flesh	1-4201-1154-X	$7.99US/$10.99CAN
___Cross Roads	1-4201-1192-2	$7.99US/$10.99CAN

Available Wherever Books Are Sold!
Check out our website at **www.kensingtonbooks.com**